I0831340

Suicide Six

Book Six

The Lone Star Series

by

Bobby Akart

Copyright Information

Other Works by Bestselling Author Bobby Akart

The Lone Star Series

Axis of Evil

Beyond Borders

Lines in the Sand

Texas Strong

Fifth Column

Suicide Six

The Pandemic Series

Beginnings

The Innocents

Level 6

Quietus

The Blackout Series

36 Hours

Zero Hour

Turning Point

Shiloh Ranch

Hornet's Nest

Devil's Homecoming

The Boston Brahmin Series

The Loyal Nine

Cyber Attack

Martial Law

False Flag

The Mechanics

Choose Freedom

Patriot's Farewell

Seeds of Liberty (Companion Guide)

The Prepping for Tomorrow Series

Cyber Warfare

EMP: Electromagnetic Pulse

Economic Collapse

DEDICATIONS

Every day, I wake up to a beautiful world filled with the undying love of my wife and the loyalty of our pups. Without them, none of my books would be possible. I wish every family could have what we have.

The Lone Star Series is dedicated to the love and support of my family. I will always protect you from anything that would disrupt our happiness.

ACKNOWLEDGEMENTS

Writing a book that is both informative and entertaining requires a tremendous team effort. Writing is the easy part. For their efforts in making *Suicide Six*, the conclusion of the Lone Star series, a reality, I would like to thank Hristo Argirov Kovatliev for his incredible cover art, Pauline Nolet for her editorial prowess, Stef Mcdaid for making this manuscript decipherable in so many formats, Sean Runnette and the folks at Audible Studios for producing the incredible narration, and the Team—Shirley, Denise, Kelly, Joe, and Jim, whose advice, friendship and attention to detail is priceless.

A special thank-you to Kevin Baron and the team at *Defense One* for providing invaluable insight into the North Korean threat and how we'd defend against it. Also, thank you to Michaela Dodge, senior policy analyst at the Heritage Foundation, Center for National Defense, for her extensive background material on missile defense, nuclear weapons modernization and arms control.

Also, enough can't be said for the efforts of Dr. Peter Vincent Pry as he continues to warn our lawmakers of the threats we face from an EMP. Dr. Pry is an unsung hero who works tirelessly to protect America and keep us aware of activities to protect the grid. Thank you sir for your kind words in the Foreword!

Thank you all!
Choose Freedom!

ABOUT THE AUTHOR

Bobby Akart

Bestselling author Bobby Akart has been ranked by Amazon as the #3 Bestselling Religion & Spirituality Author, the # 4 Bestselling Horror Author, the #5 Bestselling Science Fiction Author, and the #7 Bestselling Historical Author. He has written over twenty international bestsellers, in forty-plus fiction and nonfiction genres, including the critically acclaimed Pandemic Series, the Boston Brahmin series, the Blackout series, his highly cited nonfiction Prepping for Tomorrow series and his latest project—The Lone Star Series, which has produced six #1 best sellers.

Bobby has provided his readers a diverse range of topics that are both informative and entertaining. His attention to detail and impeccable research has allowed him to capture the imaginations of his readers through his fictional works and bring them valuable knowledge through his nonfiction books.

SIGN UP to Bobby Akart's mailing list to receive special offers, bonus content, and you'll be the first to receive news about new releases in The Lone Star Series, updates on his other series, special offers, and bonus content. You can contact Bobby directly by email (BobbyAkart@gmail.com) or through his website:

BobbyAkart.com

FOREWORD

by Dr. Peter Vincent Pry
Chief of Staff,
Congressional EMP Commission
Executive Director, Task Force
on National and Homeland Security

The recent escalating war of words and actions with rogue nations like North Korea and Iran has given rise to a new sense of urgency about threats we face—especially the existential threat that is a nuclear electromagnetic pulse (EMP) attack. I am pleased to write this foreword for author Bobby Akart as he continues to inform his readers, through his works of fiction, about the EMP threat, both man-made and naturally occurring.

With the Lone Star series, you will learn about the potential of nuclear-armed satellites flying over America daily in low Earth orbit, positioned to collapse our power grid, destroy our way of life, and possibly kill up to ninety percent of Americans.

The Congressional EMP Commission warns North Korea may already pose a worldwide threat, not only by ICBM, but by satellites, two of which presently orbit over the United States and every country on Earth.

A single satellite, if nuclear-armed, detonated at high-altitude would generate an EMP capable of blacking out power grids and life-sustaining critical infrastructure.

Yet, after massive intelligence failures grossly underestimating North Korea's nuclear capabilities, their biggest threat to the U.S. and the world remains unacknowledged—nuclear EMP attack.

The EMP threat continues to be low priority and largely ignored, even though on September 2, 2017, North Korea confirmed the

EMP Commission's assessment by testing an H-Bomb that could make a devastating EMP attack.

Two days after their H-Bomb test, on September 4, Pyongyang also released a technical report "The EMP Might of Nuclear Weapons" accurately describing a "super-EMP" weapon generating 100,000 volts/meter.

North Korea's development of a super-EMP weapon that generates 100,000 volts/meter is a technological watershed more threatening than the development of an H-Bomb and ICBM because even the U.S. nuclear deterrent, the best-protected U.S. military forces, are EMP hardened to survive only 50,000 volts/meter.

My colleague EMP Commission Chairman William Robert Graham warned Congress in 2008 that Russia had developed super-EMP weapons and most likely transferred that technology to North Korea allegedly *by accident*, according to Russian generals.

The result of this newly discovered relationship between Russia and North Korea is that the DPRK now has the technology to win a nuclear war. At the very least, a North Korean EMP attack could paralyze the U.S. nuclear deterrent and prevent U.S. retaliation, perhaps even by U.S. submarines at sea that cannot launch missiles without receiving an Emergency Action Message from the president.

However, the warning signs have gone largely ignored. Although North Korea, Russia, and China have all made nuclear threats against the United States recently, in the case of North Korea and Russia repeatedly, most analysts dismiss the war of words as *mere bluster* and *nuclear sabre rattling*, not to be taken seriously.

In the West, generations of leaders and citizens have been educated that use of nuclear weapons is unthinkable and the ultimate horror. Not so in Russia, China, and North Korea, where their nuclear capabilities are publicly paraded—missile launches and exercises are televised as a show of strength, an important part of national pride.

Then there is the issue of an EMP attack. An electromagnetic pulse attack would be perfect for implementing Russia's strategy of "de-escalation," where a conflict with the U.S. and its allies would be won by limited nuclear use. It's their version of "shock and awe" to cow the U.S. into submission. The same kind of attack is viewed as an acceptable option by China and North Korea as well.

An EMP attack would be the most militarily effective use of one or a few nuclear weapons, while also being the most acceptable nuclear option in world opinion, the option most likely to be construed in the U.S. and internationally as "restrained" and a "warning shot" without direct loss of life.

Because an electromagnetic pulse destroys electronics instead of blasting cities, even some analysts in Germany and Japan, among the most antinuclear nations, regard EMP attacks as an acceptable use of nuclear weapons. A high-altitude EMP ("HEMP") attack entails detonating a nuclear weapon at 30–400 kilometers altitude—above the atmosphere, in outer space, so high that no nuclear effects, not even the sound of the explosion, would be experienced on the ground, except the resulting EMP.

An EMP attack will kill far more people than nuclear blasting a city through indirect effects—by blacking out electric grids and destroying life-sustaining critical infrastructures like communications, transportation, food and water—in the long run. But the millions of fatalities likely to eventually result from EMP will take months to develop, as slow as starvation.

Thus, a nation hit with an EMP attack will have powerful incentives to cease hostilities, focus on repairing their critical infrastructures while there is still time and opportunity to recover, and avert national extinction.

Indeed, an EMP attack or demonstration made to "de-escalate" a crisis or conflict is very likely to raise a chorus of voices in the West against nuclear escalation and send Western leaders in a panicked search for the first "off ramp."

Axis of Evil and the entire Lone Star series are books of fiction that are based upon historical fact. The geopolitical factors in this series leading up to a potentially catastrophic collapse of America's power grid are based upon real-world scenarios.

Author Bobby Akart has written several fiction and nonfiction books with the intent to raise awareness about the threats we face from an EMP, whether via a massive solar storm or delivered by a nuclear warhead. While many books have been written about the results of nuclear war and EMPs, few have tackled the subject of using satellites as a means of delivering the fatal blow, until now.

The Lone Star series is written to be thought-provoking. It will be a reminder to us all that, as Bobby says, you never know when the day before is the day before. Prepare for tomorrow.

Dr. Peter Vincent Pry
Chief of Staff
Congressional EMP Commission
Executive Director
Task Force on National and Homeland Security

About Dr. Peter Vincent Pry

Dr. Peter Vincent Pry served as chief of staff of Congressional Electromagnetic Pulse (EMP) Commission (2001-2017), and is currently the executive director of the Task Force on National and Homeland Security, a Congressional Advisory Board dedicated to achieving protection of the United States from electromagnetic pulse (EMP), cyber warfare, mass-destruction terrorism and other threats to civilian critical infrastructures, on an accelerated basis. Dr. Pry also is director of the United States Nuclear Strategy Forum, an advisory board to Congress on policies to counter weapons of mass destruction. Foreign governments, including the United Kingdom, Israel, Canada, and Kazakhstan consult with Dr. Pry on EMP, cyber, and other strategic threats.

Dr. Pry served on the staffs of the Congressional Commission on the Strategic Posture of the United States (2008–2009); the Commission on the New Strategic Posture of the United States (2006–2008); and the Commission to Assess the Threat to the United States from Electromagnetic Pulse (EMP) Attack (2001–2008).

Dr. Pry served as professional staff on the House Armed Services Committee (HASC) of the U.S. Congress, with portfolios in nuclear strategy, WMD, Russia, China, NATO, the Middle East, Intelligence, and Terrorism (1995–2001). While serving on the HASC, Dr. Pry was chief advisor to the vice chairman of the House Armed Services Committee and the vice chairman of the House Homeland Security Committee, and to the chairman of the Terrorism Panel. Dr. Pry played a key role: running hearings in Congress that warned terrorists and rogue states could pose EMP and cyber threats, establishing the Congressional EMP Commission, helping the commission develop plans to protect the United States from EMP and cyber warfare, and working closely with senior scientists and the nation's top experts on critical infrastructures, EMP and cyber warfare.

Dr. Pry was an intelligence officer with the Central Intelligence Agency, responsible for analyzing Soviet and Russian nuclear strategy, operational plans, military doctrine, threat perceptions, and developing U.S. paradigms for strategic warning (1985–1995). He also served as a verification analyst at the U.S. Arms Control and Disarmament Agency responsible for assessing Soviet arms control treaty compliance (1984–1985).

Dr. Pry has written numerous books on national security issues, including *Blackout Wars*; *Apocalypse Unknown: The Struggle To Protect America From An Electromagnetic Pulse Catastrophe*; *Electric Armageddon: Civil-Military Preparedness For An Electromagnetic Pulse Catastrophe*; *War Scare: Russia and America on the Nuclear Brink*; *Nuclear Wars: Exchanges and Outcomes*; *The Strategic Nuclear Balance: And Why It Matters*; and *Israel's Nuclear Arsenal*. You may view his canon of work by visiting his Amazon Author page.

Dr. Pry often appears on TV and radio as an expert on national security issues. The BBC made his book *War Scare* into a two-hour TV documentary *Soviet War Scare 1983*, and his book *Electric Armageddon* was the basis for another TV documentary *Electronic Armageddon* made by National Geographic.

EPIGRAPH

A hero is an ordinary individual who finds the strength to persevere and endure in spite of overwhelming obstacles.
~ Christopher Reeve, American Actor

*****

We are building a border wall for the same reason you lock your door at night—safety.
~ Multiple readers of The Lone Star series

*****

The man who trades freedom for security does not deserve, nor will he ever receive, either.
~ Benjamin Franklin

*****

The strength of a family, like the strength of an Army, is in its loyalty to each other.
~ Author Mario Puzo

*****

"Boys, this is our world. Beautiful and terrible things will happen. Don't be afraid."
~ "Pops" Armstrong quote in *Fifth Column*

*****

Remember the Alamo!
~ Texans' battle cry in the fight for independence from Mexico

*****

Texas Free! Texas Strong!
~ Texans everywhere

Part One

CHAPTER 1

January 23, 2023
The Armstrong Ranch
Borden County, Texas

"Boys, this is our world. Beautiful and terrible things will happen. Don't be afraid."

Cooper had barely finished the words when the staccato sound of gunfire followed the bullets that tore through the wood fence rails beside them and stitched the West Texas soil in front of their horses. The startled, involuntary response of their geldings to the unexpected stimulus forced them to simultaneously rear up on their hind legs before darting forward with a burst of energy.

Cooper and Riley, wholly unprepared for an attack, were both thrown to the ground as their horses, whose reflexes were much faster than their human riders', sought to escape the danger. It was this fast-flight response that saved the boys' lives on that fateful evening.

As the guys landed on their backs, cradling their rifles as they fell, the horses bolted toward the guard towers, their hooves racing as fast as they could, acting on pure instinct to flee the gunfire.

The unknown attackers, hidden in the dark surrounds of Armstrong Ranch, didn't hesitate. The rapid fire of their automatic weapons was no match for the fleeing horses, which were both killed instantly.

As quickly as the firing started, it stopped, and the ranch became momentarily silent. Riley Armstrong, eyes wide open, was about to yell toward his brother, but Cooper quickly covered Riley's mouth with his gloved hand.

"Shhh," he whispered. "They think they've killed us. Otherwise they'd be rainin' hellfire on our heads."

Riley nodded his understanding, and Cooper removed his hand. Riley whispered back, "We have to warn everybody."

"Trust me, they've been warned. We need to get to the guard tower so we can get the high ground. Between your huntin' rifle and this AR, we can hold them off until Daddy and Preacher can get everyone to safety."

"Coop, Daddy's probably not back from Austin yet."

Cooper rose onto his knees, pointing his weapon toward the grassy hills surrounding the west side of the ranch. "Preach can handle it. Listen, we've got to get to cover. Let's run behind these mounds that Antonio and the boys built for cover. Stay behind me about twenty yards. Don't get bunched up, got it?"

"Coop, those were machine guns. Do you think it's the commandos?"

"'Fraid so. C'mon."

Cooper ran at a low crouch at first as he moved away from the fence toward the series of mounds and trenches built under Preacher's supervision with the ranch's backhoe. He said silent prayers to himself as the reality set in—he and his brother could die at any moment.

As Cooper reached cover, he glanced over his head and searched for Riley. Although it was a clear, crisp night, the new moon didn't illuminate their movements. He suspected the shooters had fired upon the horses based upon the sound of their hooves digging into the soil.

He searched through the sights of his rifle for any form of movement across the fences marking the western boundary of the ranch. Riley quickly joined him, huffing slightly, as he was out of breath, or possibly overcome with anxiety.

"Are you gonna be okay?" he asked Riley, who was now gasping for air.

Riley nodded. "Yeah, just winded. Coop, I can feel them out there, you know? They're watching us. It's like the walls are closing in on me."

"Bro, we've never been shot at. It's natural to be afraid. I am. But I'm not so danged scared that I'm ready to die. We've gotta make it to the guard tower."

"What about the shooters?"

"They're probably closing on the ranch now, so time's a-wastin'. Twenty yards separation. Don't forget."

Cooper didn't wait for a response, and he began to race across the open field toward the guard tower at the ranch's south gate. As he ran, he was thankful for two things. One, they weren't shooting at him. Secondly, he'd followed Duncan's advice to wear his Reebok sneakers when he wasn't doing ranch work. He suspected his burly brother would be building up quite a set of blisters running in his ropers.

Cooper was out of breath when he reached the base of the guard tower. He hid behind one of the power poles used as a support and fought to regain his normal breathing. Riley still hadn't arrived, so he peered around the post to look for his brother.

Riley's lumbering shadow could be seen in the distance. The physical build of the two brothers was vastly different. Cooper was taller and leaner. His body frame was ideally suited for his former profession as a bull rider. Riley was stockier and had the muscular structure of a Brahma bull. He didn't have an ounce of fat on him, but his shorter legs and heavy muscle build were not suited for three-hundred-yard sprints across an open field with the possibility of bullets chasing him.

Riley finally arrived and collapsed against the front of the post. Cooper quickly grabbed his shirt and pulled him around the back side to provide some cover from the shooters.

"Hey! Are y'all up there?" Cooper yelled in a hushed whisper to the two Slaughter ranch hands who were supposed to be manning the guard tower at this time of the evening. After he didn't receive a response, he tried it again. "Hey! It's me, Cooper. Can you hear me?"

"They ran off, Coop," said Riley in between deep breaths. "I knew they would when the goin' got rough."

"Yeah, me too." Cooper stopped talking as he heard the sounds of two horses racing in their direction from the barns.

Antonio and one of the ranch hands pulled to a stop before quickly dismounting. Antonio approached Cooper. "What happened?"

"They fired upon us. The horses got spooked and ran. The shooters must've thought we were riding away, and they shot in the direction of the sound."

"Where are the guards in the tower?"

"Gone."

"*Cabróne.*" Antonio muttered the Spanish vulgarity, which referred to an adult male goat, loosely translated to mean *bastards*. He looked around and then asked, "Where are your horses?"

"Dead, I think," replied Cooper.

Antonio grimaced. "Take one of ours back to the ranch. I'll round up the families while Pedro takes over tower watch. We'll meet back at the barns."

"What are we gonna do with everybody?" asked Riley.

"The bunker, based on what Preacher was just saying. He wants us to fall back to defend the ranch house."

Cooper helped his brother to his feet. "Okay, hurry."

It was too late. The shooters began firing upon them again. All the guys hit the ground and began to scramble for protection.

"They're comin' at us so fast!" Riley exclaimed as he crawled on his belly to another post. He chambered a round in his hunting rifle and looked through his scope for the source of the gunfire.

"It's coming from down the road near that abandoned well," said Cooper. "I saw the muzzle flash the last go-round."

Antonio turned to his ranch hand and patted him on the shoulder. He pointed upward. "Climb the ladder, and we'll cover you."

As the man ascended the stairs, Antonio turned to Cooper. "How many shooters?" asked Antonio as he glanced upward. His man had reached the protection of the guardhouse.

"Two, I—" started Cooper before more bullets ripped into the heavy-duty support posts.

"They're closer," shouted Riley. He returned fire in the general direction of where the shots had come from. That turned out to be a mistake.

Suddenly, the night erupted in a hail of gunfire coming from at least two positions surrounding the tower. The guys were pinned down, trying their best to blend in with the posts.

Antonio, Cooper, and Riley began to return fire into the darkness while the new guard opened up on the shooters' positions with his AK-47. The structure was designed to provide ballistic protection, but unfortunately, the single tower guard didn't have any backup.

The guys had never been in a gun battle like this one, and they quickly reverted to the Taliban style of shooting at their enemy—stick the rifle around the corner and squeeze the trigger.

"Guys, we don't have the numbers, and we're outgunned," said Cooper. "My extra magazines were on my horse. They could overtake us in a matter of minutes."

The ranch hand fired off another spurt from his weapon, which drew an immediate response from the well-hidden shooters. The bullets tore into the walls of the guardhouse, causing splinters to fall on the guys' heads.

"Take a horse and go. Now!" shouted Antonio.

"What about you?" asked Riley.

"I'll try to hold them off. Get back to the ranch and get our families safe."

Cooper waved to Riley, instructing him to join him at Antonio's horse.

"Cover me!" shouted Antonio to the ranch hand as he slung his rifle over his shoulder and began to climb the ladder.

His man began to shoot in the direction of the abandoned oil wells, prompting dozens of rounds of return fire. He screamed in agony before his body could be heard hitting the floor of the tower.

"Antonio, it's over," shouted Cooper. "We've gotta go."

"I can cover you," Antonio insisted as he continued to climb.

More gunshots filled the air as the bullets imbedded into the posts and ladder where Antonio was climbing. Momentarily, as if in suspended animation, his body fell backwards toward the ground.

Riley raced below him and held out his arms, hoping to break their longtime friend's fall. A second later, Antonio crashed into his arms and knocked them both to the ground.

"He's been hit!" shouted Riley, holding out his bloody arms for Cooper to see.

Cooper dismounted and raced to their side. Antonio's left hand was bleeding. A gaping bullet wound had created a hole in the palm of his hand and through the other side.

Antonio had a red bandana tied around his neck, which Cooper quickly used as a way to slow the bleeding.

"Can you ride?"

"Yeah."

Without another word, the three men scrambled for the horses, who'd remained remarkably calm during the melee. They'd been tied to the fence twenty yards away. Unlike the Armstrongs' horses, which had skipped over the bullets thrown in their direction, these two were unaffected.

Riley helped Antonio onto the back of Cooper's horse, and the trio sped off toward the faint light of the ranch house, hoping they didn't take a bullet in the back.

CHAPTER 2

January 23
The Armstrong Ranch
Borden County, Texas

"Miss Lucy, we don't have a choice," started Preacher as he frantically herded women and children toward the barn constructed over their two buried nuclear bunkers. "There's a war going on over there. At least the boys are keeping the shooters busy while we round up the families."

"Preach, if we get overrun—" Lucy Armstrong began to argue her point when more gunfire could be heard coming from the north gate.

Preacher turned away and hollered at everyone to hurry. The children and their mothers were hunched over, running toward the barn where the underground bunkers were located. He left Lucy standing alone in the yard. She frantically looked around. *Where are my children? Where is my husband?*

Major had still not returned from his unexpected trip to Austin. Earlier that day, a helicopter had arrived at the ranch unannounced. It had been dispatched at the request of Texas President Marion Burnett. Major had been whisked away in the chopper with barely an opportunity to say goodbye. She hadn't heard from him since and only assumed he'd be back soon.

While Lucy needed the comfort and protection he'd always given her, she wasn't sure it would be safe for him to arrive in the middle of an attack, or whatever this was.

Two horses galloped in her direction from the east. She immediately saw the white mare that Sook rode and assumed it was her daughter racing alongside.

"Momma! Momma! Are you okay?" Palmer shouted as they sped into the opening between the ranch house and the barn. She pulled back on the reins of her horse, bringing him to an abrupt stop.

"I'm fine, but I don't know where your brothers are," replied Lucy as she held the reins of Sook's horse, enabling her to dismount quickly.

"What can we do?" asked Sook.

"Sook, we've heard lots of gunfire coming from the area of the guard tower," began Lucy. "Palmer, your brothers were riding the western fence tonight."

Palmer quickly spun around and moved toward her horse. "I'll go get them."

Lucy reached for her daughter's arm and stopped her. "No, Palmer, you can't. That wasn't sporadic gunfire. It sounded like a war movie."

"We've gotta get them, Momma," she pleaded.

"No, we need to take cover. You and Sook need to get into the bunker for protection. The guys can take care of themselves, and Preacher's men will defend the ranch."

Sook looked at Palmer and shook her head. "I will fight."

"Me too, Momma. This is our home. I will not hide in the bunker while they steal our stuff and burn it down like they did to the Slaughters' old place."

Lucy stood firm. "Honey, the Slaughters lost their place, but at least they're alive. If these are the North Korean commandos Duncan and Sook warned us about, then we're no match for them. You've got to get inside. Please."

Palmer stood a little taller. "What are you gonna do?"

"Well, I'm gonna stay outside and wait for the boys and your father," replied Lucy.

Palmer glanced at Sook as if to confirm she was speaking for both of them. Then she bowed up. "Momma, so will we."

"Dang it, young lady. You're so stubborn."

"Helpful," Palmer shot back.

Sook stepped forward and gently put her hand on Lucy's

shoulder. In a soft, calming voice, she said with a chuckle, "She is just like her mother."

Lucy touched her future daughter-in-law's hand and returned a comforting smile. "Do you always tell the truth?"

Sook smiled and replied, "Only to my family and God. Otherwise, one never knows."

"Okay, Momma?" asked Palmer before adding, "Sook and I will cover the area around the barns while everyone gets settled. When the boys get back, the four of us will defend the house, along with you and Preach."

"I'm sure your Daddy will be along soon," added Lucy.

"Have you tried to raise Duncan on the radio he gave us?" asked Palmer.

"Your father took it with him. I don't have a way to contact either one of them."

"Good grief, Momma. We can't contact Duncan for help?"

"Honey, we're on our own. We've got to defend the ranch ourselves."

Their conversation was interrupted by the sound of horses coming between the barns toward them.

"*¡Arriba, arriba! ¡Ándale, ándale!*" shouted Preacher as the last of the ranch families arrived at the barn. He frantically waved for them to enter. Then he shouted to the women, "I hear horses! Be ready!"

Palmer and Sook raced toward the two horse pens, which provided a chute into the barn area. Any riders approaching the house from the west would have to travel between the fences around the pen. Lucy ran to Preacher's side with her pistol drawn.

Riley led the way and hollered as he approached, "It's me and Coop. Don't shoot. We need help! Antonio's been shot."

They pulled the horses to a stop, and Preacher helped his number one man off the horse. They slowly walked toward the barn, where a lantern provided enough light to see the damage.

Lucy pulled the bandana off his hand and examined his gunshot wound. "He'll live. The bullet went through and through, but we need to patch up his hand to stop the bleeding. Let me get him in the house, and Sook can assist."

"Momma, there's no time," interrupted Cooper. "The Slaughters' men ran off, and one of the hands was killed taking their place in the tower. You and Antonio need to get in the bunker. Fix him up down there."

"I'll be fine," protested Antonio. "Wrap it up again and give me a rifle." He attempted to walk away, and then his knees buckled.

"He's lost too much blood," said Preacher, who turned to Antonio. "Besides, he can be useful down there with the families. Please, my friend. Find Maria and take care of your wound. You know how to keep everyone calm and also how to operate everything. We'll hold them off until help arrives."

Reluctantly, Antonio nodded and made his way to the hatch. He held his bloodied hand inside his jacket to obscure it from the children.

"Is that everybody?" asked Lucy.

"Yes, except for our ranch hands who were on patrol at the barnyard."

Lucy moved forward to help Preacher cover the hatch with straw and hay. She turned to Riley. "Son, please fire up the bunker generator so we can get the air flowing. The lights and electrical are working off the batteries charged by the solar array."

"Okay."

As Riley departed for the side of the ranch house to start the generator, Lucy turned to Cooper. "Coop, is he okay? He seems pretty shaken."

Cooper removed his hat and wiped the sweat off his brow. "Y'all, the first shots ripped the dirt up right in front of us. The horses threw us both and took off. Seconds later, another round of bullets killed them both. If we hadn't been thrown, um, well, we'd be goners."

Lucy rushed to Cooper's side and hugged him. She couldn't hold back the tears as she considered the thought of losing a member of her family. Preacher's hand on her shoulder reminded her that they had to get ready.

"Miss Lucy," he began, "we really have to—"

Gunfire tore into the barn behind them. Palmer shrieked, and everyone ducked for cover.

"They're coming!" said Preacher. "Everyone, listen up. We need to spread out. Palmer and Sook, I need you to cover the south side past the water well and the storage shed. Coop, I've got two men watching the southwest over by the silos. Find them and send one of the guys back here."

"I'm on it," said Cooper. He joined Palmer and Sook as they raced to their posts.

"Riley, I need you to bring your truck to the back of the ranch house," began Preacher. He then turned to Lucy. "We have to assume that help isn't coming. I need you and Riley to put as many weapons and cans of ammo into Red Rover as it will hold. We have to be prepared to abandon the ranch."

Lucy protested. "No way, Preach! This is our home. We can do this! Plus, Major and Duncan will be here to help."

Preacher grabbed her by both shoulders. "We don't know that for certain, Lucy. We have to consider a plan B in case something goes wrong. Please, we don't have much time."

Lucy scowled and then relented. She hustled to the house and was inside the front door as the next rounds of gunfire erupted. Once inside, she took a deep breath and looked around the home, which had been in the Armstrong family since the 1800s.

"I will not let them take you away from our family!"

CHAPTER 3

January 23
The Armstrong Ranch
Borden County, Texas

Manuel Holloway was furious with himself for not procuring any form of night-vision device to assist in his assault on the ranch. Instead, he relied upon his commandos' superior training to sneak up on the ranchers, using the element of surprise to kill them one at a time if necessary. Unfortunately, one of the trigger-happy members of his team had taken it upon himself to fire upon the two riders along the fence row.

Based upon the lack of return fire, he assumed they were either killed in the initial volley or later when the horses were gunned down. When he was in the service, he'd had the best weapons of war the United States had to offer, including superior communications gear and night vision. Out here, in this deserted part of West Texas, they had to fight without the benefit of advanced gear, but so did their targets at the ranch.

He'd ordered his men to advance, and he learned they'd had some success at the guard tower, killing one and apparently wounding another. All of his teams had crossed the ranch's border fencing and were advancing in the faint glow of light emanating from the area where the ranch house and two barns stood.

This ranch was his prize. It was going to be a place for Holloway and his gang to hang their hats while they terrorized West Texas for years to come. He knew the long-term impact of a grid-down scenario. All of North America would struggle to survive and later rebuild. Those who died would leave behind items of value that

Holloway would use to set up his future.

By the time the dust settled and ninety percent of the population disappeared, *ashes to ashes*, as they say, he'd be settled in, secured, and hopefully rich.

There was a second incentive for him to take this particular ranch. He firmly believed that the soldier boy who'd been a pain in his neck since Winslow, Arizona, was connected to this place somehow. With a little luck, Holloway would get his revenge on the man tonight. At the very least, he'd pile the bodies in a heap out by the pigsty for soldier boy to find later.

Holloway studied the area through the monocular, using his only eye to determine what type of activity was occurring around the house. At first, the ranch house was lit up like a Christmas tree. The occupants clearly didn't understand the concept of light discipline. They never imagined being attacked.

Kudos to them, he thought to himself as the premature shooting by his men drew reactions from the ranchers. Within seconds after the gunfire, the lights were doused except for the faint glow of a lantern in the barn nearest to him.

Based upon his surveillance, he suspected the ranch house and the barns were surrounded by a dozen men or less. That was assuming, of course, they didn't put rifles in the hands of women and children. He doubted that was the case, as the Texans would be too proud to enlist the weak to defend against the strong. No, these cowboys were too arrogant for that.

That said, he thought to himself, they obviously had no intention of giving up the ranch. Holloway leaned back against the Ford truck that had been his ride for the last couple of weeks. He considered his options.

Holloway could allow his men to continue their advance under cover of darkness, but they were in the open and in unfamiliar territory. The ranchers, now that the element of surprise had been lost, would be dug into defensive positions. They'd be prepared in anticipation of an attack.

His men were trained killers and most likely possessed superior firepower. However, they were also the visitors on this field of play, and the home team had a lot to live for.

Once again, he observed the buildings through the monocular. There was no activity except the swinging lantern in the nearest barn. It was time to break their spirit and end this thing.

"Bring me the last RPG!" he shouted to one of his men. "I'm not a patient man, and I don't intend to be sitting out here in case they've called for the cavalry."

His best rocket-propelled grenade gunner arrived at his side.

Holloway handed him the monocular. "Can you find the barn? Look for a barely visible light."

The commando took the monocular and placed it over his eye socket. He quickly pulled it down and wiped the moisture onto his shirt. Holloway was prone to sweating profusely regardless of the outside temperature.

"I see it," he replied. "This is my target?"

"Yes, but nothing else. The barn and its contents are expendable. We have an extra barn, and from what I can tell, those hiding inside won't really do us any good."

"Yes, sir," the gunner replied nonchalantly as he affixed Holloway's last grenade to the launcher and looked through the sights to identify the target. After a tense moment, he announced, "I've got the target in my sights."

"Well, let her fly!"

CHAPTER 4

January 23
The Armstrong Ranch
Borden County, Texas

Lucy noticed the sudden silence of the gunfire while Riley finished packing Red Rover. Her curiosity overcame her, so she walked through the house toward the front porch. The high-pitched whistling sound was unlike anything she'd heard before. It was eerie and ominous at the same time.

The ripping and crunching sound of the rocket-propelled grenade crashing into their barn, coupled with the intense bright light and heat, momentarily mesmerized Lucy. She was frozen on the front porch for a brief second before the gust of energy, air, and debris knocked her backwards and into the foyer.

Her ears were ringing when suddenly she found Preacher hovering over her. She tried to lift her arm, and the pain seared through her, bringing her back to the present. She knew he was talking to her, but she couldn't hear, nor comprehend, what he was saying.

Lucy glanced over to her left arm, which was on fire. Her eyes widened, unable to grasp what had happened to her. Preacher was swatting at her arm with his jacket in a desperate attempt to douse the flame. The wound she suffered turned out to be superficial first-degree burns, but they scarred her to her core.

She looked to her right arm at a piece of wood sticking out of her forearm. The barn-red paint color mixed with her blood to a near perfect match. Her senses began to return, and then she understood what was stuck in her body—part of the barn.

Lucy found her voice and screamed in pain.

Riley was by her side now, and he touched her face. His hands comforted her, but his wiping the smoke and soot from her cheeks didn't take away the searing pains in both of her arms.

She just wanted to sleep.

Maybe I'll take a little nap, and when I wake up, this terrible nightmare will be over. Maybe I'll mosey up to the barnyard and gather some eggs. Yep, that's just what I'll do.

Lucy's eyes grew heavy, and then she drifted away.

*****

"Momma, wake up! Wake up!" begged Riley as tears streamed down his face. He was wiping her face, trying to stir his mother awake.

Gunfire erupted again, forcing him to listen to Preacher's instructions, which had fallen on his deaf ears. His entire focus had been on his mother.

Finally, Preacher shook Riley back into the moment. "Riley! You have to get her to safety. Boy, can you hear me?"

"But-but," Riley stammered. Then he recovered. "Yeah. Okay. What should I do?"

"Riley, take her to the east woods, down where you guys hunt hogs."

"In the truck?" Riley still wasn't thinking clearly.

Preacher took a deep breath and forced himself to remain calm. They had only a short time to survive or die at the hands of the North Koreans. "Yes. Take her to the truck. I'll fetch her medical bags and meet you there. Drive Red Rover down the ravine to the woods and take care of her wounds."

"But, but, um, I don't—"

"Riley, just stop the bleeding and make her comfortable. I'm gonna find Palmer and Sook. They'll be right behind you, okay?'

Riley looked through his teary eyes and nodded. He stooped over his mother and easily scooped up her limp body in his arms. While he carried her outside to the rear of the ranch house, Preacher grabbed a couple of gallon jugs of water and Lucy's medical bags, including the one she'd created especially for trauma injuries.

Within minutes, Riley was on his way, and Preacher raced back toward the destroyed barn.

He had been watching the north driveway when he heard the incoming RPG. He'd never been to war, but he'd seen enough war movies to know what the sound probably meant. Instinctively, he'd leapt between two large rolls of hay and covered his head. The explosion had been deafening.

After it hit, he immediately exited the barn and saw the devastation. The RPG had struck the horse pen in front of the other barn, which housed the underground bunker. The impact leveled the barn, caught it on fire, and sent burning debris in all directions. When he saw parts of the barn on the front porch lying in flames, he immediately ran to the house. His concern was for Lucy and Riley at that point because he assumed the ranch families in the bunker had perished.

Now, he had to go see. Preacher covered his face with his arm and ran toward the structure, which was fully engulfed in flames. As he approached, Palmer and Sook came from his left, riding at breakneck speed toward the house. He stopped and ran toward them.

"Preacher!" shouted Palmer. "Oh my God!"

Preacher ran to meet them, and he held his hands high in the air to prevent the girls from getting closer. Palmer was about to dismount when he stopped her.

"There's no time to get off. Listen to me, please, and do as I say, quickly."

To reiterate the sense of urgency, more gunfire was exchanged between the commandos and the guys firing back from the silos.

Preacher continued. "Go to the other barn and take two of the horses that are tied to the posts. They're already saddled up from earlier. Please be careful. They'll be agitated."

"Okay, Preacher. But where's Momma and Riley?"

Preacher was about to answer the question truthfully but caught himself. He needed Palmer to remain calm. He'd already assessed Sook and was impressed with her stony demeanor in the face of danger. Palmer was more emotional out of concern for her mother. He chose to tell a half-truth to prevent an accidental injury from exacerbating the situation.

"They took Red Rover to the east woods. You know, where you guys go huntin'. Do you know where they would go?"

Palmer nodded, as did Sook. Both had kept their adventure in the east woods a secret from the others.

"Okay, go, and be careful. I'm gonna round up Cooper and see if it's possible to help the folks underground."

This caused Palmer to turn her horse toward the barn. She took in the scene and covered her mouth. Tears began to flow from her eyes. "Oh. God, no!"

Preacher grew concerned as the gunfire stopped once again. This probably meant the commandos were advancing. "Palmer, please. You've got to go now!"

The girls reacted and dug their heels into the horses' sides. They took off for the barn that was miraculously still standing, as it had for many decades.

Preacher once again turned his attention to the destroyed barn. The fire had subsided somewhat, which enabled him to get closer. Through the crackling of burning timber, he heard horses racing in his direction. It was Cooper and one of his ranch hands.

Cooper pointed in Preacher's direction to acknowledge his presence, but the guys raced past him toward the house, where they could safely tie off their horses. Preacher ran toward them, meeting them halfway in the middle of the yard.

"Dang it, Preach! They're gonna get buried alive under there!" exclaimed Cooper.

Preacher looked back toward the barn and saw that it was beginning to shift towards his left. "It's gonna collapse!"

Slowly at first, and then succumbing to the weight of the burning roof structure, the barn built to conceal their underground bunker gave up. It toppled over in a mass of shooting sparks and flames rising high into the air.

"What do we do?" Cooper shouted as he walked closer to the

burning pile of debris. He shielded his face from the heat to get a better look.

Preacher joined his side, and the two inched closer. More gunfire erupted from the north side of the ranch, reminding them that they were standing out in the open and vulnerable.

"Boys, come with me!" shouted Preacher as he darted toward the other barn. His ranch hand and Cooper quickly followed.

"We've gotta do something to help them!" yelled the ranch hand, who turned his attention back to the flames. "They'll die in there!"

Cooper grabbed him around the shoulders and led him back toward Preacher and the other horses, which were nervously pacing in their stalls.

"Boys, listen up." Preacher began to issue his instructions. "Saddle up two of the horses, and then let the others go. Shoo them out of the barn in case the fire spreads."

"Okay. What do we do with the saddled horses?" Cooper asked as he grabbed a saddle off the rack and handed it to his helper.

Preacher walked over to his horse and pulled out his rifle. After the two horses were saddled, he tapped his ranch hand on the shoulder. "Take my horse around back and tie it off to a post. Then come back here. Hurry!"

The young man untied Preacher's horse. He mounted the stallion and took off.

Preacher then addressed Cooper. "Can you handle leading these two horses down the ravine?"

"Yeah, sure. But—"

Preacher held up his hand to cut Cooper off. "Coop, we can't hold out much longer. They'll be coming for us now, so we've got to go."

"Are you saying we've gotta give up the ranch? And what about those people in the bunker? They'll die."

"Listen, Coop. Even without power and a source of fresh oxygen, they can survive in there for up to twenty-four hours. As for the ranch, we're not giving it up—permanently."

"Whadya mean?"

"Coop, we're gonna live to fight another day. We're gonna save ourselves and figure out what to do next. But if we take a last stand, we're both gonna die."

Preacher buckled his knees slightly and looked directly into Cooper's eyes. "Do you understand what I'm saying? This battle is lost. But tomorrow is a new day."

"Okay. Okay. Where do we go?"

Preacher patted him on the shoulders and smiled. They walked briskly, leading the two horses into the front yard, and approached the house.

"Coop, take these two horses and lead them down the trail. I've sent everyone to the woods. Join up with them, establish a secured perimeter, and take care of them. You're in charge, Coop. Can you handle it?"

"Yessir," Cooper replied respectfully. "But why aren't you coming?"

"I'm gonna hold them off and give you time to get a clean getaway. I don't want them to see you leading the horses away."

"But let me—"

"Nope, scoot. We're out of time. Go!"

Cooper spontaneously hugged Preacher before he took the reins of the horses, which were saddled and ready to go.

Only Cooper's horse remained. "Preach, the kid took off. You're alone. Maybe I should—"

"No, Coop. I got this. Now git!"

Preacher followed him to the front of the house and held the reins as Cooper mounted his ride.

Cooper tipped his hat, and Preacher did the same. As Cooper pulled on the reins to leave, Preacher shouted after him, "Texas strong!"

Cooper nodded his head upward in agreement. "Texas strong!"

CHAPTER 5

January 23
The Armstrong Ranch
Borden County, Texas

Cooper had only been gone a minute, leaving Preacher standing alone on the front porch of the ranch house. With the ranch hand taking off after leading Preacher's horse to the rear of the house, Preacher knew he was on his own. The Armstrong Ranch had been his home since his fall from grace as the minister to a small congregation. When Major and Lucy had taken him in, with no questions asked about his past, he'd rewarded them with a loyalty that only a member of the family could bestow. He'd dedicated his life to the operation of the Armstrong Ranch, and now, as he stared at the scene before him, the place he called home was partially in flames. It was under attack by an unseen enemy from a foreign land. And he was the last man standing.

He allowed himself too long to reminisce about his life as a former preacher and now the man who ran the Armstrong Ranch. The bullets that ripped into the railing and post next to him were a reminder of the task at hand. He ducked for cover and scrambled inside.

He swept the still-smoldering debris out of the way and closed the door. There were no locks to lock. This was the Armstrong Ranch, and it hadn't needed to be locked up since it was built—until now.

He leaned against the thick walls built of oak and mortar mix. The windows had been shattered and forced inside from the RPG blast. As more bullets hit the front façade of the ranch house, Preacher knew the commandos were closing in.

They were firing at the house in short bursts of five or six rounds each. They had no apparent target. The shots were meant to intimidate and induce surrender. Preacher would not surrender. He'd likely be tortured and killed anyway. His adversaries were animals—not human.

His mind raced. *How can I distract them and keep them focused on me?*

If he used the upstairs windows overlooking the barn and the front yard, he'd have the high ground, but if they penetrated the downstairs, his means of escape would be cut off. He thought about the drop from the roof of the kitchen. The expansion of the kitchen years ago had included a lean-to tin roof to cover firewood from moisture.

That's it! Preacher bolted for the stairwell and took the steps two at a time. The gunfire ceased, allowing him to steady his nerves. First, he glanced out the window at the end of the hallway, which overlooked the front porch roof. He didn't see any movement and noticed the fire was dying down somewhat. *Fire fueled by dry hay burns fast*, he thought to himself. He was glad he'd made a habit of storing chemicals and fuel in a separate block building a hundred feet away.

He then confirmed his memory by glancing into the bedroom located above the original kitchen. He could slip through the window and then slide off the tin roof to the ground. The eight-foot drop would not be painful.

Preacher removed the magazine from his AR-15 and checked the ammunition. He'd spent about half of this thirty-round magazine. He had two more. Duncan had taught him a method to keep up with his ammo count. As Preacher loaded his magazines, he inserted three tracer rounds first. During a battle, Duncan suggested, you'd know when your mag was about to empty. This helped the shooter mentally prepare to change magazines quickly and efficiently.

He slammed the half-spent magazine back into the AR-15's receiver and pulled the charging handle. He was ready. He made his way back to the front window and peeked around the corner. He waited for the commandos to advance upon the house. With a little luck, they'd assume that everyone had run off, abandoning the house to them. He could pick off a few of them before he hauled his cookies away too.

He waited. There was no movement. He ran to the master bedroom and peered through the curtains to look for an assault from the rear. The surroundings appeared to be still.

Then he heard the sound of crunching glass coming from downstairs. *How did they slip past me? Crafty devils!*

Preacher was fully aware of the creaking sounds the ranch house made. He didn't want to give away his position, but he needed to be prepared to shoot anyone who came up the stairs. Walking slowly, heel-to-toe, he moved along the hallway toward the front of the house. He pointed his gun over the railing as he went, prepared to fire upon the first sign of movement.

He heard hushed voices in a language that sure as heck wasn't Texan. *Dang*, he thought to himself, *I hate it when I'm right.*

Then he saw one of them. A man, dressed in camouflaged clothing, moved through Preacher's field of vision and into the kitchen. Another began to climb the stairs. Preacher slowly slipped backwards to get a better shot at the stair-climber and the man in the kitchen, who'd most likely appear after hearing the sound of the gunfire.

He slipped his finger on the trigger and exhaled. He thought of Cooper as he readied himself to ride a two-thousand-pound bull into the ring. Coop's muscles would tense. He'd get that look of determination on his face. When he was ready, he'd say, "Here we go, boys!"

I'm ready!

Preacher calmly fired two rounds into the commando's head, splaying blood and brain matter all over the decades-old wallpaper installed by Miss Lucy the week she'd moved in after marrying Major.

As predicted, the shooter who'd entered the kitchen rushed out to assist his comrade. His loyalty earned him two bullets to the chest, killing him instantly.

Preacher didn't hesitate. He rushed to the front window and opened fire upon the men who were racing toward the house. He missed wildly at first, but then finally found his mark as the tracer bullets emerged from the magazine. One of the four men in the front yard was knocked to the ground.

Preacher dropped the magazine, and it hit the floor with a thud. His nervous hands momentarily failed him as he fumbled with the replacement. Not having sufficient practice swapping magazines took precious seconds away, and it allowed the attacking commandos to gain the upper hand.

Bullets tore through the open window and ripped into the plaster ceiling. Preacher finally inserted the second magazine and was preparing to shoot back when more gunfire splintered the window frame, causing debris to pepper his face. He wiped away the splinters, which had embedded in his skin, and stuck his rifle around the window frame to fire back. This caused the commandos to back down, or so he thought.

The crunching of the glass gave away their position downstairs. Preacher moved to the top of the stairs and trained his rifle on the first step. One of the men started to turn the corner, and Preacher fired prematurely. Had he waited a split second longer, he could've had a bigger target. Instead, his four-round burst only managed to knock the rifle out of the shooter's hands.

Then the unexpected happened. Gunfire erupted once again, and this time the bullets were ripping through the floor beneath his feet. Powerful NATO 7.62 rounds were erupting out of an AR-10, turning the wood floor into kindling.

One bullet went through the flooring and embedded in his left foot. The impact startled Preacher, who recoiled and attempted to flee for cover. As he lost his focus, the trained commandos sensed an opening.

Screaming something in Korean that Preacher couldn't understand, one of the men bolted up the stairs and fired at him, striking him in the right arm and shoulder. He got knocked backwards into the wall but reflexively managed a shot at his attacker.

The bullet found the attacker's knee, which caused him to fall and roll back down the stairs. Preacher had an opening to escape.

He hobbled toward the bedroom window, allowing one leg to carry the bulk of his weight. His right arm was incapable of carrying weight, so he abandoned his rifle to give him more mobility as he climbed through the window. He'd almost cleared the window opening when he heard shouting and the heavy footsteps of men racing up the stairs.

Preacher had to hurry. They'd follow the blood trail. He tried to make his way down the tin roof, but he slipped on his own blood, causing him to crash to the roof and roll off to the hard ground below.

Landing on his right shoulder, the excruciating pain shot through his body, causing his eyes to roll into the back of his head. But Preacher didn't give up. He wasn't going to die here. He clawed his way to his horse and lifted himself up using the post where the reins were tied off.

"I can do this," Preacher mumbled, encouraging himself to survive. He untied his horse and took a deep breath. He tried to put weight on his left foot, and it caused him to spontaneously scream in pain.

"*I bangbeob! I bangbeob!*" shouted one of the North Koreans.

Preacher didn't have to understand the language to know that his escape route had been discovered. With a renewed sense of urgency and will to live, Preacher inserted his right foot in the stirrup and used his left arm to pull himself onto his horse. He allowed himself a slight chuckle as he thanked God for not getting him shot with the wrong combination of arms and legs to mount his horse.

"Hah!" Preacher encouraged his horse forward with exuberance and a squeeze of his legs. His beloved stallion, a high-spirited horse, immediately responded, and they were off.

Preacher managed a prayer in those brief seconds as he raced away from the carnage.

Heavenly Father, thank you for Your protection. Please deliver me to your Rock of safety.

At that moment, more bullets were delivered to the body of Preacher Caleb O'Malley, striking him in the back as his horse galloped into the darkness.

CHAPTER 6

January 23
The East Woods
The Armstrong Ranch
Borden County, Texas

After a rough ride down the ravine, Riley found a suitable hiding spot for Red Rover that he knew his siblings could find as well. The east woods bordering the Armstrong Ranch had been a favorite place for the three rodeo kids to play together before their lives became immersed in the rodeo lifestyle. They'd hunt and fish, in addition to playing hide-and-seek, in those early formative years. Their constant companionship resulted in a bond between the three that didn't include their older brothers, Dallas and Duncan.

They all knew the woods well, and Riley was certain they'd find this clearing in the middle, where they'd built numerous forts as kids. Using leftover lumber from projects that had been built around the ranch, Riley, Palmer, and Cooper would build elaborate structures in the oak trees and on the ground below.

They'd spend a day fishing and then cook on an open fire. Palmer was a dead-eye hunter with her .22-caliber rifle. She'd shoot squirrels, rabbits, and other small game. Riley and Cooper became adept at skinning the animals and preparing them for their campfire. It was a routine the kids learned from playing, but it was a useful survival skill they could employ now that they'd grown up.

"Someone's comin', Momma," started Riley, as he could hear the horses descending the trail toward their camp. He quickly jumped to his feet, grabbed his rifle, and positioned himself to fire upon anyone that wasn't his family.

Their camp was enveloped in darkness, as the tree canopy blocked out any ambient light that emanated from the sky. Riley craned his neck over the fallen tree he used as cover and stared up the trail, hoping to catch a glimpse of movement. The slow approach of the riders gave him some comfort. He doubted the commandos would ease up to their camp on horseback.

"Four horses but only two riders," mumbled Riley to himself as they got closer. He decided to take a chance, but with his rifle ready. "Who's there?"

Palmer cautiously replied, "Riley, is that you? It's me and Sook."

"Yeah, come into the clearing," he said as he emerged from behind the tree to show himself on the trail. "Momma needs y'all's help."

Palmer, leading the way, entered the clearing first. "What's wrong with Momma?"

"She got hit with debris from the blast," replied Riley. "I've stopped the bleeding on one arm, but she made me wait until y'all arrived to pull the barn board out of her other arm."

"What?" asked Palmer as she quickly got off her horse. "Where is she?"

"I've got her over here inside the sleeping bag to keep her warm." Riley led Palmer to an area he'd cleared when they arrived. He'd created a two-inch layer of pine needles on the ground to add insulation between the cold surface and the sleeping bag. Lucy was wrapped up in the one-person sleeping bag like a burrito.

Palmer rushed to her mother's side and fell to her knees. She began to well up in tears. "Momma, are you okay?"

Lucy was weak, but she managed a response. "Yes, honey. I'll be fine. But I'm glad you're here. Sook too?"

"Yes, Miss Lucy. I am here too." Sook felt Lucy's forehead.

"Fever?" asked Palmer.

"Not yet," replied Sook. She turned her attention back to Lucy. "We need to see your wounds."

Lucy provided an imperceptible nod, causing Palmer and Sook to give each other a concerned look. Palmer slowly unzipped the sleeping bag, allowing the cool night air to surround Lucy's body slowly. Once her arm was exposed, they asked for a flashlight.

Riley provided a battery-operated lantern, which had several levels of light settings. "I'm gonna stand watch, okay. If you need me, I'll be at the entrance to the woods."

"Thank you, son," whispered Lucy. She looked at Palmer. "He's a good boy, but he doesn't need to tackle this arm. You girls will know what to do."

Palmer turned to Sook. "The bleeding has stopped, but see the redness around the wound? Soon, it will become infected."

Lucy raised her other arm to get their attention. "My medical bag is next to that tree stump."

Sook jumped up and retrieved the trauma kit that Lucy had built years ago but never had an occasion to use. She began pulling out certain essentials like gauze dressing, medical tape, and Betadine to cleanse and disinfect the wound.

"Girls, you have to get the entire piece of wood out of my arm." Lucy managed the strength to give Palmer and Sook instructions. "Sook, you do it. Palmer will be too emotional out of fear that she is hurting me. This needs to be removed quickly. Don't worry about my pain. Palmer, you be prepared to flush the wound with the bottled water over there."

Sook searched through the bag and laid out the tools she'd need. After locating three sizes of tweezers to extract various parts of the splintered barn board, she searched through the outside pockets of the bag.

"What are you looking for?" asked Palmer.

"Needles and sutures."

"Keep looking in the side pockets," interjected Lucy.

Seconds later, Sook was satisfied she had everything necessary to proceed.

"I know what to do, Miss Lucy," said Sook as she leaned over Lucy's face. She handed Palmer a large bulb syringe and another syringe-looking device out of the bag. "Palmer, I will need you to keep the wound clear so I can see, okay?"

Palmer held up the larger device. "It looks like a turkey baster."

"It is, honey," said Lucy. "It's perfect for larger wounds like this one."

Sook leaned over Lucy and whispered, "I am sorry if I hurt you. It has been a long time since I practiced on the pigs at home."

Lucy managed a smile and a chuckle before grimacing in pain. "I guess I'm stuck like a pig already. Can't get any worse. You'll do fine."

After they donned sterile gloves, Palmer and Sook worked together to extract the board from Lucy's arm. Lucy, to her credit, remained calm during the process. She groaned a little here and there, but otherwise she was a real trooper.

Sook put on a single-light headlamp, which had been packed in the medical kit. This helped illuminate the wound and allowed her to remove all the splinters she could find.

"I am also worried about these paint flakes in her body. Palmer, I will continue to flush the wound while you suction. Okay?"

For the next several minutes, they continued to wash out the wound until Sook was satisfied.

"Miss Lucy, I will use the size four suture thread with the thin, curved needle. Your skin is much softer than the pigs'."

Lucy, who had a few tears streaming from her eyes, smiled at Sook and Palmer. "Nicest compliment I've received all day."

"Yes. Miss Lucy, this will hurt worse than the removal of the board. I am sorry."

"Go ahead, my angel," said Lucy as she closed her eyes and prepared herself for the suturing process.

With the wound cleared of debris and the bleeding stopped, Sook set about the process of suturing. First, she wiped Lucy's skin around the open wound with antiseptic wipes. Then she knelt next to Lucy so that the wound was parallel to Sook's body.

She threaded the needle with the suture thread and began the process from the middle of the laceration outward. Leaving one-eighth of an inch between each stitch, Sook methodically sewed up Lucy's arm and used basic suture knots to ensure their stability.

Finally, she used triple-antibiotic ointment to dress the wound and wrapped bandages into place with medical tape to protect it.

When she was finished, Sook leaned back on her heels and removed the sterile gloves. She nodded to Palmer and pointed to the zipper on the sleeping bag. Palmer took her cue and immediately zipped it closed.

"Thank you, Sook," said a teary-eyed Palmer. She bent over to look into her mother's face and immediately grew concerned.

"Momma! Momma!"

CHAPTER 7

January 23
The East Woods
The Armstrong Ranch
Borden County, Texas

Lucy slowly opened her eyes and looked at Palmer. "Sorry, I was just resting my eyes."

Palmer wiped away her tears and then burst into laughter. "Don't scare me like that, Momma!"

Sook, puzzled by the reaction, studied them both and then began to laugh as well.

Palmer explained the inside joke. "Sook, after Daddy retired, we bought him a leather recliner for the family room. He called it his retirement chair, but really it became like a second bedroom. We would be watching a TV show and notice that Daddy had fallen asleep. Sometimes he would jolt himself awake and look around. He'd always say *I was just resting my eyes.*"

Lucy managed a smile. "Your daddy was always up well before dawn to tend to the ranch. He'd tell me to sleep in, but I felt obligated to at least make him coffee and a little something to eat. Because he worked hard, he deserved to go to sleep at nine o'clock every night, but he tried to stay up with the rest of us."

"Hey, look who I found!" Riley announced his presence into the clearing with Cooper.

Palmer leapt up from her crouch and ran to give him a hug. She examined him for injuries, much like her mother would have done if she could.

After their hug, Riley stood aside so Cooper could see his mother. He knelt down next to Sook and gave her a hug with his left arm, followed by a thankful smile.

"Hey, Momma. Riley told me what happened. How're you feelin'?"

Lucy, who was mummified in the sleeping bag, couldn't move, but her smile spoke volumes. "I'll be fine, Coop. I have a couple of damaged wings, but they'll heal with the help of these young ladies."

Cooper touched her cheek with the back of his fingers. It was a simple gesture, but one that caused the waterworks to open up on Palmer and Sook.

He choked back the tears and tried to be reassuring. "It's gonna be okay, Momma."

"Son, where's Preacher?" Lucy asked.

"He stayed to stall them. I had to lead two horses down here, and he wanted me to have a good head start. I'm sure he'll be along shortly."

Riley had been pacing around the clearing, listening to the conversation. He needed to get back to watching the trail, but he was clearly agitated. "Y'all, I ain't givin' up the ranch. I think we need to talk about fightin' back."

Cooper touched his mother's face one more time and stood to address his brother. "Preacher's last words to me were *live to fight another day*. It makes sense, and we need to regroup before we go charging back up that hill."

"I think the longer we let them stay in our home, the harder it'll be to get 'em out," Riley shot back.

"What about the families in the bunker?" asked Palmer. "They're gonna be buried alive under the barn."

Cooper circled around and held his hands out, urging calm. "Please, everyone. It would be suicide for three or four of us to go back up there now. We need to take care of Momma and wait for Preacher to return. Plus, Daddy should be arriving back at the ranch at any time. We don't want to do anything that might jeopardize him."

Lucy spoke up. "If I remember correctly, the bunker will provide enough oxygen for up to twenty-four hours."

"That's what Preacher said," interjected Cooper. "There are a lot of people inside, and I don't think we should risk waiting that long if we hope to save them. With no generator forcing air inside, they'll use it up quickly."

Riley was unconvinced. He stomped around the campsite, kicking at defenseless pinecones. "So I reckon we'll just sit around the fire and roast marshmallows. I mean, sure, let them get comfy and cozy in my dang bed."

"Young man," said Lucy sternly, "that's enough. Preacher was right and so is your brother. This thing has just started. Let's get our heads on straight and wait for the right time."

Dejected, Riley hung his head after the rebuke. "Okay, Momma. I'm gonna go watch the trail."

As Riley walked into the dark woods, Lucy looked to Palmer. "Honey, go with your brother. You have the ability to calm him down better than any of us. You know how he gets. We're gonna need his head in the fight. Okay?"

"Yes, ma'am." Palmer leaned over her mother and kissed her on the cheek. She grabbed one of the rifles out of the back of Red Rover and jogged after Riley.

Lucy summoned Cooper by her side. "I need you to take charge, son, until your daddy returns. For years, he and Preacher rode around the ranch envisioning scenarios like this one. He'll know what to do."

She turned her attention to Sook and smiled. "Plus, we have Duncan home, who is an expert, and from what I've seen, Sook can hold her own too. We can do this, but everybody has to be pullin' in the same direction. Right?"

"I understand, Momma. I'll give Riley his space. Why don't you try to get some sleep? Sook, would you mind sitting with her while I get all the weapons ready and magazines loaded with ammo?"

"Yes, Coop. She is my best patient."

Lucy and Cooper chuckled at her response as he made his way to the back of Red Rover. With Sook watching over Lucy, the matriarch of the Armstrong family felt secure and comfortable enough to *rest her eyes* for a while.

CHAPTER 8

January 23
The East Woods
The Armstrong Ranch
Borden County, Texas

"It's been too long, sis," said Riley as he continued to fidget on the sandstone rock he'd been sitting on for nearly an hour. Full of nervous energy, he'd alternated between checking on his mother, walking up the trail to dig out another cache bucket, and forcing himself to sit on the rock.

Palmer didn't want to admit it, but she had a bad feeling about Preacher. He should've been fifteen minutes behind Cooper at the most. They were a long way from the ranch house, which muted the earlier sounds of gunfire somewhat. But there hadn't been any shooting for at least twenty minutes.

"Riley, I agree, but we're kinda stuck at this point. If something has happened to Preach, then we just find a way to meet up with Duncan and Daddy to decide what to do next."

"How long?"

Palmer had asked herself the same question. "I don't know," she replied truthfully. She didn't want to jump to conclusions, but the realization of losing the ranch was beginning to set in. Worse yet, Palmer began to think of everyone inside the underground bunker, desperate to get out but dying of asphyxiation.

The two sat in silence until they heard the sound of rocks tumbling down the trail. Somebody was approaching.

"Stay here," whispered Riley. "I'll duck behind that rock

outcropping and wait until I can see who it is. Don't shoot until I do, okay?"

"Yeah, go!"

Riley hustled across the trail and wound his way through the boulders that lined the narrow path barely wide enough for Red Rover to fit through.

Each second seemed like an eternity as the sounds emanating from the darkness grew louder. To Palmer, the shuffling of feet and tumbling rocks resembled an old drunk who'd lost his way out of a saloon.

"Palmer! It's Preacher! Oh no!"

Palmer slung her rifle over her shoulder and ran up the trail, stumbling slightly on the loose stones. She immediately recognized Preacher's chestnut horse with its white stripe that descended from his eyes to his nostrils. Only something was wrong. The beautiful white snout was stained.

"He's been shot, sis! Help me!"

Palmer reached the horse's side and saw the cause of the stain. Both horse and rider were covered in Preacher's blood.

Palmer tried to remain calm as she gave instructions to her brother. "Leave him on the horse, and let's get them both to the clearing. Hurry, but be careful."

Riley had a better idea. "I've got this, don't worry. Run ahead and get Cooper to stand watch. Tell Sook to get ready. Sis, he's still alive, and we can save him!"

Palmer ran like she'd never run before, dodging low tree branches and ignoring the unsure footing of the forest floor. Before she reached the clearing, she was shouting ahead.

"Coop! Coop! Come quickly! Preacher's been shot!"

She continued running. Her heart was pounding, and the beats were thumping in her head from the exhilaration. She never heard Cooper running toward her in the dark, wooded canopy—until they crashed into one another.

Cooper, who'd kept his wits about him after he heard her shouts, managed to bear hug his sister. The two spun around but avoided hitting the ground.

Cooper remained calm. "You and Sook get ready. I'll guide Riley back through the woods."

"Go!"

Palmer took a deep breath and walked briskly toward the clearing. As she regained her composure, she realized the importance of avoiding a twisted or broken ankle on the dark path. Plus, she didn't want to overly alarm her mother. At this point, she didn't know how bad the gunshot wounds were.

When she arrived in the clearing, Sook was standing.

"What is it, Palmer?"

"Preacher's been shot. Many times, I think. There's a lot of blood, Sook. All over his body and his horse."

Sook spontaneously hugged her best friend and future sister. "Palmer, we will pray and do our best with God's help."

Palmer allowed herself a smile and nodded. "Get what you need ready. I've got to break the news to Momma."

While Sook gathered the medical supplies necessary to treat gunshot wounds, Palmer approached her mother. She could hear the guys coming through the woods, so she had to hurry.

She dropped to one knee and brushed her mother's hair. Before she could speak, Lucy opened her eyes and said, "Something's happened, hasn't it? Is it Preacher?"

"Yes, Momma. He's been shot, and I think it's bad. We're going to try to fix him up, but he's lost a lot of blood."

"Okay, honey. Bring him over by me. I will help you as I can. Is he conscious?"

"No, I mean, I don't think so. They're coming now."

Lucy nodded toward Red Rover. "There are blankets in the truck. After you treat him, you'll need to wrap him up to keep him from going into shock."

Palmer stood and joined Sook at Red Rover. The two young women were being challenged, and they found themselves up to the task. Life in a post-apocalyptic world was about a test of a person's will to survive. It didn't matter if you were young or old, male or female. Every individual had the inherent ability to rise up and deal with these challenges.

For the next hour, Palmer and Sook worked at a feverish pace to save Preacher's life. Even Cooper scrubbed in, so to speak, by donning sterile gloves and handling the wound-irrigation duties.

Using a combination of the advanced trauma supplies purchased by Lucy, which included Celox blood-clotting granules, two HALO chest seals, and an Israeli bandage battle dressing, the young women managed to get Preacher's bleeding under control.

Lucy stopped them from attempting to remove the bullets from his body. His left foot had a gaping hole in the forefoot, with the bullet embedded somewhere amongst the tendons. His right arm had been grazed with one bullet, but a second was lodged in his triceps muscle.

However, it was the three gunshot wounds in his back that caused the most damage. There were only entry wounds, which meant the bullets inside him would begin to cause an uncontrollable infection. If Preacher didn't get to an emergency room soon, he'd likely die under the stars of the West Texas sky.

CHAPTER 9

January 23
The Armstrong Ranch
Borden County, Texas

Holloway was surrounded by silence except for the occasional popping sounds of the barn burning behind him. He stood alone in the front yard, taking in the fruits of his labor. *Just what the doctor ordered*, he thought to himself as he admired his conquest.

He glanced around at the smoldering fire, which was quickly burning itself out. One of his lieutenants jogged out of the house and gave him a report. "The house is clear. One old man escaped on the back of a horse, but he was shot up pretty bad. At least four or five rounds. Do you want me to send a team to look for him?"

"Nah, there's not a hospital for a hundred miles," replied Holloway. "If he's been shot that many times, he's got a foot or two in the grave anyway. Make sure that fire doesn't burn down the other barn, and set up a perimeter security. Nobody's coming to the rescue for these people. If they ran off, which is likely, they won't be stupid enough to return."

"Yessir," his lieutenant replied before he jogged towards the barn. He was shouting in Korean for his men to join him.

"Also, fire up the generators!" Holloway smiled and took one final look at the front of the house. "Now, let's go in and check out my new digs."

He strutted up the porch stairs with confidence, touching every piece of railing and wall as he entered the family room. The smell of a burned-out fire in the fireplace reached his nostrils, as did the smell of his three dead soldiers killed by Preacher.

He flipped on the light switch and took it all in. The house was a mess of broken glass, splintered wood, and death. The first order of business would be to clean up his new home.

Holloway hollered out the front door for two men to come inside and dispose of the bodies, followed by a thorough clean-up of the debris. His men immediately responded, which gave him the opportunity to take a self-tour of the Armstrongs' home.

For the next thirty minutes, Holloway turned on all of the lights in the house. He entered every room and rifled through every closet. No drawer or cabinet was left unopened. He wasn't looking for anything in particular. Holloway just wanted to see what the former owners had.

The initial excitement of his victory began to wear off as he became disillusioned at the lack of spoils normally afforded the conqueror. *Where are the weapons?* Ranchers were gun-totin' cowboys, so he assumed, anyway.

Where are the hidden bags of gold? None of these people trusted banks. It shocked Holloway that money wasn't stuffed under every mattress.

He picked up the Armstrongs' family Bible and thumbed through it. There were records of old weddings and babies being born dating back to the 1800s. He examined the worn pages and the old entries in varied styles of handwriting. Obviously, it had been handed down from generation to generation.

"Their name was Armstrong," he mumbled before tossing the Bible on the floor in the corner of the family room. *Of course they were Bible-thumpers*, he thought to himself.

Holloway looked at the pictures that hung in the hallway leading to the back bedrooms. Decades of Armstrong photos had been carefully positioned on the wall, from oldest to most recent. Holloway studied them for a moment. Then he slowly reached out and stuck his fingers underneath a picture frame. One by one, he flipped them off their hooks until they fell to the wood floors, causing the frames to crack and the glass to break. Without regard to the family's history that adorned the wall, Holloway's heavy frame and steel-toed boots walked on top of the photos, further scarring the Armstrongs' legacy.

He made his way through the kitchen and was pleased to find a well-stocked pantry. The food provisions would supplement the food supplies they'd accumulated over the last couple of weeks.

Upstairs, he immediately discovered the master bedroom. This space intrigued him the most. To Holloway, the ranchers' bedroom was their most personal space. This was their comfort zone where they laid their heads at night. This was the bed where they made the babies that Holloway had observed in the pictures.

These thoughts caused his mind to race. Holloway slid a chair to the corner of the room and sat down. His legs were sprawled out in front of him, and he clasped his fingers across his stomach. He'd never contemplated having a family. Since he had been discharged from the military, he'd led a life of mercenary activities and criminal enterprises. The apocalypse was his opportunity to shine, and now he'd fulfilled his dream.

Seeing the photos and the evidence of family life, which filled every room of the house, he had a sudden sense of emptiness inside. *Should I consider finding a wife? Have kids? Raise them on a ranch like this family has done for nearly two hundred years?*

A light tapping on the door startled him out of his daydream. "What is it?" he growled, annoyed at the intrusion.

"Sir, I have two men assigned to clean up," advised his top lieutenant. "The fire is contained and will burn itself out soon enough. Perimeter security has been established. We do have one unfinished matter to address."

"What is it?" asked Holloway as he stood to address his subordinate.

"During the initial gunfight, sir, the two men in the guard tower ran toward the oil and gas facility to our south. They appeared to have automatic weapons. May I send a team to eliminate any threat they might pose?"

Holloway looked around the master bedroom one last time and then considered his options. It was a loose end that could come back to haunt them. Their earlier surveillance indicated a small number of people at the petroleum facility, but they had a significant number of cows in what appeared to be a makeshift dairy operation.

"Yeah, go ahead," ordered Holloway. "However, if there are any young women over there, bring them back alive. And a cow too. I'd like to cook a steak."

CHAPTER 10

January 23
The East Woods
The Armstrong Ranch
Borden County, Texas

Sook was exhausted from working on Preacher's gunshot wounds. After another change of Lucy's dressings, she curled up to sleep in the front seat of Red Rover while Palmer took a shift watching over their two patients. Cooper and Riley continued to maintain a watch over the trail, which was the only direct means of ingress and egress from the ranch house to the east woods.

Palmer struggled to stay awake and periodically caught herself nodding off. She kept the fire going to keep her mother and Preacher warm. The guys agreed that the flames couldn't be seen from the trail due to the dense underbrush of the woods.

She was able to keep Riley calm, and he came back periodically to check on their mother. The better she rested, the more convinced he became to wait for help. This was for the better, they all agreed, because none of them needed the stress of an overly emotional member of the group during a time of crisis. There was a reason for the axiom *cooler heads prevail.*

Palmer had just returned from gathering more kindling from the woods when she heard Preacher moan. He was stirring back to consciousness. Since his horse had delivered him down the trail, Preacher had been unable to respond to their voices or any type of stimuli. They thought he might be in a coma but weren't sure. Sometimes, when traumatized, the body forces the brain into a coma in order to rest. A loss of consciousness was similar and required constant monitoring.

Palmer and Sook had taken great care to keep Preacher warm, but dehydration was a big concern. They didn't have the benefit of intravenous fluids. They kept his mouth moist with a damp cloth and a small syringe. They didn't risk trying to force water down his throat for fear it would enter his lungs.

Palmer dropped the wood and ran to Preacher's side. She took the wet cloth and held it against the gallon jug of water, allowing the moisture to soak in. After patting his forehead and face, she whispered in his ear, "Hey, Preach. It's me, Palmer. Can you hear me?"

A slight smile came over his face, and he nodded, which caused him to wince. "It hurts."

"I know it does. You were shot several times, so try to stay still, okay? Can you take in a little water?"

"Yeah."

Preacher was too weak to lift his head, so Palmer gently slid her left hand behind his neck and assisted him. She squeezed the water out of the cloth into his mouth, allowing him just enough to eliminate the dryness in his mouth and throat. After she was comfortable that he could swallow, she allowed a small amount of water from the jug to enter his system.

He took some in and then nodded his head that he'd had enough. "Lucy?" he whispered.

Palmer gently laid his head down and turned it toward her mother. "She's gonna be fine. See? She's been sleeping since we finished working on you."

"The boys?" he whispered.

"Coop and Riley are standing watch. Sook's asleep in the truck. She did a great job on both you and Momma."

"The others?"

"Not yet. Don't worry about them, Preach. You need to focus on fighting, okay?"

With a considerable amount of strain and effort, Preacher lifted his left arm and motioned for Palmer to come closer. She leaned down and put her ear near his mouth.

"God will be taking me soon. I need to say goodbye to Miss Lucy."

Palmer's eyes filled with tears. She didn't think it was possible to cry so much, but two people whom she loved dearly were both lying on the cold ground in the middle of the woods, and one of them was preparing himself to die.

"No. There will be no goodbyes. I've been praying for you to live. God will not take you now!" Palmer raised her voice slightly, which stirred her mother awake.

"Palmer, is everything okay?"

"Momma, Preacher's awake, and he's asking for you."

Lucy turned her face toward her old friend and smiled. His eyes locked with hers, and the man who'd been like a brother to Major returned her smile.

"Hey there, Preach," she began. "Glad to see ya back among the living."

"Miss Lucy, it will be my time soon."

He began to cough, and a little blood came out of the side of his mouth. Palmer quickly wiped it off so neither Preacher nor her mother could see it. The tears flowed again as she realized that this was a sign of internal bleeding, and Preacher didn't have much longer.

"Maybe so, but not yet, mister. I'm pretty sure my husband will be mighty pissed off if you leave without saying goodbye!"

Preacher chuckled, which caused him more pain than joy. "Water, please."

Palmer quickly provided him another drink.

He nodded his appreciation and turned his attention back to Lucy. "You helped me when I was at the lowest of lows. I've thanked God daily for you both and prayed for the safety of all of us. I am sorry this has happened."

He began coughing again, but this time it was deeper and guttural. More fluid was coming up out of his lungs.

The door to Red Rover opened as Sook emerged from inside. She rushed next to Palmer and immediately felt Preacher's forehead.

She whispered in his ear, "Hi, Preacher. You must rest."

He nodded but ignored her as he continued. "Miss Lucy, tell the boss man thank you for everything he has done for me. I've never said it enough myself."

Sook dug through the medical bag and located the thermometer. She slipped on a sterile probe cover and inserted it into Preacher's mouth. "This will keep you quiet for a moment." She could see the crow's feet lines appear on the outside corners of his eyes, indicating he appreciated her friendly admonishment.

Lucy finally responded to Preacher. "He will be here soon enough. We'll get you to a hospital, and you'll be back in the saddle in no time. You need to stay positive and fight for your life, Preacher."

He smiled again, and then his eyes closed as he lost consciousness.

Sook immediately felt for his pulse. "It's high but good. He needs more rest, and so do you, Miss—"

Before Sook could finish her sentence, Cooper rushed into the clearing. "We've heard more gunfire from the direction of the Slaughters' place. I feel bad, but we can't help them. They're on their own."

"I agree, son," said Miss Lucy. "We have our own troubles."

Suddenly, Riley emerged into the clearing as well. "Coop, come back. There's more gunfire. This time it's coming from the north side of the ranch."

"Daddy?" asked Palmer.

"Or Duncan," said Cooper. "Either way, you and Sook keep alert. It could be the commandos searching the ranch for us."

Palmer reached over and squeezed Sook's hand. "Let's get ready to fight."

Chapter 11

January 23
The North Gate
The Armstrong Ranch
Borden County, Texas

Major Armstrong glanced down at his watch for the tenth time since they'd left Austin. The entire day had been a whirlwind of activity since the helicopter dispatched by President Marion Burnett had arrived at their ranch. He was naturally disappointed when he learned that the chopper had been sent away on other presidential business, which required him to ride in the back of a specially equipped Ford Police Interceptor utilized by the Texas Highway Patrol. His two-man escort rode in the front seat, remaining quiet for the majority of the ride back to the ranch. This suited Major fine, as he had some weighty issues on his mind.

President Burnett had formally offered him the job as her second vice president of the newly formed nation. Under the circumstances, Major was naturally cautious about the offer. Her first vice president, Montgomery Gregg, had died at the receiving end of a highly-trained-sniper's bullet. Major was not interested in suffering a similar fate.

During the ride back, he considered the pros and cons. The situation in Texas had changed dramatically since the initial EMP attack had struck the rest of the United States. The former state was blessed to have been spared from the direct effects of the power grid collapsing and the subsequent nuclear war between North Korea and the States.

His family was together once again, and they seemed to be ready for the long haul, until the unthinkable had occurred. As Duncan warned, North Korean commandos were on North American soil, and they were coming for Texas. The attack had resulted in breached borders, the collapse of the ERCOT grid, and now the threat the Lightning Death Squads posed to ordinary Texans.

Major knew what the safe approach was. Mind his own business, protect the ranch, and most importantly, protect his family. To be fair, he considered the option of taking the position. The president had made him her first choice. She'd given him a short time frame to respond because it meant she'd move on to a second choice, or even a third.

He didn't necessarily consider Marion to be in a position of weakness, but he knew that he had the opportunity to write his own meal ticket. The president would not deny him any reasonable conditions he proposed.

So what were they? Under what conditions would Major risk danger to his family, and himself, by becoming Texas Vice President Armstrong?

First and foremost, he'd insist upon protection for the ranch. A full security detail, possibly platoon size, even if it was on the low end of sixteen to twenty troops.

Second, he would reside at the residence and utilize a helicopter for the less-than-three-hundred-mile ride from the ranch to Austin. He could get a lot of paperwork done in that hour or so flight back and forth each day.

Third, he would become the daily point of contact for the military. With Duncan's assistance, he'd make sure the forces were loyal to Texas and not their former employer, the United States. This aspect of secession had concerned Major from the beginning. Despite his dislike of Gregg, Major understood the importance of his presence in Marion's cabinet. Before he was assassinated, Gregg had been the glue that held the military in place.

Finally, there were other perks that went with this position of power, including food and medical care. The aggravation of becoming a politician might be worth the comfort of knowing his family had an increased chance of survival.

All of these scenarios swirled through Major's mind as he directed the troopers toward the north gate of the ranch. As they approached, their headlights shone on two unfamiliar figures. Major leaned forward and grasped the back of the front seat to get a better look.

"Guys! Something's not—"

He never got to finish his sentence as a hail of gunfire obliterated the windshield and killed his escorts instantly. It was pure luck or a gift from heaven that allowed Major to survive the volley.

He fell backwards into the rear seat and ducked to avoid the ricocheting bullets and flying pieces of glass. He forced himself to think as the gunfire continued to riddle the Ford with bullets.

Major looked up and realized the vehicle was still inching forward. The driver was slumped over the steering wheel, but the truck was still in gear. This was his opportunity to escape. He immediately remembered that he didn't have a rifle with him. He felt for his sidearm, which was still secured in his holster.

He planned on opening the door while the truck was still moving to utilize the distraction. Just as he reached for the handle, he realized he'd forgotten his radio. That was his only lifeline to Duncan and help.

As the truck continued to roll dangerously close to the shooters, he fumbled through the darkness, feeling his way along the seat and then the floorboard of the truck. Finally, his hand reached underneath the driver's seat and he felt it. Major grunted as he reached for the radio until he had it firmly in his grasp.

The gunfire continued, and the noise was deafening. He had to go. Major threw open the right-side door and rolled onto the hard gravel surface. He regained his footing. He gripped the radio and began to run away from the shooters, attempting to keep the truck between them and himself for protection.

His feet clumsily slipped on the loose gravel again as he tried to flee his attackers. Once on his feet, he tried to find the speed-dial button on the satellite phone as he ran. That was when the commandos' laser sights found him. He began running in a zigzag pattern in attempt to avoid their aim.

Major cut to the right, and bullets tore up the ground to his left. He emulated a tailback well past his prime being pursued by tacklers as he darted back to the left, once again cheating death.

His adrenaline kept him going toward the narrow bridge that crossed the Colorado River on the north side of the ranch. He glanced down again and found the speed dial on the phone. He had to call Duncan before he was killed so he could get help for his family.

More gunfire erupted behind him as he heard Duncan answer the phone. "Son! Help! We need you—"

Major wasn't able to finish the sentence as a bullet knocked the phone out of his hand, causing it to break into a dozen pieces. Frightened, Major lost his composure as he ducked another volley and started down the hill toward the river crossing. He rolled an ankle in a pothole and toppled off the hard-packed surface toward the shoulder. He tumbled over and over, banging his body against rocks while scraping his hands and face on underbrush.

The gunfire continued, but they were shooting in the direction of the bridge. He'd managed to evade and escape his pursuers. Major took a moment to recover from the chase. He needed to catch his breath in order to make it across the river in these low temperatures. One misstep and he could slip under the water and most certainly succumb to hypothermia.

Major knew his land. He knew where the best points to cross the river were. He had to hurry to sneak under the bridge, where the men would be looking for him, and get past the beaver dam, which he'd built with his sons before the world went to crap. Due to the drought they'd suffered for years, this would be the shallowest point at which to cross.

He knew the way along the grassy riverbank, as he'd ridden the perimeter many times with Preacher. The cold weather did have its benefits. He closed his eyes and said a silent prayer to God, thanking Him for the cold weather of January, as opposed to the heat of summer, when these marshy areas would be full of copperheads.

It took Major thirty minutes or more to pass the back side of Miss

Lucy's barnyard. He stopped for a moment and contemplated walking toward the back of the barn to take a look around. Then he heard the North Koreans' voices. They were near the barnyard. That was when the realization came over him that his ranch was lost.

Grief immediately overcame him. *Is my family dead? Have these animals overrun the ranch and murdered my wife and children?* Dread and then anger built up inside Major. He wanted to run up the embankment, past the windmill that had become a symbol of the ranch's history, and shoot everything that moved.

Then he remembered a conversation he'd had with Preacher while they'd moved cattle down through the ravine toward the abandoned ranch to their east. Preacher's words had been *live to fight another day.*

He had to have confidence in Preacher's and Lucy's abilities to make the right decisions in order to stay out of harm's way. He trusted Preacher to remember his own words.

Major fought back the emotions and gathered himself up off the wet ground. He needed to get to safety, and now his only hope was to flag down his son as he approached from Lubbock. If he didn't intercept Duncan, he'd be driving straight into a *Hornet's Nest.*

CHAPTER 12

January 23
Boys Ranch, Texas

Duncan and Espy had reached Boys Ranch north of Amarillo an hour and a half ago. The number of refugees who'd broken through the northern border of Texas was larger than initially reported. Plus, the number who were armed astonished Duncan as he made his initial assessment. As his unit reported the findings of their reconnaissance, Duncan began to wonder whether the people who'd infiltrated the community made up primarily of orphaned children and their counselors were part of a larger orchestrated effort. These men were armed with AR-15s and AK-47s. They weren't trained to do battle with Duncan's Texas Quick Reaction Force, but with kids as human hostages, his team had to attempt to negotiate before the TX-QRF escalated the standoff to the next level.

Another hour of the standoff had passed, and Duncan was growing impatient. "Espy, we've tried negotiating," started Duncan as he observed the small town from a nearby hillside. "It would be impossible to know how many of them are inside the community and where the hostages are tucked away."

"We could wait them out," offered Espy. "Maybe they'll get nervous and give up."

"I don't know. They seem entrenched. They've got a roof over their head and food in their bellies. All we can do is keep them contained and be prepared to respond to any hostile move on their part."

One of Duncan's lieutenants approached the front of the Humvee. He was holding out a map of Boys Ranch, which was covered with a number of circles, arrows, and numbers. He opened it up on the hood of the truck and used his flashlight to illuminate the details.

"Whadya have, Lieutenant?" asked Duncan.

"Sir, the best we can tell, there are a total of seventeen armed gunman and another half-dozen females accompanying them," started the lieutenant. He began to point to various highlighted locations on the map. "They are positioned in the areas marked with circles. The number next to the circle corresponds with the quantity of gunmen."

"Commander," started Espy, who always referred to Duncan by rank when they were in the presence of other members of the military. He began tracing his fingers around the map. "If we change our tactics from containment to a stealth attack on their positions, we might be able to slowly pick them off. They're spread around the town, and it's doubtful they're working with comms. We can pick them off, free the hostages, and encircle the remainder of the hostiles."

Duncan thought for a moment. This was a risky maneuver because the eruption of gunfire could throw the entire operation into chaos. However, he wasn't in a position to conduct a prolonged standoff. He'd already been told that his unit was on its own by his superiors at Fort Hood. They were overwhelmed with border control and dealing with chaos in the larger cities of Texas as a result of the power outage.

"Let's do it, Sergeant," said Duncan. "Break your men up into teams. Keep the comms open, and I'll act as a rover to respond to hot spots as needed."

"Yessir," said Espy, who rolled up the map and led the lieutenant down the hill toward their temporary encampment. Ten minutes later, the teams were traveling to their point of entry to begin the operation.

Duncan studied the town through his night-vision field glasses. The ATN military-issue night-vision goggles used the best night-vision technology in the world. He especially liked the head-strap system, which allowed hands-free use.

He studied the perimeter and observed his teams getting into place. He returned to the driver's seat of the Humvee and turned up the volume on his radio.

"Alpha team, ready!"

"Bravo team, ready!"

Each of Espy's teams were in position, awaiting his orders. Duncan was reaching for the microphone above his head when his satellite phone rang.

He pressed the receive button and immediately heard automatic gunfire fill the cab of the truck. He had to take a second glance through the windshield to make sure Espy hadn't already engaged the hostage takers. Then he realized it was coming from the phone.

"Hello?"

"Son! Help! We need you—"

Duncan heard his father's voice through the earpiece as the gunfire continued before the signal went dead. He frantically tried to redial, but the phone rang continuously.

Duncan jumped out of the truck and walked in circles as he ran his fingers through his hair. His dad was in trouble, but he had no idea where he was.

We need you. We! He said we. Dammit! The ranch was under attack, and he was two hundred plus miles away!

"Commander, on your orders, sir."

It was Espy's voice coming through the radio in the Humvee. Duncan had to make a decision. He had a duty to his country, but he'd vowed to always place his family first.

"Sir?"

"Roger, Sergeant. There is an emergency at home base."

The line remained silent for a few seconds as Espy analyzed the statement. Duncan deliberately used the word *home*, hoping Espy would pick up on the reference.

"Shall we abort, sir?"

Decision time.

"No, Sergeant. You're a green-go. You are now in charge of this op. Heads up and eyes open, boys."

Duncan fired up the Humvee and tore off down the highway toward Amarillo and beyond. The military Humvees he'd driven in the Middle Eastern theater had a top speed of seventy miles per hour. He'd pushed this Texas National Guard model to nearly ninety. He was about to find out what this truck was capable of.

*****

Duncan's mind processed all of the scenarios as he sped through Gail toward the last dozen miles to the ranch. He'd reached out to Camp Lubbock to refresh his memory on their manpower status. Much of his unit was at Boys Ranch with Espy while only a skeleton crew remained to protect the TX-QRF facility. Pulling a two-man team would create gaping holes in their security, which would leave the base vulnerable to attack. He had no idea whether the ranch was under assault by Holloway and his seasoned commandos or not. He couldn't afford to lose Camp Lubbock on a hunch.

He considered calling in air support and troops through Fort Hood. However, the show of force might result in getting his family killed. If they were under attack or held hostage, panicked gunmen might decide to kill and run rather than fight the Texas military.

As hard as it was not to call upon the assets at his disposal, Duncan knew it was best to gather more information and assess his options with a full picture of what he was facing ahead.

He turned off Willow Valley Road and took the shortcut across the hilly terrain that ran parallel to the Colorado River. This was the quickest way to FM 1205 and the long driveway into the north gate of the Armstrong Ranch.

Duncan caught himself strangling the steering wheel with both hands. He loosened his grip, flexed his fingers, and wiped his sweaty palms on his desert-night camouflage fatigues. Designed for use by the Marine Corps Combat units in the Middle East, Duncan had ordered the unit to wear the mixture of black, dark blue, and light gray for their mission to Boys Ranch.

After turning on the packed gravel and clay driveway, he forced himself to slow down. In the quiet darkness, his vehicle could be heard from the north gate, and he wasn't certain who'd be manning it. Knowing the driveway well, Duncan turned off his headlights and affixed his night-vision goggles to his head.

The flat, arid lands of West Texas turned bright green as he continued forward. As he rolled slowly toward the gate, an occasional set of beady eyes appeared on both sides of the road. Curious black-tailed prairie dogs or rock squirrels would emerge from their hides to take a look using natural night vision as reliable as his eight-thousand-dollar device.

Duncan hit an unexpected pothole, which jerked the steering wheel to the left as he passed through a chute of boulders. He attempted to correct his course, and then it happened. In the darkness, he never saw the trip wire that triggered the improvised explosive device set up by Holloway's men.

A massive blast underneath upended the three-ton Humvee and sent it tilting toward the right. Duncan flew against the passenger side of the truck as it swerved its way toward the side of the road and then toppled onto its side. The windows had exploded outward from the pressure, but bits of glass still flew about the interior of the truck.

His body fought to maintain consciousness as the Humvee took one final roll until it wedged on its roof against a large boulder. The blast under the enclosed truck had produced overpressure within the cab, which had immediately impacted Duncan's brain. His head pounded. He temporarily lost his hearing, and his vision became blurred.

He was having difficulty breathing, as the blast had effected his lungs. With the grenade directly between the hard surface of the driveway and the bottom left side of the Humvee, the blast pressure had exerted itself upward toward the bottom of the truck. The sudden, violent movement had caused Duncan's internal organs to shake uncontrollably inside his body.

Duncan was in incredible physical shape, and he'd experienced similar attacks during his service in the military. An average man would have succumbed to the blast or at the very least fallen unconscious. Duncan's physical ability to withstand the blast effects saved his life.

The Humvee was about to catch on fire as the fireball created by the grenade burned under the fuel tank. He had to get out of the truck. He crawled through the windshield and found his way to the rocky soil in a dry creek bed adjacent to the driveway.

His head was pounding, and his vision was blurred, but he kept dragging his body forward. The ringing of his ears prevented him from hearing the armed commandos running up the driveway toward him. All he knew was that the Humvee was about to blow.

Duncan found a rock and attempted to pull himself up. He closed his eyes and willed his vision to come back. Looking ahead, he could make out the two shapes approaching him, but he couldn't see anything with sufficient clarity to react. His knees buckled, and he fell to the ground again. Then he heard the distinctive sound of a charging handle being pulled on a battle rifle.

Not good.

Duncan Armstrong closed his eyes and knew it was over. In those milliseconds as his brain processed the prospect of his final days on Earth, visions of his parents, siblings, and the sweet face of Sook flashed through his mind. He took solace in knowing that he'd done his duty to God, country, and family.

Content with his fate, his body relaxed as he heard two shots reverberate through the night.

CHAPTER 13

January 23
The Armstrong Ranch
Borden County, Texas

Holloway ran onto the front porch of the house with a can of garbanzo beans in one hand and a spoon in the other. The explosion could be heard inside over the crackling fire, which he'd built to stay warm. He found his men scrambling out of the barn, where they were forced to sleep temporarily.

"Somebody out here want to tell me what the hell is going on?" he barked at no one in particular.

One of his men rushed to his side with a two-way radio. "Sir, as instructed, the perimeter security patrols set up IEDs at each entry to stop incoming vehicles. The north gate device was triggered."

Holloway nodded and scooped out another spoonful of the delectable chick peas mixed with Tabasco sauce. He realized he didn't have his radio and reminded himself that this might not be over yet. He checked his watch. It was just after ten.

He motioned for the commando to hand over his radio, which Holloway clipped to his gun belt. "Give me that and find another. Then take a couple of guys to check it out. Raise me on the radio when you know something."

Holloway glanced toward the pile of smoldering debris where the barn had stood. His plan was to get up bright and early in the morning to supervise the cleanup. He was ready for day one of life as a Texas rancher. As for tonight, he looked forward to a well-deserved rest mixed with spending a little quality time with the woman captured by his men after they had killed the dairy farmers to the south.

The pickup truck pulled out of the yard and headed north up the driveway. Holloway wandered around as he was left alone to his thoughts. He had a nose for trouble and could sense that this battle wasn't over yet. He and his men needed rest. They hadn't slept since the night before the assault on Camp Lubbock. Between fleeing their pursuers and conducting reconnaissance on the ranch, they'd only enjoyed a restless nap of an hour or two.

He'd taken his prize, and now he was anxious to enjoy it. But something in his gut told him these Armstrongs weren't going to go away quietly. He found his way closer to the destroyed barn and took a deep breath. It reminded him of war. The smell of burned-down buildings and death.

Holloway took a last scoop of garbanzo beans into his mouth and licked the spoon clean. He tossed the empty can into the smoking debris, and it landed with a clanking, metal-on-metal sound. Finding this odd, he tilted his head momentarily. Holloway took a step forward and then stopped as the radio crackled to life.

"Sir, I'm passing through the north gate. There appears to be a wrecked Humvee up ahead."

Holloway grinned. *I knew it.*

CHAPTER 14

January 23
The Armstrong Ranch
Borden County, Texas

Major was a quarter mile downriver when he heard the explosion. He quickly turned and saw the fireball, which rose into the sky, followed by the sickening sound of steel scraping against the rocks. His heart immediately sank. A heinous trap had been set, and his gut told him that Duncan had been ensnared in it.

As he raced through the scrub oaks that lined the north side of the river, he could hear shouts coming from the bridge to his left. The commandos were still searching for him, but they'd taken the time at some point to booby-trap the driveway leading to the ranch. Somehow, they'd expected more visitors like himself.

He entered the clearing overlooking the drive, and he immediately recognized Duncan's Humvee. He fought back the urge to run to his son's aid, as the commandos had their rifles raised and were slowly walking toward the vehicle.

That was when Major saw a man slumped over a large rock. It was too dark to determine if it was Duncan, but the flames underneath the Humvee illuminated the area enough for Major to know that he had to move quickly to save the man's life.

He drew his weapon and moved in, periodically glancing toward the ranch to make sure no one else was approaching. With the distracting noise coming from the burning oil out of the truck's engine, Major was able to close on the gunmen.

The men stood over the helpless figure and raised their rifles to shoot, when Major expertly fired two rounds into the base of their skulls, killing them instantly. He quickly moved forward, and then he saw Duncan.

His son rose to his knees and held his hand up, grasping for the large rock in front of him.

"Son, it's me!" Major holstered his weapon and helped Duncan off the ground. "Are you hurt?"

"They rattled my innards, Dad," Duncan replied with a muted chuckle.

"Let me help you stand." Major lifted Duncan up by grabbing under his armpits, and then he steadied him against the boulder.

"Better. Dad, what happened?"

"They've taken the ranch, son. I don't know anything about your mother or the kids. I approached the north gate with two state troopers, and they were gunned down. I barely made it out alive when I tried to call you. They shot the radio out of my hand."

Duncan was beginning to regain his composure and looked around. He raised his head and sniffed. Gasoline was pouring out of the fuel tank.

He forced himself to stand. "I've got to get my rifle and the night vision."

His wobbly legs rejected that notion. Major helped his son back to a seated position on the rock, and then he walked toward the Humvee, shielding his eyes from the light and heat as he approached.

A reflection in the ditch caught his eye. The flames were flickering on a shiny object. Major rushed forward and crawled on his knees the final ten feet to avoid the heat from the flames. The reflections showed themselves again, allowing him to retrieve Duncan's goggles.

Major then turned his attention to the truck. It was too risky to crawl inside the cab and search for the rifle. Duncan had done a great job of stocking the ranch with weapons over the last two weeks. They could make do with what he'd procured, but he wasn't gonna let them make do without a father.

He scrambled to his feet and rushed back to Duncan. The sound of an approaching vehicle gave him a new sense of urgency. His eyes searched for his son, but he couldn't see him. Once he approached the rock, he found out why.

Duncan had found the strength and the presence of mind to strip the dead North Koreans of their weapons, radios, and extra ammunition. He was tucking things into his cargo pants pockets when Major caught up to him.

"Dad, they'll be coming. We've got to go."

"They're already on the way. I just heard their truck going over the bridge."

Duncan stood and wiped the dirt off his sleeves and hands. "I'm glad you heard them. My ears are still ringing." He handed Major a gun belt, who slung it over his shoulder. Then he added, "What is it they say about your ears ringing?"

Major was puzzled at his son's nonchalant attitude and became immediately concerned for his mental well-being. "You mean right for spite and left for love?"

"Yeah, that. I seem to have equal numbers on both sides of the love-hate spectrum. Come on, let's hide so we can figure out what to do next."

Major put his arm around his son and helped him across the road and into the woods. As they walked together, he told Duncan more details of what he'd observed earlier. Their conversation reinforced what Major always knew about his son, the warrior. He'd never met a man as coolheaded under pressure.

"Dad, I'm not gonna accept that they're dead. Worst case is they're being held hostage. The best case is they escaped. Where would they go?"

"East, I think. Either to the ranch where we moved some cattle the other day or even the woods where they could seek cover. Lucy and the boys were hiding buckets of food, guns, ammo, and huntin' clothes near the trail that led down the ravine."

Duncan rolled his head around his shoulders and neck. "My eyesight's coming back, and the haters and lovers must've taken a break, because the ringin' has subsided."

"Are you up for a hike?"

"Yeah, it makes sense that they would flee the point of attack. It was smart to move the caches to the east in the direction of their bugout. Lead the way, but take us as close to the house as you can so we can get a feel of what we're up against."

Major started ahead, and then Duncan stopped him by touching his shoulder. Major turned and locked eyes with his oldest son.

"Dad, thanks for saving my life."

"You're welcome, son. None of us are going to die today."

CHAPTER 15

January 23
The East Woods
The Armstrong Ranch
Borden County, Texas

"This should be the last one," said Cooper as he slowly walked up the trail toward the first cache bucket he and Riley had hidden with their mother the other day. Little did they know at the time that they'd need the contents already.

"Coop, should we take these others back first?" asked Riley as he stopped thirty feet behind his brother. He leaned over and heaved for air. Tromping up the ravine on the uneven trail had taken its toll on the heavier of the two brothers.

"Wait here if you want. I remember where we buried it, and I can dig it out quickly."

Riley didn't hesitate as he immediately stopped. "I ain't gonna argue."

Cooper could hear the sound of the plastic buckets being set aside by Riley, so he quickly turned and made his way toward the oak tree that was lined up with the corner fence post. He was almost there when he heard the sound of shuffling feet. He quickly turned off the SureFire flashlight and readied his rifle.

Cooper had to think fast as the sounds of the rocks tumbling down the trail grew louder. *Should I backtrack and rejoin Riley? If I warn him, whoever is coming down the trail might hear. Should I take them on by myself?*

Suddenly, the noise stopped. Crap! Did they discover me already?

He tried to move quietly behind a rock to gain cover. It seemed like an eternity as he listened in the darkness for any hint of noise.

Was I wrong? Was it Riley kickin' rocks and the direction of the sound was distorted?

His heart was beating out of his chest. His ears strained, and his eyes sought any form of movement.

He waited.

"Quiet, Coop!" a voice hissed in his ear as a strong hand covered his mouth at the same time.

Cooper's eyes grew wide, and he tried to turn around, but the grip on his mouth and arms prevented any movement. He furiously nodded his head up and down. He turned and saw the night-vision goggles a few inches from his face.

"Duncan?" asked Cooper.

"Yeah. Dad too. But you have to be quiet and careful. There's a patrol just above us on the fence line. I saw you and Riley as you came up the hill, but I couldn't warn you. Coop, y'all talk way too much. Seriously."

Cooper didn't respond to the admonishment and instead gave his brother a hearty hug, one that was long overdue between the two brothers, who'd spent the last several years at odds over the death of Dallas in the war.

Major fumbled through the dark, pushing tree branches out of the way to move alongside them. "Coop, where's your momma and sister?"

"We have a camp, Dad. Down in the east woods. Listen, there's more."

"Shhh," Duncan warned. "They're right above us." The sound of men walking along the ridgeline could be heard as their heavy feet gave away their position.

"Wait. I'll be right back," said Cooper as he walked toward the fence post and quietly uncovered the last cache bucket. He knelt down to avoid detection, but it also enabled him to follow the dark silhouette of the commandos against the starlit sky.

Once the patrol had walked out of sight, he returned to the guys.

"I'll carry the bucket," instructed Major.

"Thanks, Dad. I'll go find Riley before he hollers up the trail. He's only forty feet or so down this slope."

Duncan moved ahead while Major followed in his footsteps. Duncan had a flashlight in his chest rig, but he was afraid for Major to use it. Fortunately for Cooper, the timing of their encounter had forced him to turn his light off. Had Duncan not intentionally made himself known by kicking a few stones, Cooper would've been discovered by the patrol.

Moments later, they joined Riley and Cooper before moving to the bottom of the ravine as a group. At one point, Cooper stopped and pressed the button on his flashlight to signal Palmer, who was standing guard alone while Sook tended to the wounded.

As they approached her position, the brothers stood to the side to allow Major to greet his daughter first. He'd reached the bottom of the trail when Palmer emerged from behind a rock outcropping.

"Daddy?"

"Yes, honey. It's me and Duncan."

Palmer ran into his arms, and the force of the embrace almost knocked them both over. Major, who was still sore from his own encounter with the North Korean gunmen, winced but didn't care. There was nothing better than holding his baby girl in his arms again. Twice, he'd thought he'd lost his kids, and twice, they'd been reunited. The joyful reunion once again brought tears to his eyes.

Duncan joined them and gave Palmer a hug. "How're ya doin'?"

"I'm fine, but—" Palmer's voice trailed off, and she began to cry again. "Dang it, I really need to stop crying."

"Honey, what is it?" asked Major.

Palmer shouldered her rifle and took her father by the hand. She looked over to Cooper and Riley, who waved her on. They hid the buckets behind their lookout position and prepared to take the watch.

"Daddy, Momma's been hurt. Preacher, too. Come with me."

She led him by the hand into the woods alone as Duncan stayed behind to give the guys his night-vision goggles and a quick tutorial.

The night vision provided them a significant advantage over anyone descending the trail toward their camp.

He also separated his brothers so they could cover both sides of the natural choke point the trail created with the outcroppings. By moving up the trail slightly, there was a narrow passage that would block most vehicles and cause patrols to move single file through the rock walls. Also, by climbing on top of the rocks, they'd have a better vantage point and the high ground against any intruders.

While Duncan positioned them, Cooper filled his brother in on Lucy's and Preacher's injuries. He also assured him that Sook was safe and doing an incredible job of nursing her patients.

Duncan walked carefully down the woodsy trail after Palmer and Major had entered the clearing. He overheard Palmer explain what had happened as she prepared her father for what he was about to see.

Major dropped the gun belt and radio obtained from the commandos and rushed to his wife's side. Tears streamed down his face as he touched his love's face. She looked so peaceful in his eyes, but he couldn't resist the urge to awaken her.

"Lucy, are you awake? Lucy?"

Slowly, she opened her eyes, and a smile came across her face. "You're late for supper. Bad day at the office?"

Major and Lucy laughed tears of joy as he leaned down and kissed her cheeks.

Palmer and Sook, who'd stepped to the side, hugged one another and began crying again. The waterworks were pouring out of the Armstrongs' eyes as Major and Lucy told each other how much they loved each other.

Major leaned up and smiled. "Yeah, traffic was horrible. I'm just glad to be home. How are you holdin' up?"

"I'm fine. No, actually, I'm healed up now that you're by my side. Major, the uncertainty. I thought they'd shoot you when you stepped off the helicopter. But, you know, I never heard it."

"I came back with a couple of state troopers. We can talk about that later. Preacher's in bad shape, isn't he?"

"Yes, dear. I was counting on the chopper to possibly take him to a hospital. He's probably not gonna make it."

Major touched her face one more time and then looked at his longtime friend, who'd run the Armstrong Ranch for years. Preacher was sleeping, and Lucy advised her husband to let him rest.

Just as Major rolled off his knees to sit beside his wife, Duncan entered the clearing. Sook gasped for air and covered her mouth with both hands. Almost in shock, she stood wide-eyed as tears streamed down her face.

Duncan dropped his gear. He walked straight to her just as she regained her composure and ran into his arms. He lifted her into the air and swung her around until he became slightly dizzy. He immediately set her down and held his head.

"Oh, Duncan. I'm sorry. Are you okay?"

"Yeah, just a little headache." He pulled her close and kissed her before touching his face to hers. The warmth of her cheeks revived him, and suddenly the pains of the attack disappeared.

Sook whispered into his ear, "You must go to your mother. She has been worried for you."

Duncan smiled, kissed her briefly again, and walked toward Lucy, who was still zippered up in the sleeping bag.

"Cooper told me what happened," started Duncan as he glanced over to Preacher, who was still asleep. "How're you feeling?"

Lucy smiled as her oldest son planted a kiss on her still-moist cheek. "I feel like I'm ready to take our ranch back now that our war hero is here."

Duncan reared back and chuckled. He looked over to Preacher and gently patted his chest. "This man's a hero. From what Riley and Cooper told me, there isn't a better field general around that could accomplish what Preacher did. We're all safe because of him."

"Well said, son," said Major as he rose. Duncan joined his side. "Whadya say? No rest for the weary, right?"

"Dang straight," replied Palmer.

"Yes, I agree," added Sook. "Whatever that means."

The group shared a laugh.

Duncan patted his father on the back. "Good. There's work to be done."

CHAPTER 16

January 24
The Armstrong Ranch
Borden County, Texas

Duncan faced a little bit of resistance when he announced he was going back up the ravine to scout the ranch alone. He needed to determine the number of men who'd taken the ranch and whether Holloway was in fact leading them. Major objected on the basis of his health following the blast that had overturned his Humvee. His mother demanded that he not go alone, insisting that one of the guys go with him.

Sook insisted that she go with him because she understood the North Korean dialect and had spent time with Duncan learning some of his cloak-and-dagger methods. She also had medical training if he needed help. *Plus*, she argued, *I can kill as quickly and silently as they can.*

In the end, Sook's argument prevailed, and she immediately changed into dark clothing retrieved from the cache buckets. After confirming their plans for surveillance with Major, Duncan and Sook set out into the darkness.

Equipped with rifles, sidearms, knives, and night vision, Duncan and Sook made their way up the hill with only one stop for Duncan to catch his breath. He didn't want to overly concern his parents, but his chest was still feeling the effect of the blast impact. All of his faculties were fine, although he was still having some difficulty breathing when his body was strained.

As they reached the top of the ravine, Duncan had a fairly clear line of sight to the ranch house. Only one light was turned on that was visible from the rear, and that appeared to be in his parents' bedroom. Everything else surrounding the barns and home was pitch black.

This suited Duncan fine because that meant ambient light wouldn't interfere with his night-vision capabilities. He reached into his cargo pocket and retrieved one of the North Koreans' two-way radios.

He turned it on and adjusted the volume so it could only be heard if the receiver was placed tightly against his ear. He looked down at the illuminated display and made a note of the default channel. Duncan was sure the dead bodies had been found by his Humvee, and most likely the commandos had noticed they'd been stripped of their gear. Now that they were up on the flat ground surrounding the ranch house, they could scroll through the channels to listen in on the commandos' communications activity.

Sook was his secret weapon in this regard. He gave her instructions on operating the radio and told her to stay close by his side. He would continue to use his night vision as they walked along the fence line and toward the rear of the house.

Duncan proceeded under a few manpower assumptions. Most likely, the commandos would adopt similar sentry positions as they had prior to the attack—two near the tower, two at the north bridge, and one or more roving patrols.

It was a brilliant move on the part of Preacher to release all of the horses, not just for their safety, but so they couldn't be used by the commandos. This forced them all to patrol on foot or use their vehicles, which could be both seen and heard.

The unknown for Duncan centered around the ranch house and one remaining barn. Before they left, he and his parents had discussed the possible fate of the ranch hands' families locked in the bunker. The consensus was the air would start to dwindle by eight in the morning, with noticeable effects happening a couple of hours before that.

The clock was ticking on their lives in two respects. They could die from lack of oxygen, or they might panic and attempt to exit the bunker despite the threats aboveground. There might be burning wood over their heads or the barrel of a rifle in their faces. Either way, the options weren't good.

Major was convinced that Antonio, despite being wounded himself, would keep a level head and make the right decision. Hopefully, those within the bunker would follow his instructions and remain calm as they awaited a rescue.

Duncan knew there were a lot of *hopefullys* and *maybes* under these no-win circumstances. As a result, the timing of the rescue was one of the factors in his decision to mount a predawn attack.

The other advantages included using cover of darkness and familiarity with the ranch. The Armstrongs had spent their entire lives on this land. They knew every fence post, hill, watering hole, and oak tree. The commandos did not. Also, Duncan had night vision, which gave him a tremendous advantage, especially if he got into close-quarters combat at the ranch house compound.

He took Sook by the hand and helped her over the wood-rail fence. They used sporadic scrub oaks located behind the house to provide cover as they moved from one trunk to another. At one point, he stopped behind a larger tree and removed the goggles so Sook could take a better look. He explained his goal of moving to the back side of the old smokehouse and storage buildings on the kitchen side of their home. From there, they'd stop, watch, and listen.

They cautiously moved closer, but still proceeded with a sense of urgency. Duncan would have less than an hour to study the commandos' movements. Thus far, there had been no radio contact between them unless they'd missed a brief communication on another channel. If the patrols did not check in with one another often, that would work to his advantage.

A few minutes later, they'd reached the back side of the smokehouse. Sook reached out for Duncan's hand and pulled him close to her. She caught him off guard with a kiss.

"Well, thank you," he said with a big smile.

Sook stood on her toes and whispered in his ear, "This is exciting."

Duncan furrowed his brow and then smiled. *Yes, in a way it is. It always has been.*

He gave her a quick kiss and nodded. "It is exciting, but dangerous." He gently tapped on her forehead, reminding her to stay focused.

They found four fifty-five-gallon drums, which were used to burn trash, near the building, and they quickly made their way behind them before falling to their knees. Duncan had a clear view of the front yard and the barn.

He counted two men smoking, the red cherry at the end of the cigarettes increasing in intensity as they inhaled. They were speaking in hushed voices that Sook could not discern. There were several pickup trucks parked in front, two of which were pointed toward the north gate, and the other three were spread haphazardly on the front lawn.

Next, he focused his attention on the barns. The big barn was still standing, and he could make out a faint light coming from a lantern in the hayloft. He suspected some of the men were forced to sleep outside.

The smaller barn, which had been built to house younger horses and to cover their underground bunker, had completely collapsed into a pile of black, charred ruins. An occasional spark flew into the air when a gust of wind kicked in, but for the most part, Duncan determined the fire to have burned itself out.

They spent another thirty minutes watching the front of the house, and there were no changes other than one occasion when the two men walked into the barn and were replaced by two others. Duncan didn't observe them using their radios, nor did Sook pick up anything by listening.

Duncan considered everything he'd observed and formulated a plan in his mind. The biggest variable was the number of men in the barn and how he could deal with the north and south sides of the ranch in a coordinated attack.

He took a deep breath and exhaled as he thought about their odds against trained commandos who'd been schooled in the art of warfare as part of the elite Lightning Death Squads. Men who were also mentally prepared for operating in a criminal enterprise by a one-eyed marauder named Holloway.

Duncan chuckled, shook his head, and looked down at the West Texas soil that had belonged to the Armstrong family for nearly two centuries. His odds weren't good.

I have an army of six. This is suicide.

CHAPTER 17

January 24
The Armstrong Ranch
Borden County, Texas

Just after midnight, Duncan and Sook had returned to their camp in the east woods to a group of anxious faces. He'd led men into battle and fellow operatives into impossible missions—like the assassination attempt on Kim Jong-un. This was much different. The faces looking to him for guidance and direction were his family and the first woman he'd ever loved.

Duncan was their leader now, and the results of his leadership would not be determined by what he did in the coming hours, but rather, what he could inspire his family to do.

He gathered everyone around the campfire and cleared an area of the forest floor of debris. They intently watched Duncan as he gathered twigs, stones, and a curved vine.

He began to create a three-dimensional rendition of the ranch and the location of its buildings. The curved vine marked the northern boundary along the river, and a piece of bark off a fallen oak tree was used to depict the bridge. He stacked small twigs along the river to mark the barnyard. The south side of the ranch was marked by a long twig, and the guard tower was indicated by a rectangular standing stone. Finally, he laid out the buildings surrounding the ranch house.

The group watched with great interest as Duncan first removed the magazine from the Daniel Defense AR-10 and dropped the 7.62 mm ammunition out of it. He stood the bullets upright at various parts of his makeshift map. Then he removed his sidearm and removed its ammunition as well. He rolled these shorter bullets through his hands as he spoke.

He paused to study the faces and found what he was looking for—determination. Even his mother insisted upon being unburdened by the sleeping bag and leaned upright against a tree stump protruding from the ground near the fire. Despite her burned arm and the wounds in the other, she'd had a remarkable recovery since Major returned. The strength his parents exuded together played a factor in the assignments he was about to make.

"Our primary goal is to retake the ranch house because Holloway is there, and the families are buried underground nearby. If we had the luxury of time, Sook and I could've surveilled the ranch house and gotten a better head count. This is a gaping hole in my plan, but it's not insurmountable, and I'll show you why."

Now fully engaged, everyone scooted closer to the map, being careful not to obstruct Lucy's view. Duncan continued.

He placed two of the nine-millimeter rounds from his pistol near the guard tower. "We're all going to approach on horseback, although it will be important to dismount before the point of attack. Your horses are your fallback position and the means of escape. Regardless of what I'm about to lay out, if you have to retreat, do not lead them back down here. Ride away from your target and make a roundabout way back to our camp."

"Makes sense," said Major, who gave Lucy a knowing smile.

Duncan then placed two of the taller 7.62 rounds outside the boundary fence, which was represented by a long twig. "These two rounds represent Cooper and Riley. Guys, I need you to circle around past the Slaughters' place and approach the guard tower from that direction. Most likely, there will be a two-man team focusing their attention on the west side of the ranch where they originally came from. As you pass through the Reinecke operation, look for signs of life. Based upon the gunfire you heard earlier, I suspect the Slaughters are dead. But watch out for hostiles too."

"Should we take them out if they show themselves?" asked Riley.

"No, it'll ruin the element of surprise we need to succeed. Don't be seen, and make your way to the guard tower. Position yourselves to fire upon the commandos in the tower, as well as any others that may show up in vehicles."

"How will we know when to shoot?" asked Cooper.

Duncan replied with a sly grin, "When all hell breaks loose. You'll see."

"Dang straight!" added Riley as he sat a little taller in his spot.

Duncan handed Cooper one of the North Koreans' radios. "Sook and I have been monitoring these all night. We haven't heard them check in a single time. It's odd, actually. They're almost complacent already. Surprising, but that's fine by me. Anyway, I have the channel preset to match the radio I'll be giving Dad."

Major leaned forward as Duncan handed him the other radio. Then he placed two bullets near the north bridge. Duncan looked to Palmer and his father as he did so.

"Dad, Palmer, you're going to take out the sentries at the north gate and possibly any reinforcements who respond from the barnyard, although I suspect they'll already be at the gate or near the bridge."

"I like working with Sook," interrupted Palmer. "Um, no offense, Daddy."

"Consider me offended," mumbled Major somewhat jokingly.

"Daddy! You know better than that."

"C'mon, you two, focus," Duncan chided his recruits. "Palmer, your silencer plays a big role in all of this. We need to take out the commandos at the north gate without warning the others. Besides, I need Sook for something else."

"Okay," Palmer said with a pout. She reached over and squeezed Sook's hand. "You can have her for this mission only."

"If we execute as planned, this will be our only mission," replied Duncan curtly. He was all business.

"Son, how will we know when to begin?"

Duncan exhaled. "It has to be done by timing and speed. You two know the area surrounding the bridge well. You need to get the jump on the guards and eliminate them with Palmer's silenced H&K. Once you have, grab their weapons and head for the silos, here." Duncan pointed out the location of the silos, which were between the ranch house and the south gate tower.

"We can do that. Then what? The barnyard?"

"It depends," replied Duncan. "I need you in position at the silos at four a.m. If you can make your way to the barnyard undetected and eliminate any threats, then all the better. I seriously doubt there will be more than a couple of men there, but it's worth a try."

"Got it," said Palmer.

"Everybody, I can't stress enough the importance of keeping your movements and activities undetected. Okay?"

Everyone acknowledged Duncan's statement before he continued.

"Once in position, you contact the guys on the radio and let them know," replied Duncan. He turned to his brothers. "When you get Dad's signal, light 'em up."

"Finally!" said an exuberant Riley.

"Well, don't get too excited," started Duncan. He spread five round pebbles around near the front of the ranch house. "When the gunfire erupts, the commandos are gonna come screamin' out of the barn, get in these five cars, and take off toward you guys. Once you open fire, if you don't kill both guards, you need to move toward the east down the fence row."

"Why?" asked Riley.

"Two reasons. First, these guys are trained well, and they'll know where you were firing from by both sound and visually due to your muzzle flash. Second, the approaching vehicles will head straight for the guard tower. If you're in position down the fence row, you can catch them off guard as they drive by. If they make it that far."

"Whadya mean?" asked Palmer.

"That's where part two of your responsibilities kick in," replied Duncan. He pointed to the silos. "Here, you've got the perfect cover to ambush them as they leave the house and head toward Cooper and Riley's position. If you miss them, then the guys can engage. If everybody misses, they'll be turning around soon enough anyway."

"Why?"

"Because Sook and I will have them chasing their tails," replied Duncan as he hugged his fiancée and pulled her close to him. He looked her in the eye. "Tonight, we fight side by side again."

"And we'll win," she said with a smile.

"Yes, we will."

CHAPTER 18

January 24
The East Woods
The Armstrong Ranch
Borden County, Texas

"Daddy! Preacher's awake." Palmer leaned backward and waved to her father, who continued to discuss tactics with Duncan around the battle map. He patted his son on the arm and quickly came to his friend's side.

Major dropped to Preacher's side and leaned down to speak into his ear. "How're ya doin', old man?"

"Not bad for Swiss cheese," the bullet-ridden former minister replied. "Glad you made it back, boss."

Preacher began to cough, causing Sook and Palmer to hover out of concern. He managed to raise his left arm, indicating he was okay.

"How about you let me do the talkin'?" said Major.

"Just one thing," started Preacher as he struggled to regain his breath. "The bunker. My idea. Please save them."

Major squeezed his friend's hand. "Duncan has a plan to take back the ranch and rescue the ranch families. We're gonna leave soon, and when it's over, I'll be back to take you to a hospital."

Preacher began to cough again, and Major comforted him. "You hang on, buddy. We're gonna get you fixed up."

Preacher smiled and nodded. "Don't put dirt on my grave just yet."

Major offered his friend more words of support and strength, but he'd already drifted off to sleep. Major exhaled and his head dropped as he closed his eyes to say a quick prayer for Preacher. Then the anger began to build up inside him. He wanted revenge for what those animals had done to his family and the Armstrong Ranch.

He joined Cooper and Riley, who were going over potential scenarios that might arise. They all agreed that another pair of night-vision goggles would've helped, but in the final analysis, Duncan needed them the most. All three guys agreed that Holloway, the head of this evil snake, had to die. When he did, the remaining commandos who survived the attack would scatter.

"Everybody don't forget that we know this ranch and they don't," said Major. "That's a huge advantage."

Duncan added something else. "Also on our side is commitment and desire. We're fighting for our home. They're fighting for a criminal madman who's hell-bent on stealing what isn't his. These guys are far different than the Lighting Death Squad commandos who are fighting for their country and Dear Leader. Don't get me wrong. They're fierce fighters. I just don't believe they'll be willing to risk their lives again for Holloway."

Meanwhile, Palmer and Sook took the time to change the dressings on their patients' wounds. Lucy was feeling better and insisted that Palmer give her a pistol and a rifle, just in case.

"If they get past you all, then I'm gonna take out as many of them as I can."

"Momma," interjected a concerned Palmer, "that's suicide. They may just leave you be."

"I don't care. I'd rather die fighting than let them take my family, my ranch, and me."

As Palmer and Sook finished up, Duncan instructed Riley and Cooper to ready the horses with extra weapons and ammo. Each of them would carry a holstered sidearm as well as ankle holsters on Duncan and Major. Hunting rifles would go in the saddle scabbards, and each would carry their battle rifles over their shoulders. Riley finished loading all of their additional magazines, which were stuffed into saddlebags or their cargo pants.

Duncan was proud of their preparations. They might not be seasoned soldiers, but they looked the part, and all of them had adopted the mindset of a warrior. It's not the strength of your weaponry that makes you a warrior, it's what's in your heart and soul.

"Son, is that what going off to war was like?" asked Major as he joined Duncan in staring down at the map he'd created.

"Honestly, Dad, it's worse. When I used to leave for a tour of duty, it was because it was my job. When I became an operator, things changed slightly. What I used to do was not war, which was made up of losses and gains on the battlefield. It was, however, a necessity."

"Was there a difference? I mean, when you had to leave on a mission, was your thinking different from going to the Middle East?"

"Not really. I mean, the quandary was the same. How do you love your family and go on a mission, or off to war, for that matter, knowing full well that you might not return? I've faced death many times, Dad. When I got on those military transports, I always knew that my ticket could be punched and I'd return via Andrews in a casket."

He turned to his Dad and patted him on the chest. Then Duncan wandered off to the edge of the woods alone to stare off into the darkness.

"Dear, is he all right?" Lucy asked.

Major joined Lucy and the girls.

"Maybe I should go to him," said Sook as she stood from her crouch.

Major gently took her by the hand and held her by his side. "No, he's fine."

"But—" Sook tugged slightly in protest.

Major pulled her closer and put his arm around her. He reached out to Palmer, who hugged him as well.

"Let me tell y'all about Duncan. Every once in a while, you'll meet a man who doesn't feel anything. He can kill and fall asleep the moment his head hits the pillow without giving it a second thought. Duncan is one of those guys. That said, it's his feelings that separate him from those animals who took our ranch."

Major paused and looked into Lucy's eyes. "Your son has to

become a different person right now. He has to become that unfeeling animal. He needs to morph into a beast that kills without hesitation or feeling. Trust me. Our success depends upon it."

CHAPTER 19

January 24
The Armstrong Ranch
Borden County, Texas

Cooper and Riley were the first to set out. Their circuitous route to the south gate guard tower required them to ride through the shooting range, around the Slaughters' property, and through the oil well field. The longer ride was more treacherous as well, but it was one the guys had made all their lives.

They emerged from the ravine and slowly made their way to the Reinecke operation, which the Slaughters had called home. The guys were still sore at their ranch hands who'd abandoned their posts when the shooting started. Duncan had halfheartedly defended the men on the basis they were concerned for their own families, but Cooper and Riley were not swayed. In their minds, the Slaughters had made a deal, and they should've stuck to it.

If they had stayed in the fight, as Riley put it, the attackers would've been delayed, and the ranch's defenses could've held in place.

"Woulda, shoulda, coulda," said Cooper, cutting off the debate. "Duncan said to look for signs of life, and that's all we'll do. Maybe we can talk them in to covering us if we have to hightail it out of there."

"Aren't we supposed to avoid contact?" asked Riley, who then went on to remind Cooper of Duncan's plan.

"Yeah, but I don't see the harm in asking for their help. They owe us, Riley."

The guys rode closer to the block and stone caretaker's house, which Mr. and Mrs. Slaughter had called home since their own place had burned down many weeks ago. As they approached, Riley pointed out a darkened shape lying in the dirt.

Cooper quickly dismounted and readied his rifle. Walking as quietly as possible, he slowly placed the heel of his foot down and then quietly rolled his foot toward his toes. His hips rotated back and forth, which allowed him to respond to movement on either side of him. Cooper's eyes darted from the house, to the body, and then to nearby points of cover. He found himself at his highest state of awareness since he'd ridden One Night Stand on the night of the EMP attack.

When he arrived at the body, he rolled it over to identify it. The man's face was missing, as it had been shot several times. However, the red plaid shirt confirmed it was one of the Slaughters' ranch hands.

Cooper fought the urge to vomit. He quickly moved to the house, abandoning his quiet approach in favor of speed. As he went, he wondered, *Am I running toward the house or away from the dead guy?*

He reached the back wall of the house and listened for any indication of sound. There was none. The door was open, but not voluntarily. It had been shot off its hinges. He glanced inside but didn't feel the need to go further. The automatic gunfire they'd heard earlier in the evening emanating from this direction was just confirmed. The Slaughters had been slaughtered.

Cooper shouldered his rifle and ran back to where Riley was patiently waiting. "What did you see, Coop?"

"All dead or missing. Let's go."

The guys made their way past the improvised cattle pens used for the dairy cows. As they rode past, the cows shuffled somewhat and let out an occasional bellow.

"There's the gravel road through the wells up ahead," said Riley, pointing toward the dusty gray road past the cattle pens. "This one is kinda over the river and through the woods, but it'll lead us to the south gate."

Cooper looked down at his watch. They were ahead of schedule, but he wanted to get in position nonetheless. He thought about picking up the speed to a slow trot, but their horses' hooves striking the packed surface would be too loud. He rode along in silence with an anger building up inside him.

An anger his brother could sense. "Hey, Coop, you all right? What did you see back there?"

"Death, Riley. But it was different. Listen, I get war is hell and all that. We're gonna shoot at them, and they're gonna shoot back. I'm prepared for that."

"I'm with ya, but I'm not afraid, are you?"

Cooper scowled. "I was a little, earlier. Now I'm pissed. Riley, they shot that man's face off. He had already taken two bullets to the center of his chest. But then one of these guys felt it necessary to shoot several rounds into the guy's face until it was gone. What's the point in that?"

Riley didn't immediately respond, as they had taken a second turn toward the gate house and were getting closer. After a moment, he responded.

"That's why we're here," he began. "If we don't end this, they'll end us."

CHAPTER 20

January 24
The Armstrong Ranch
Borden County, Texas

Palmer and Major were the last to depart the east woods. Duncan and Sook had to walk a significant distance in order to avoid detection, so they left soon after the guys. Their goal was to be in position behind the ranch house before Major and Palmer initiated their attack on the north gate. Palmer waited patiently while Major spoke with Lucy.

"I'll take care of Preach the best I can," started Lucy as she propped herself a little higher on the tree stump. She grimaced in pain, and Major quickly moved to assist her.

"Are you sure sitting up like this is a good idea?" he asked as she got settled in to a comfortable spot.

She reached for her rifle and cradled it in her lap. "Yeah, I'm fine," she replied as she looked up at her husband's face. "Each arm has a different kind of pain, you know? But those pains will pale in comparison to losing you."

"You're not gonna lose me," interjected Major as he gave her one more kiss on the cheek.

Lucy smiled and laughed a little. "I remember when we first got married. I tried to be a big girl as you left for work every day. Back then, you were in the field more and had several dangerous encounters. You'd come home that night, tell Pops and me the stories of your heroic efforts, and I always acted proud. In reality, it scared me for years. I never wanted you to know that I was frightened for your safety because I was afraid it might cloud your judgment."

"I'm sorry, Miss Lucy. I should have known better."

"No, don't get me wrong. I'm bringing it up because you *always* came home to me. After all of these years, and the dangers you've faced, I could count on you to come home safely."

"Tonight will be no different," he said with another reassuring kiss. The hardest moment of the evening for Major was right now. He wanted to give the love of his life one more kiss, one more hug, and one more promise that it would be all right.

"I know, and I also can tell by the looks of my impatient daughter that you've got to go," said Lucy.

"I do. Remember this. You know I'll be back, and you can start counting down in your head when I'll return for you. Just a couple of hours, you'll see."

Lucy leaned up and gave her husband one last kiss. Then she made him a promise and asked for one in return. "I'll do everything I can to keep Preach alive until you get back. Major, I need a promise from you."

"Of course, darling. I promise to come back to you in one piece."

Lucy glanced at Palmer and then looked her husband in the eyes. "Promise me you'll bring back our kids alive too."

He touched her face and kissed the tears as they flowed down her cheeks. "Absolutely. I promise."

Major gave her yet another peck on the cheek and then left with Palmer. They had to ride along the lake until they reached the point where the Colorado River poured into Lake J. B. Thomas. Working along the riverbanks, they'd locate the crossing he and Duncan had used earlier in the evening when they had escaped the commandos investigating his overturned Humvee.

The water was shallow enough for them to walk the horses across to the other side. Using the north side of the river, they could easily access the north gate of the ranch without running across any sentries posted at the barnyard. There'd be time for them later, Major hoped.

Forty-five minutes later, they were in position. The bridge

appeared to be unguarded, but Major insisted upon walking across to look for tripwires first. He and Duncan surmised that this form of triggering device had been used to set off the grenade blast that had overturned his Humvee. The armor had protected Duncan from death. Nothing could stop the blast from killing their horses, and them, for that matter.

Hugging the guardrail, Major slowly moved across the bridge, which had stood as the unofficial entrance to the ranch for decades. Built in the fifties out of hand-hewn beams and supports, it provided a distinctive thumping sound as vehicles crossed it. If the bridge was clear of IEDs, he and Palmer would have to walk the horses across to avoid unnecessarily raising the attention of any guards manning the gate a quarter mile away.

Finding the bridge to be safe, he hustled back to Palmer, and they readied their weapons as they entered the battlefield. They tied their horses off to a signpost, which read Armstrong Ranch, and proceeded surreptitiously toward their targets.

The north gate to the ranch rested in the midst of a stand of pecan trees, which lined the driveway for a hundred yards on each side of the entry. In normal times, the wrought-iron steel gate remained open during the day and closed in the evening. A keypad allowed entry, as did the keyless remotes assigned to their vehicles. Tonight, the gates were open, but the driveway was partially blocked by a white Ford pickup truck.

"Follow me," whispered Major as he darted from tree to tree. He wasn't able to identify the guards with particularity, only detecting shadowy movements. "We need to cross over the fence and get behind them."

Palmer followed his lead, and the two of them found the four-rail fence that marked the perimeter of the Armstrong Ranch. They easily climbed over and crouched to one knee to determine if they'd been detected.

The commandos were talking to one another in English, which was out of character from what Duncan had told them. Despite the fact that these men had lived in the U.S. for many years, they still seemed to use their native North Korean when interacting in battle or conducting conversations. Major shrugged this off and became hopeful that they might reveal information that would give him a tactical advantage.

One of the men raised his voice slightly, enabling Major to hear every word.

"Seriously, how long do you think we can hold this ranch? I mean, Holloway is delusional if he thinks he can squat here and get away with it."

"Man, that crazy dude is delusional and psycho. Look, don't get me wrong. He took me in when I was just street hustlin' dope for the Fullerton Boyz. Holloway turned that operation from a bunch of gangbangers to a real street gang."

"Yeah, at platoon strength too."

"No doubt. I can't fault him for what his goals are, but this seems a little nuts to me. For now, it's all we've—"

Palmer had had enough of the chatter. While the two men were ignoring their duties and distracted by their conversation, she'd quietly approached from one tree to another until their silhouettes stood out against the tailgate of the white pickup.

As Duncan had taught her, she quickly fired two rounds into each of the men's bodies, who immediately dropped to their knees as if to pray. Palmer never gave them the chance as she skillfully punctured each of their skulls with a nine-millimeter bullet.

Major quickly ran into the clearing with his weapon ready for any type of movement. Palmer checked the truck bed to look for anyone hiding, and Major likewise cleared the front and back seats of the cab. Satisfied they'd removed the threat, both of them put away their weapons.

Major turned to Palmer. "Go get the horses while I dispose of their bodies. Let's not tip off any roving patrols we may have missed."

"I'm on my way."

While she was gone, Major stripped the dead of their weapons and a single two-way radio. He programmed it to the same channel he'd be monitoring with his sons. Then he dragged the two dead commandos into the woods behind a pile of fallen tree limbs. Lastly, he reached into the pickup, took the keys, and manually locked the doors. He didn't want the truck to be used by any fleeing commandos.

When Palmer arrived, he quickly mounted his horse and handed her the extra radio. Major checked his watch. Their efficiency had paid off.

"Let's check on your mother's barnyard. Maybe we can take out a couple more."

They urged their horses forward and rode along the well-worn path that lined the outer perimeter along the fence. It was a path he and Preacher had taken many times over the years.

Major fought off the melancholy feelings about his old friend. He knew Preacher was likely to die before they could get him medical help. He'd lost too much blood, and despite the heroic efforts of Sook to control his fever, the bullets lodged within his body were taking their toll.

First, he and his youngest child had a job to do. Step one was accomplished. Removing any reinforcement threat at the barnyard would help Duncan and Sook as they went after Holloway. Also, it would lower the number of commandos they'd have to account for after it was over.

"Daddy, we should stop well short of the barnyard. The chickens will sense our approach. If they get riled up, our cover will be blown and so will the whole operation."

Major chuckled. "You're starting to sound like Duncan."

"Yeah, I reckon I am. Up ahead, Daddy. Just before the small barn would be best."

Palmer took the lead and slowly made her way to a broken-down wagon, which had found its final resting place many years ago, but nobody had the heart to give it a proper burial.

After dismounting, Palmer moved toward the back of the barn, with Major just behind her. He pointed out another one of the pickups parked near the hog pen. They knew one or more commandos would be here, but the question was whether they were in the smaller utility barn or in the larger hay barn on the other side of the chicken coops. Out of concern for disturbing the chickens, they tried the small barn first.

Palmer knew the side door creaked when it was opened, so she whispered to her father, "Daddy, guard this entrance. I'm gonna slip around to the front and see if I can identify them. If they come out this way, well, you know what to do."

Major nodded and gave her a thumbs-up. In this moment, he had never been prouder of his daughter. She had grown up to be a well-rounded, astute young woman. Now, she had the presence of mind to take on trained killers without fear. He wasn't afraid for her as she rounded the corner of the barn alone.

He leaned against the barn and tried to see through cracks in the boards. It was dark inside, and his view was partially obscured by a tractor, but he was able to catch a glimpse of a shadow moving from right to left.

Frustrated by his inability to see, he moved to the other side of the door and searched for a knothole or gap in the barn board. There was nothing, so he took a deep breath, steadied his rifle, and listened.

Spit-spit. Spit.

It was the distinctive sound of a silencer doing its job. An excruciating minute passed as Major's palms became sweaty. He assumed Palmer had killed her target, but the deathly silence unnerved him. *Where is she?*

Another minute passed, and Major felt fear for his daughter for the first time. His confidence in her abilities was being pushed back inside him—replaced by apprehension.

He followed her path inside, using the front entrance to avoid the squeaky hinges. While his curiosity and concern got the best of him, he also needed to be careful not to get shot by her deadly aim by mistake.

The tension was building within him, and he decided he'd call out to her in a whisper. "Palmer! Palmer!"

"Over here!" Palmer responded calmly from across the hog pen near the side door to the other barn. "We're clear, Daddy. I got the one guy. Will you grab his gun while I get the horses?"

Major fell against the barn and breathed a sigh of relief. He swallowed hard and tried to moisten his mouth, which had dried out of nervousness.

"Okay," he finally responded and went about the same routine as before. He gathered up the commando's weapon and fumbled through his pockets, where he found the truck's keys. This man did not have a radio.

Not concerned about disrupting the chickens, Palmer rode into the barnyard with her father's horse. Once again, he checked his watch.

"Palmer, I'm very proud of you."

She began to laugh. "Thank you, Daddy. Can I have a raise in my allowance now? It's been years since y'all put quarters under my pillow for lost teeth and such."

Major leaned off the side of his saddle and extended his fist toward his daughter. She promptly provided him a fist bump.

"I think you've certainly earned a bonus. How about a shiny new Ford truck? We've got a white one and a red one to choose from."

"I'll take white. There's already one Red Rover in the family."

Major laughed and pulled on the reins to turn his horse toward the silos. "C'mon. We've got less than ten minutes to get to the silos. Your trigger-happy brothers are probably gettin' antsy."

CHAPTER 21

January 24
The Armstrong Ranch
Borden County, Texas

Duncan and Sook spent a furtive hour together as they circled the ranch house in preparation for their attack on Holloway. All of the lights were off inside, and the same two guards were milling about the front lawn. The vehicles were still parked in the same position as earlier, and there was no indication of any type of change in their security measures. All of these factors contributed to Duncan's earlier conclusion that the North Koreans had become comfortable in their surroundings.

Our surroundings.

The men were smoking and talking in hushed tones. Occasionally they'd laugh and slap each other on the back. Also, rather than patrolling the grounds with their rifles at low ready, now they'd slung them over their shoulders, and a bottle of liquor emerged in place of their weapons.

Duncan thought about the disciplined soldiers he'd encountered near the nuclear-testing facility in Kusong. When he and Park had been stalked following the failed assassination attempt, those men had been intense, alert, and followed orders. The two guards laughing and drinking on the front yard of his family's home were North Koreans by birth, and perhaps trained with the Lightning Death Squads, but they'd lost their edge as commandos.

They were criminals, just like Holloway. Drunk ones at that.

Without having radio contact with his dad, Duncan was unable to determine whether they'd been successful at the north gate. Two things gave him confidence in their efforts. One, he hadn't heard any gunfire as of yet, and based upon the time, if something had gone awry, the night air would've exploded in gunfire all around the ranch.

Secondly, there had been no radio communications between the two guards they'd been observing and the outposts. While there was a time and place to maintain radio silence, when performing perimeter security, *all silence, all the time* was not a good idea.

Duncan assessed his options. The men were too far away from the house to take them quietly by using his knives. In their inebriated state, he considered drawing them around toward the smokehouse with some type of noise, similar to the tactic Park had used as they'd approached the military base in Kusong.

Duncan's new secret weapon was soft-spoken Sook. He'd seen her in action on Sinmi-do when, by using her charm, she'd disarmed the North Korean soldiers searching for him. He could employ her again for this task, but even these near-drunk men would be astonished that a North Korean girl had found her way to West Texas.

The silenced H&K was the best option, but he had to get close enough to fire upon the men without missing. From his hidden position two hundred feet away from the guards, he would have to eliminate two threats with a single shot each without them uttering a sound. Even with his skill set, it was very risky.

It was time to make his move. He and Sook made their way to the corner of the house. Duncan took her silenced sidearm and prepared himself by whispering his final instructions to Sook. She was prepared to use the Kel-Tec PLR-16 he'd obtained from the armory to shoot at anyone who exited the house. She'd only had minimal training with the short, lightweight equivalent to an AR-15 rifle, but this weapon was easy to use and control.

"Are you ready?" Duncan whispered to Sook.

She smiled and nodded. "I have your six."

Duncan, who'd remained focused during the last hour as he mentally prepared for their against-all-odds battle to regain their home, managed to snicker. "Where did you learn that?"

"Preacher told me I needed to learn to talk like a soldier. He reads many army books."

"Okay, well, he's right," said Duncan. Then he grew serious as he prepared to ambush the sentries. "Sook, things will happen very fast now. Pay close attention to me and my signals. We will have to move quickly and quietly. Okay?"

"I am ready. Move!"

Again, Duncan laughed to himself and responded, "Moving."

At a low crouch he entered the front yard, where the Zoysia and Bermuda grasses were dormant for the winter. His soft approach coupled with the cushioning effect of the lawn allowed him to get within forty feet of his targets—deadly close for the former operator and trained killer.

Duncan, who was right-handed, always chose to eliminate the left target first when training. It was more comfortable to swing his barrel away from his body rather than across it, especially when he was wearing a full kit with extra magazines and a compact sidearm stowed in it.

He continued walking toward his targets, closing a few additional feet as he studied their movements and reactions. The drunken guards were oblivious to his approach and were blissfully unaware as the bullets silently flew into the back of their skulls.

Duncan immediately sped to their side and felt for a pulse. They were both dead. He swerved his body from the barn to the main house, looking for movement. All was quiet. As instructed, Sook placed herself at the corner of the porch with her weapon raised toward the stairs descending onto the front lawn.

Comfortable that she had him covered, he holstered his weapon and dragged the two men across the grass into the dark side of the house. He turned the commando's radio off and slid it into his cargo pants pocket.

He quickly rejoined Sook at the house. With a final glance at his surroundings, he realized he'd left the liquor bottle lying in the grass. It would be visible to the men who were likely sleeping in the barn, but in the frenzy created by the attack on the south gate, he was sure the empty liquor bottle wouldn't be spotted. Dead bodies, on the other hand, would've been noticed, which was why he disposed of them.

"Stay here," Duncan whispered before he darted across the front of house to the other side of the porch. Being careful to avoid the glass and debris that still littered the porch following the RPG attack, Duncan snuck up to the living room windows and peered inside. Snoring immediately caught his attention as the apparently exhausted men crashed from two days of battles from here to Lubbock.

There was a man asleep on each end of the sofa, another one sprawled out on the settee, and a fourth leaned back in his dad's recliner. He and Sook would have to work together to kill the four men and not wake up the other occupants of the home.

As he moved back toward her, he contemplated the stealth approach or whether to go in there with *guns a-blazin'*. Duncan grimaced as he led her around the side of the house. He dreaded the dangers of close-quarters combat with his beloved Sook by his side.

CHAPTER 22

January 24
The Armstrong Ranch
Borden County, Texas

Duncan and Sook entered the kitchen door nearest the smokehouse. He carefully turned the knob and gradually pushed the door open to minimize the creaking sound it made. Fortunately, the already cold air inside the house wouldn't be affected by their entry. Once the door opening was wide enough for him to slide through, he pointed the barrel of his rifle inside and allowed it to lead the way.

Sook tapped Duncan on the shoulder. "Let me go first. I know the floors better."

He and Sook were in familiar territory. They knew where the furnishings were located, which doorway led where, and what boards creaked as they walked on them. Sook had spent every day at the ranch house since their arrival back at the ranch. Duncan, on the other hand, had been away for long periods of time, including the years when he had been deployed abroad.

Duncan admired her fearlessness and had total confidence in her abilities. Despite his misgivings about including her in this perilous task, he relented and slid to the side as she passed.

They entered the family room, and the low light of the dying fire confirmed the number of commandos asleep on the furniture. Sook pulled a Morakniv Bushcraft survival knife from its sheath. The knife had been given to her by Preacher to be used as a multipurpose tool in survival or defensive situations. The sheath came with a diamond sharpener and an integrated fire starter, which had come in handy at their campsite the evening before.

Duncan pointed to the right, indicating Sook would take the man in the recliner and the man whose neck was exposed on that end of the sofa. Killing with a knife was a brutal, personal act. It required personal contact between the killer and the victim. Oftentimes, it resulted from extreme hate, revenge, or payback of a vendetta. Tonight, for Duncan and Sook, it was all business.

They were careful to avoid any debris on the floor as they approached. At one point, Duncan's heavier frame caused them both to pause in their tracks, watching and listening for a change in movement of their prey, which would necessarily result in weapons being drawn.

None of the commandos stirred. Duncan nodded to Sook, and they moved closer. When they arrived at their mark, the two moved in unison and quickly sliced into the throats of the men who'd attacked the ranch.

Earlier, Duncan had explained the art of slitting the throat of another human being. It didn't always result in instant death, which was typically portrayed on television and movies. It was actually a slower process, and it was not necessarily a quiet one. The victim typically gasped for air and flailed about in an attempt to stop the bleeding.

Duncan had pointed out the location of the external carotid artery, which provided the blood supply to the face and neck. Immediately behind it was the internal carotid artery, which provided blood to the brain. In order to achieve a quick, silent kill, the attacker had to slice deep enough into the throat to sever both arteries. Even then, it would take the target a few seconds to pass out due to the lack of oxygenated blood to the brain.

He'd warned that it took a certain amount of expertise to make the perfect cut, but Sook assured him that she was capable. He also described the resulting mess. When the deep cut was made, the jugular vein was likely to be severed. Blood would pour out of the victim's throat in spurts as this happened.

The act would require Sook to clamp her hand firmly over her victim's mouth to prevent him from screaming, hold firm while she made her cut, and then be patient while the target died. Then she would need the presence of mind to move to her next victim without stumbling or slipping on the blood.

After Duncan described the details of a kill to Sook, he studied her lack of emotion and steely resolve. She had a coldness in her voice that troubled him somewhat. Despite her outwardly warm and loving manner, Sook was capable of killing, just like he was. As they prepared to make their first kills, he had no doubt she'd adopted the mindset of a deadly assassin.

In choreographed-like unison, they eliminated the first two commandos. Working in tandem, they moved toward the sofa, where the second kills were quicker. It was over in seconds as the four men lay dead, their throats laid bare by the sharp knives of their assassins.

Duncan returned his knives to the specially designed pockets in his cargo pants and moved against the wall adjacent to the back bedrooms. Sook joined him, her chest heaving from exhilaration.

"Are you okay?"

"Oh, yes. Now what?"

Duncan tapped on the PLR-16. "Ready your weapon. I'm going to clear these rooms, and then we'll head upstairs."

She nodded, but Duncan didn't see her as he slipped down the darkened hallway toward the two downstairs guest bedrooms. He drew the silenced pistol and moved slowly across the floor, which had shards of broken glass on it. Duncan was puzzled initially, as there were no windows in this part of the house, and then he found the pile of broken picture frames swept into an open closet.

He instantly recalled what the photo frames contained, and he became enraged. "Animals," he muttered as he entered the first room and skillfully delivered two bullets to the brain of the occupant of the first bed.

Returning to the hallway, he made his way to the second bedroom. He turned the knob of the closed door. A piece of furniture was blocking it.

"Crap," he muttered to himself. Whoever was located in this bedroom had had the presence of mind to barricade the door, as none of the interior doors to the house had locks on them. If he forced his way in, they'd be alarmed, and a shoot-out would ensue.

Duncan pushed the door inward a little more, moving it forward slightly with each effort. After a minute, he was able to see the foot of the bed. He was taking up precious time as he deliberately created a wider opening. He glanced at his watch. It was approaching 4:00—the time when all hell was going to break loose.

He nudged the door again as he created a wider gap. More of the sleeping man could be seen on the bed. Another push and his head would be in view. Duncan closed his eyes, focusing all of his senses on his movements and the sounds in the deathly quiet ranch house. One more time and he'd have the angle to take a shot.

There! That's all I need!

Duncan slid the silenced barrel of the gun through the crack and took aim. The spitting sound preceded the bullets entering the body of the commando, which rose off the bed with each shot. Duncan fired twice into the man's torso and placed a third shot in the head. The downstairs was clear.

Even though this magazine still had a few rounds in it, he quickly replaced it with a full one. He had another one available in his kit, but he hopefully wouldn't need to use it. He made his way back to the family room, where Sook was waiting.

"Good?" she asked.

"Very good," said Duncan as he nodded toward the stairwell. "Stay a few steps behind me."

As instructed, Sook followed as Duncan readied his rifle and led the way. If Holloway or any of his men upstairs heard them, knives and pistols would be insufficient from this point forward.

Just as Duncan reached the third step of a dozen, gunfire erupted on the ranch.

CHAPTER 23

January 24
The Armstrong Ranch
Borden County, Texas

Major knew his sons well, especially the emotionally charged Riley. Cooper would have to muster all of his patience and convincing abilities to keep his brother under control. As kids, Riley was never one to enjoy fishing with Palmer and Cooper. He was too hyper, but not in a pump-the-kid-full-of-Adderall sort of way. Riley liked to do stuff, and the concept of baiting a hook, dropping it into the lake, and waiting was not for him. He'd rather grab his Daddy's shotgun and blast the dang fish out of the water to get instant gratification.

His approach to staking out the south gate guard tower was no different. Several times, Cooper had to talk him out of running to the tower, climbing up the stairs, and *tearin' into those guys*, as Riley put it.

Duncan checked his watch, and it was approaching four a.m.

"It's almost time, Riley. Get ready. You spray the sides of the guardhouse with automatic fire while I focus on the first head that pops up over the rail."

"Like Whac-A-Mole," said Riley with a laugh.

"Exactly. One at a time if necessary. But we'll get 'em."

A few minutes later, Cooper's radio squawked to life. It was their dad.

"Boys, it's time. Light 'em up!"

Riley immediately obliged. He rose to one knee and took aim. In quick spurts of a few rounds each, he found his distance and splintered the walls of the building.

Still a few hours away from sunrise, Cooper studied the reaction of the commandos the best he could in the minimal amount of light afforded by the stars. They'd caught the two men off guard, as indicated by their return fire. Rather than stand and shoot, both of them reached their rifles over the top of the wall and fired into the sky well above Cooper's and Riley's heads.

"Again!" shouted Cooper, prompting Riley to spray more bullets along the side.

"I think they're afraid," said Riley, who stopped shooting.

The quiet was interrupted by the sound of approaching vehicles from the ranch house. As Duncan had predicted, commandos were being dispatched from the ranch house compound to assist their comrades. Cooper was comforted in knowing that his dad and sister would ambush them, but he and Riley weren't in position as required to take them out completely.

"This ain't workin'!" exclaimed Cooper.

"I'm gonna keep pouring rounds into the space between the boards," Riley shouted as he opened fire once again.

Cooper stood against the rail of the fence and blocked out the approaching vehicles. He waited for an opportunity. One of the shooters finally revealed himself, and Cooper was ready. Cooper's quick reaction sealed the commando's fate.

In the blink of an eye following the squeeze of the trigger on the powerful .308-caliber hunting rifle, Cooper shot the man in the neck and threw him against the other half wall of the structure.

Cooper immediately shouted instructions to his brother. "Move! We've got to stop the cars headed our way."

The boys turned and ran down the fence row toward the point where they were across from the silos a couple of thousand feet away. From this distance, their shots at the vehicles, which were traveling equidistant between their position and the silos, might not be accurate, but they would serve to distract and pull the commandos away from the ranch.

Riley bolted past his brother with his fully automatic battle rifle courtesy of the Camp Lubbock armory. As he did, Cooper had a thought as there was a momentary cessation of gunfire. He slid to a stop and returned to the edge of the fence. He pulled the bolt mechanism and inserted a round into the chamber. He pointed his rifle at the guard tower once again and prepared to fire.

His gut instinct was right. The commando, most likely curious about the approaching trucks or out of a false sense of security, stuck his head above the rail to get a better look. It was all Cooper needed, who had been an expert marksman with a hunting rifle since he was a teenager.

The unexpected retort of the rifle caused Riley to stumble behind him, but the bullet found its mark, accomplishing the first part of their mission. Both of the guards were dead or seriously wounded.

Cooper finally caught up to Riley, who had opened fire upon the vehicles. The lead truck had been disabled and stopped dead in its tracks with the headlights burning. Another continued toward the guard tower, but gunfire from the direction of the silos caused them to slow. Riley's continuous assault on the commandos forced one of them to veer off the driveway and head in their direction.

When the truck stopped bouncing across the rough terrain and found a smoother surface, its headlights illuminated Cooper and Riley near the fence.

"Dang it!" shouted Riley as he continued to fire from a crouch. The commandos began to return fire.

"We gotta go!" shouted Cooper as he slapped his brother on the back and began to run toward their horses.

Riley ignored his brother and continued to fire at the truck. He managed to shoot out one of the truck's headlights before he ran out of ammunition. He released the magazine, pocketed it, and began to run after his brother while he slapped another magazine into the rifle. He tugged on the charging handle and dove behind an oil well for protection as shots tore up the ground beside them.

"We gotta take a stand, Coop! There's no way to outrun them."

Cooper looked around him. The oil wells were their only source of cover but not a bad option. The steel and concrete structures gave them plenty to hide behind as they engaged the oncoming shooters. The key was to stop them before they enjoyed the cover of the oil wells too. Then the guys would be at a distinct disadvantage against the men with superior training and automatic weapons to counter Cooper's hunting rifle.

"Okay, right here. Stay spread apart. We've gotta stop them in their tracks."

"You shoot out the radiator, and I'll focus on the tires," Riley shouted back.

Riley immediately began to fire at the vehicle's wheel wells, resulting in the metallic sound of bullets colliding with the fenders of the truck.

Cooper did his part, sending round after round toward the massive front grille of the pickup. Their efforts were rewarded, as a loud hissing sound could be heard followed by an explosion as the truck began to swerve back and forth. Both of the guys had found their mark.

"Should we shoot out the headlights?" Riley hollered his question to his brother through the oil field.

Cooper quickly responded, "No! Now we can see them comin'."

He focused on movement around the truck. *Why aren't they bailing out? How many are still inside?* He waited and listened.

When he heard the sound of breaking glass, he realized that he and Riley were blinded to any activity inside or to the rear of the truck.

"They're going through the rear window, Riley. Let 'em have it!"

Both guys began shooting at the front windshield, easily blowing it backwards into the cab. The sounds of screams and groans encouraged them to continue.

Riley yelled to his brother, "Coop! Get the horses! We're gonna have to chase them, or they'll run straight for the silos. Daddy and Palmer would be outnumbered."

Cooper responded as he shouldered his rifle and ran back toward the horses. "Shoot out the headlights so they can't see us! I'll be back!"

Riley rained bullets onto the truck, destroying the headlights and killing one of the commandos as he attempted to exit the front seat and shoot back. Cooper quickly returned to his side and held Riley's rifle while he climbed onto his saddle.

After Cooper returned his rifle, Riley slung it over his shoulder. "Coop, we've got to hurry. C'mon!"

Riley took off, and Cooper shouted after him, "Pistols? The rapid gunfire will spook the horses."

"Yeah," replied Riley, who was putting some distance between his horse and Cooper's. "Old West style!"

Cooper pulled his gun, dug his heels upward into his horse's sides, and hollered, "Hee-yah!"

Soon, the guys were racing toward the abandoned pickup and chasing two men who'd split apart but were both running in the direction of the third pickup, which was slowly approaching the silos.

"We're gainin' on 'em!" shouted Riley before the men turned and fired in their direction. Riley returned fire with his pistol and caught one of the men in the arm, who promptly dropped his rifle. He took off toward the right, and Riley gave chase.

"I got this guy!" shouted Cooper, who shot the man in the leg, causing him to tumble head over heels to the ground. Cooper leaned over his horse's neck to speed forward toward the fleeing man. Suddenly, the commando rose out of the tall grass and fired in Cooper's direction, spooking his horse and causing him to abruptly stop.

Cooper dismounted and crawled on his hands and knees toward the commando, who was now rolling in the tall grass. He was moaning in pain. Cooper chose to remain low to prevent the wounded man from having a better target.

He continued to move closer to the sound of the man's groans until he saw him. Cooper didn't hesitate as he raised his gun and fired. It took five shots to find the man in the tall grass, but the last two trigger pulls were successful.

Riley continued to chase the last commando as a gun battle ensued between his dad and sister and the commandos who'd turned toward the silos. He needed to help them, but this guy needed to be finished off first.

Riley was close and was able to get a steady aim on the commando. He squeezed the trigger to finish him off, but his gun jammed. He pulled the trigger again to no avail. Riley's instincts kicked in, so he defaulted to what he knew best.

After holstering the pistol, he repeatedly kicked his heels into his horse and bore down on the man who was running for his life. He pulled alongside the commando and jumped from his horse, grabbing the man around the neck. Executing a perfect tackle as if the man were a steer, Riley rolled him over onto the ground, pulled his hands behind him, and placed him into the disposable cuffs given to them by Duncan.

The man tried to wiggle loose despite the pain Riley was inflicting upon him. The man's efforts only served to aggravate Riley more, who pistol-whipped the man unconscious. Then he used a second set of cuffs to truss the man together, locking his legs to his wrists behind his back.

Cooper ran to his side. "C'mon, we need to help them at the silos. The third truck only had one guy, and he was dead, slumped over the steering wheel."

Riley gave the gunman a kick to the ribs and said, "I'm ready."

The guys pulled their rifles over their heads and began to run toward the silos, where the shooting continued. As they ran, Cooper asked his brother, "Why didn't you just shoot him?"

"I don't know. I guess I miss steer wrestlin'."

CHAPTER 24

January 24
The Armstrong Ranch
Borden County, Texas

After the guys opened fire on the guard tower, it took the rest of the commandos about five minutes to get into their vehicles and head for the south gate. Major's goal was to take out the lead vehicle, hoping to cause a wreck and add to the confusion. He and Palmer focused on this task and successfully shot out the tires, bringing the truck to an abrupt halt. When the driver rolled down the passenger-side window and began firing toward the silos, Major sent several well-targeted rounds in return fire and killed the lone occupant of the vehicle.

"Daddy! One of the trucks is turning our way!" Palmer swung her rifle in the direction of the pickup, which swerved to avoid a collision with the lead vehicle and then drove toward the silos.

"I see it! The other one is headed toward the boys. Hang tough, honey. This is what we wanted."

Suddenly, bullets tore into the tall grain silos that flanked their position. By design, the silos were to be used as a rally point after the four of them engaged the sentry guards and any reinforcements. From this point on the ranch, they could run through the oak trees toward the two horse training pens and directly past the barns.

If Major and Palmer were successful, they would distract the reinforcements while Duncan moved on the ranch house. Eliminating the threat altogether was not expected but would be a plus.

After five long minutes in this firefight, Major was concerned that the men were flanking their position. The silos, while large, were cylindrical. They didn't provide the best cover because he and Palmer had to expose themselves to gunfire during the battle.

In the opening minutes of them exchanging rounds with their attackers, Major and Palmer had held their own although they had only scored one casualty in the lead vehicle. Now, Major determined they were facing three or four of the commandos, who were making their way through the tall grass to ambush them. They felt pinned down and were unsure of their next move.

"Daddy, we can't fall back. Coop and Riley might walk right into an ambush."

Major took a deep breath and looked around them for a solution. "The other problem is that I can't tell the difference between the commandos and the boys approaching us from the south. I don't wanna shoot one of them by mistake."

Palmer glanced around the silo. The gunmen had stopped firing for the moment, as did Riley and Cooper.

"Daddy, we can't abandon our position or the guys. Let's raise them on the radio."

"I don't know, honey. That's risky. In the tall grasses, they might get exposed by the sound."

The stalemate continued for another moment until the sounds of gunshots startled them.

"That's coming from the house!" exclaimed Palmer. "What do you wanna do?"

Major peeked around the curved structure. He saw movement in the grasses. Several men appeared to be running toward the razed barn. He motioned for his daughter to follow him.

"C'mon! This is our chance to cut them off."

Major moved past the last silo and ran through the trees toward the horse pen. The shortest route to the house was along the outside of the fence toward the location of the burned-out barn. They'd always kept a ten-foot-wide strip mowed so the horses penned up in the enclosure wouldn't attempt to reach the grasses. The commandos would naturally seek the path of least resistance, and Major planned on being ready for them.

"Here they come," said Palmer in a whisper.

"I'll take the front guys, and you take the ones to the rear," Major instructed as he drew his aim on the clearing.

As the gunfire coming from the ranch house subsided momentarily, they could hear the rustling sound of the men running through the hayfield. The shuffling of their heavy footsteps grew louder, which indicated they were getting closer.

He whispered to Palmer, "Wait until they all hit the clearing, and then fire after I do."

"Okay," she muttered.

The hunters stalked their prey. The first man appeared, shuffling through the grasses. Then like the ballplayers in *Field of Dreams*, two more emerged. Major had to decide. If he didn't shoot now, they'd get past their position. He slid his finger on the trigger and thought, *Is there a fourth man?*

He couldn't wait any longer. As soon as he began to empty his magazine on the first two men, Palmer opened fire on the third, who spun around in a pirouette, firing his rifle into the air until he dropped to the ground.

Major walked toward them. "Be careful. There could be one more."

Swinging the barrels of their rifles side to side in a sweeping motion, they advanced on the commandos. Major placed his focus on the back side of the silo. Palmer focused on the men who were sprawled out on the ground.

Just as they arrived at the now dead gunmen, a shot reverberated through the steel structures behind their position. They both swung their guns around just in time to observe the fourth commando tumbling into a tree before he died.

Cooper's voice could be heard from the trees. "Hey, don't shoot! It's just us."

He and Riley emerged into the clearing by the fence. Palmer ran to Riley and hugged him. Cooper walked backwards as he covered the group's back in case they had missed one of the North Korean shooters.

"Everybody good?" asked Major.

Cooper turned to his father. "Yeah, you guys?"

Before Major could respond, Riley interrupted, "Y'all, the shooting's stopped at the house."

"Do you think it's over?" asked Palmer.

"We're fixin' to find out," replied Cooper as he walked briskly toward the house.

Their fast walk changed to a sprint as gunfire filled the air once again.

CHAPTER 25

January 24
The Armstrong Ranch
Borden County, Texas

Duncan realized he was behind schedule. His plan required that he eliminate Holloway before the attack on the south sentry post. Now he had to deal with Holloway and any additional commandos without drawing the attention of the armed commandos who were shouting instructions as they emerged from the barn.

He motioned for Sook to stay in place and watch the front door. Before he climbed the stairs in search of Holloway, he adjusted the night-vision goggles on his head. He drew his sidearm and quietly made his way up the stairs. On the landing at the top of the stairs, he pointed it in the direction of the master bedroom, assuming that was where Holloway was sleeping.

He moved down the hall and slammed the door open with his left hand and fired repeatedly into the bed. The bullets tore through the cover and ripped into the feather pillows, which were stuffed under the covers in an attempt to deceive any intruder. Duncan realized his mistake at the last second when Holloway tackled him from behind.

The much heavier man knocked the breath out of Duncan as the two fell onto the wood floors. His night-vision goggles had been knocked off, and he'd lost control of the pistol as he hit the floor. Duncan's chest, still tender from the IED blast under his Humvee, gasped for air as Holloway began to pummel his head.

Using his arms to fend off the onslaught of punches, Duncan heard gunfire downstairs and knew Sook was exchanging fire with someone in the front yard. The shots periodically rang out, but Duncan had to focus on defending himself.

Duncan tried to turn his body sideways to throw Holloway off balance, but the crazed man slugged Duncan twice in the ribs. With all his effort, Duncan responded by raising his hips, which forced Holloway forward and toward Duncan's head. This had the effect of shifting Holloway's weight horizontally and less directly on top of Duncan.

No longer pinned down, Duncan lifted his butt higher into the air, taking a cue from the bulls Cooper used to ride. Holloway flew over Duncan's head and into a nightstand. Duncan searched for his pistol in the darkness, and then he saw it near the foot of the bed. But so did Holloway.

Like two kids scrambling for doubloons at Mardi Gras, the men crawled on all fours and lunged at the same time for the weapon. Duncan's fist hit the gun first, but it caused it to slide under the middle of the bed, placing it effectively out of reach for both of them.

Duncan scrambled backward and started to pull his rifle over his neck and shoulders. However, Holloway didn't hesitate as he swung his legs around to kick Duncan in the ribs with a heavy blow that knocked him to the ground.

Duncan abandoned his efforts to unsling his rifle and pulled one of his knives. As Holloway lunged for him, Duncan stabbed him in the upper left arm, which forced a guttural groan from Holloway.

Holloway quickly recovered and growled at his adversary. He grabbed Duncan by the wrist and then twisted Duncan's arm, forcing him to release the knife, which was still embedded in the stronger man's bicep. Holloway was crazed now. He ripped the blade from his arm and yelled at Duncan, "Ready to die?"

"Are you?" Duncan yelled back as he quickly slid his hand down his pant leg to retrieve his other knife.

The men both rose to their feet and circled one another. Duncan contemplated removing his rifle and shooting Holloway, but his adversary was far too quick. Holloway would pounce on Duncan before he could use the quick release on his sling and point the weapon.

"Just give it up, pal! I'll let your family live, but you, you gotta go."

"Screw you! Hear that gunfire? That's the sound of your men dying." As if on cue, Sook fired off several more bursts as she continued to exchange gunfire with one of Holloway's men.

"Really?" growled Holloway as he continued to circle the room with Duncan. "Sounds to me like you and the other guy are trapped in here. Last chance, hero. Give it up!"

While Holloway was focused on making speeches, Duncan had reversed the knife within his grip. He had the benefit of the darkness to prepare a side-body throw to embed the knife in Holloway's chest.

Duncan continued the circular dance with the killer until Holloway had reached the open doorway. At that moment, Sook fired off several more rounds, which momentarily caught Holloway's attention. That was the opening Duncan was waiting for. With a slashing motion, he let his knife fly. Silently, it flew across the room with a swooshing sound until it struck Holloway in the sternum.

Surprised, the large man looked down at the blood pouring out of him and reached to remove the knife. Duncan didn't hesitate and bum-rushed Holloway. The impact of the two men colliding served to force the knife deeper into Holloway's chest and caused him to drop Duncan's other knife. Duncan quickly scooped it up and plunged it into Holloway's heart, ending the former warrior-turned-criminal's life.

He leaned over the dead man's body for a few seconds to catch his breath. The shooting had stopped, and the night fell silent once again. Duncan stood and moved to the top of the stairs. He called for Sook.

"Sook, what's happening?"

"One shooter in the hayloft. All others left in the trucks."

Duncan returned his knives to his pants and finally was able to put his rifle to use. He moved to the front window overlooking the front yard. He focused his attention on the two windows facing the ranch house. In the darkness, he was unable to detect any movement.

"Hold him off, Sook!"

He ran back into the bedroom and searched for the night-vision goggles, finding them in the corner of the room. Duncan affixed them to his head and made sure they were working properly. Then he raced back to the front window.

The illuminated field of vision was helpful, but he still couldn't identify the location of the shooter. After a few tense minutes in which Duncan became concerned the man might have escaped toward his family, who were in the area of the silos, he came up with an idea.

He walked over to the railing and whispered loudly to Sook, "Begin shooting from right to left from the corner of the barn to the first window. Understand?"

"Yes!"

Duncan moved back to the window as Sook began firing. An illuminated silhouette moved past the first window toward the middle of the barn.

"Keep going toward the center!"

She continued firing, and Duncan readied the powerful AR-10. As soon as he saw the man emerge in the second window, he opened fire. Bullets ripped into the barn board and sailed into the window, where the body twisted until it hung over the opening. Sook continued to fire, ensuring the final commando was dead.

Using his night-vision capability, Duncan made out four figures racing through the horse pens in their direction. He readied his rifle and allowed them to get closer to the burned-out barn. He waited, hoping they'd bunch up and make his work easier.

Almost. Almost. Come on, suckers.

Duncan slid his finger onto the trigger as they came closer.

CHAPTER 26

January 24
The Armstrong Ranch
Borden County, Texas

"Hold fire. Hold your fire, Sook!"

He spotted the ponytailed hair of Palmer as she reached the taller man leading the contingent. He quickly assessed the body shapes of the four once they arrived in clear view and realized it was his family.

Duncan shouted out the window, "Hey, it's me. Are y'all okay?"

"We got 'em all, son! We think we got 'em all!"

"Clear the barn! I'll be right there."

Before Duncan descended the stairs, he moved toward the last bedroom at the end of the hallway where Holloway had emerged earlier. He entered the room with his rifle ready, and that was when he discovered another body.

Duncan removed his night vision and flipped on the bedroom lights. Lying partially clothed on the floor was the battered, dead body of a young woman. Duncan shook his head in sadness and disgust at what had happened to her. He shouldered his rifle and removed the duvet cover from the bed. He knelt down next to the woman and gently covered her. He took a deep breath, closed his eyes, and then exhaled.

"So senseless," he muttered as he stood.

Duncan marched out of his room with his right hand on the pistol grip. He paused at his parents' bedroom and almost drew the weapon to shoot Holloway in the head out of spite, but then the bloody mess on the floor reminded him that they'd have enough to clean up already.

He started down the stairs, but Sook reached him halfway and rushed into his arms.

"Is it really over?" she asked as her tough exterior broke down into a flood of emotions.

"Almost," Duncan replied. "The sun will be up soon, and we'll need to sweep the ranch. But first, we need to help the people in the bunker."

She gave him a long kiss and whispered, "I love you," into his ear.

"I love you back, Sook. I am so proud of you right now."

She shook her head from side to side. "I want this to be over and everyone to be safe. Then I will be proud too."

Duncan understood. His family had been forced to become killers. This was a loving, caring group of people who followed Christian principles in leading their lives. The circumstances and the assault upon their home had forced them to take up weapons against their fellow man to protect themselves. It was not necessarily a proud moment, but one born of necessity. Duncan only hoped it was the last.

"Barn's clear!" shouted Riley from the front yard.

"C'mon, Sook. Let's go dig out the rest of our family."

They walked into the front yard and were immediately greeted by an enthusiastic Palmer. She and Sook cried tears of joy as Major joined them. He and Duncan gave one another a hearty hug until Duncan reluctantly pointed out his injuries to his father.

"Sorry, son. I'm glad you're okay."

"I'm good, Dad," he said as Riley and Cooper joined the reunion. Everyone took a moment to offer congratulations and thanks to God for protecting them during the fight. Then Duncan forced them to get down to business once again.

"Guys, we've got lots of work to do," started Duncan as he began to dole out the assignments. "I wanna believe that we've taken them all out, but you never know for sure. Until sunrise when we can canvass the ranch, we need to be aware of our surroundings and possible stragglers who are dumb enough to attack us again."

"Agreed," said Major. "Tell us what to do."

"Dad, I think you and Riley should ride down to the east woods. They've been alone down there, and as tough as Momma is, I'm sure she's worried out of her mind."

"Okay, I'll round up our horses," said Riley.

Duncan continued to address his father. "Dad, I have to warn ya. The house is full of blood and dead bodies. There'll be cleanup to do, but I just thought you might want to warn Momma before she sees it for herself."

Major chuckled and placed his hand on Duncan's shoulder. "She won't care, son. I can assure you of that. Now, she might start to grumble here and there, but deep down, she'll be glad we're all safe."

Duncan turned to Cooper and the girls. "We need to dig out the families. Let's go."

Cooper and Duncan walked briskly toward the barn. Palmer and Sook followed close behind. Duncan posted them to stand watch while the guys began to remove charred debris from the burnt-out barn.

Ten minutes later, Cooper came across the empty can of garbanzo beans. "That's weird. I wonder why this didn't burn." He reached down, and that was when he found the hatch to the bunker.

The hatch measured thirty inches in diameter and featured a steel wheel embedded in its lid. A flap-style cover could be set to the side, revealing the wheel, which required several turns to open.

"Duncan! I found it."

Duncan quickly joined Cooper, and they frantically cleared a path from the hatch to the other barn. In the darkness, they didn't want one of the kids to step on a blackened nail or piece of metal.

Cooper removed the flap and tried to turn the wheel. It wouldn't budge. Duncan gave it a try and was unsuccessful.

"The intense heat from the fire must have welded it shut," Duncan surmised.

Suddenly, Cooper jumped up and ran toward the other barn. "I've got an idea."

He was gone several minutes, and he returned with his hands full of tools.

"First, let's pour this motor oil around the wheel. It might help lube the threads. Then we'll use this Council Tool crowbar to break the weld."

It was a five-foot-long heavy carbon-steel crowbar used for prying and moving heavy objects. It had a round, tapered handle and a pinch point to create maximum leverage on the wheel.

The guys worked together to lube the wheel and then determined the best way to angle the tool into the wheel without breaking it. Once they agreed on the process, Cooper took a deep breath and leaned his shoulder into the council tool. The long crowbar began to bend slightly as he gave it more effort, and then with a final push, the seal broke and the wheel moved slightly.

"Yeah!" shouted Duncan as he caught his brother, who'd lost his balance during the sudden shift of the wheel. "Now let's try it."

Duncan's shout grabbed the attention of Sook and Palmer, who ran to the hatch to assist. The wheel was still difficult to turn, so the guys alternated until the hatch seal finally succumbed, releasing a rush of stale, hot air.

"Antonio! Antonio! It's Coop. It's over!"

Duncan opened the hatch all the way, and everyone crowded around to looked inside. It was pitch black, and they couldn't hear anything.

No shuffling. No voices. No crying. No breathing.

Duncan tried. "Hey, it's over! You can come out now!"

Nothing.

Palmer was the first to break down. "Oh my God! Please, Lord, no!"

Cooper, leaning on one knee, buried his face in his hands as he began to sob. "We're too late. Oh no, we're too late."

Tears streamed out of Sook's eyes as she tried to comfort Palmer and Cooper. Duncan's eyes welled up in tears as he consoled the others, but he knew that someone had to go down and investigate. He pulled his shemagh out of his kit. Then he wrapped it around his nose and mouth in anticipation of encountering the stench of death. With his SureFire flashlight leading the way, he descended into the dark bunker.

"I'll come with you," said Cooper, leaning over the hatch as he tried to fight back the tears that soaked his face.

"Nah, Coop. I got this. I'll be back in a minute."

Duncan took a deep breath and held it as he found his way down the final rungs of the ladder to the bottom. He turned and illuminated the room with his flashlight. He turned to his right, pushed open the slightly ajar utility closet door, and found the room to be empty. Stepping deeper into the underground bunker, he looked into the bedroom to his left. It had been slept in, but now lay empty.

A chill came over Duncan's body as he fought off the feeling that ghosts were all around him. As he passed the galley kitchen and the seating areas, he looked for any trace of the ranch families, whether dead or alive. There was none.

Finally, he reached the hallway that connected the two bunkers together. He stepped through the portal to the steel, cylindrical tunnel and shined his light on the other bunker. The door was shut. He approached cautiously and tried the access handle. It wouldn't move.

He carefully moved forward, leaned against the door, and placed his ear against it. The sound was subtle, but it was recognizable. A baby was crying inside.

Duncan removed his knife and used the ringed end to begin tapping on the hatch. Nothing happened. He tried it again.

There was a clanking sound followed by a high-pitched squeak. The handle was moving, and Duncan stood back, allowing the flashlight to brighten the hall.

"Hello? Antonio? It's me. Duncan."

The door slowly pushed open, and Duncan used his flashlight to look inside. Crammed into the smaller bunker were frightened, crying round faces. Babies, children, and mothers all looked at him with wide-open, confused eyes. They clutched one another and began to cry as they tried to process what was happening. Duncan wiped the tears from his eyes, and then he smiled.

"You're safe now. It's over."

Only Antonio stood up among them, his eyes tired from lack of sleep. He shuffled toward Duncan and hugged the taller man.

"*Gracias Dios. Gracias, Duncan.*"

They were a disheveled bunch, but they were alive. He and Antonio helped everyone to their feet and lit up the walkway to the next bunker with his flashlight. Duncan led the way until he reached the bottom of the ladder.

"Hey, y'all!" he shouted with a laugh. "You wanna give me a hand in getting these folks outta here? They're all alive!"

The trio above immediately stopped sniffling and began to holler with joy. Cooper leaned over the hatch and helped lift the kids out first. Palmer greeted them while Sook ran into the house to retrieve blankets and bottles of water.

One by one, the families of the ranch hands, some of whom had given their lives fighting Holloway's gang, emerged from the depths of the bunker to breathe in the fresh morning air. Preacher's quick thinking had given them the opportunity to live through the attack. The Armstrong family's will to survive had defeated a more powerful enemy, which allowed the innocents emerging from the bunker to live another day.

CHAPTER 27

January 24
The East Woods
The Armstrong Ranch
Borden County, Texas

Major and Riley arrived at the bottom of the ravine, where they dismounted and walked their horses toward the campsite. Major lit up the path and was sure to announce himself as he approached. He was certain his lovely wife would follow the axiom *don't shoot 'til you see the whites of their eyes*, an order first given by American Colonist William Prescott at the Battle of Bunker Hill during the War for Independence. Under the tense circumstances, he thought it prudent to speak out to her before she could get a clean shot at him.

"Major, is everyone okay?" a concerned Lucy shouted back before they could see one another.

"Everybody's fine," he replied as he handed the reins to Riley and rushed to his wife's side.

He gingerly held her and whispered into her ear, "I love you."

Lucy, who was exhausted, whispered that she loved him back. Throughout their marriage, a day hadn't passed where they didn't exchange a kiss and a promise of love. This day would be no different.

Major immediately became concerned for her well-being. "Darlin', you look so weak. Let me get you some water."

Lucy didn't object as her husband began to take care of her. Major propped her up further and retrieved a water bottle from the truck. He held it for her as she thirstily drank it down.

"I tried to give some to Preach, and it slipped out of my hands and rolled under the tree over there. My arms hurt too much to crawl around him."

"It's okay. We're here now," said Major as Riley approached his mother's side. Always emotional, tears streamed down his face as he hugged her. They held each other for half a minute before Lucy spoke.

"All the kids are safe? You promise?"

"We promise, Momma. We did great up there. They stayed behind to help the families out of the bunker."

Lucy nodded, and her eyes shut for a moment.

Major knew she was physically drained. He whispered to Riley, "Son, get the truck ready. We need to get your mom in a place where she can rest and we can watch over her. I'm gonna see about Preacher."

Lucy raised her arm slightly. "Major, he's in a bad way. He only woke up one time to moan and speak incoherently about being sorry for what he'd done. I couldn't make most of it out."

Major took her hand and kissed it before placing it back on her lap. He stood to walk around the two prone patients and knelt down next to his best friend. Major looked around for a towel near the medical supplies and found a washcloth. He poured some water over it and gently wiped the sweat off Preacher's brow.

"He's burning up from fever," mumbled Major as Lucy watched.

The cool water stimulated Preacher, who slowly opened his eyes and looked up to Major's face. "How'd we do?" he asked in a raspy voice before having a coughing fit.

Major held his head up and allowed some of the water to trickle into his mouth and throat.

Preacher managed a smile and nodded his appreciation.

"We got 'em, Preach. Thank you for saving our family."

Preacher tried to shrug, but the wince on his face showed it was too painful. The moisture in his mouth and the presence of Major by his side granted him the ability to find his voice. "We could've run away and left it all behind, but the ranch is a part of us all."

"Well, thanks to you, my friend and brother, we saved the ranch and our family's lives. Now my job is to get you fixed up and back in the saddle."

A tear flowed from Preacher's right eye as he shook his head from side to side. "Nah. It's my time now. God's ready to take me, I hope."

"No, Preach. Please hold on until I can get you some help."

Preacher lifted his left arm and reached for Major's hand. Major took it in his and squeezed, urging his friend to be strong.

"Listen up, boss. Goodbyes aren't the end. You and I will meet again in Heaven."

"Of course we will, Preach. All of us will, but not yet. Can you hang on?"

Preacher ignored his question and continued. "We both knew this day would come. Life's about changin', 'cause nothin' ever stays the same."

Major realized Preacher was slipping away. There was so much to say, and he didn't know where to start. All he could do was encourage his friend to embrace his fate.

"I know, Preach. God brought us together, and I know He has plans for us both. I want you to know how thankful I've been to have someone like you in my life. That's what makes saying goodbye so hard."

Lucy was leaning on her son, and both were sniffling as tears poured out of their eyes. Preacher looked over to them and smiled before he turned his attention back to Major.

He managed his final words. "I was born a Texan and I will die on Texas soil. God blessed Texas, and he blessed me with your friendship and brotherhood. Stay Texas Strong."

Preacher Caleb O'Malley gave Major's hand a final squeeze, lowered his head against the ground, and closed his eyes for the final time. He was at peace.

CHAPTER 28

January 24
The Armstrong Ranch
Borden County, Texas

The dawn of the new day brought a hectic combination of cleanup, rejuvenation, and, finally, a time to mourn those lost in the battle for Armstrong Ranch.

Palmer and Sook took control of their home. Several of the women who had survived in the bunker joined them in cleaning up the mess left behind. The bodies of the dead commandos were dragged off the ranch property and piled on the north side of the river. Then they were burned without ceremony or any words on their behalf.

Holloway, at Duncan's insistence, was the last one thrown on the pile. "Let the dead lie at his feet," he'd said as he supervised the funeral pyre. As the flames shot into the sky and the smell of flesh filled the air, Holloway's eye stared at Duncan, who glared back at the man who'd caused so much death and destruction in his life. Holloway was a disgrace to his country, his military career, and himself. He'd surely rot in hell.

As Duncan mounted up and began his ride back to the ranch, he heard the sound of vehicles approaching from the gravel road leading toward Gail. He rode up a slight hill where he could get a better look. It was the cavalry, so to speak. A little late, but there nonetheless.

Espy had arrived with his men from Camp Lubbock. They'd taken all night to round up the gunmen who'd held the counselors and kids at Boys Town hostage. Only one of Espy's men had suffered a minor flesh wound, and he was pleased to report all of the hostages were safe.

Duncan thanked him for coming and insisted he get back to Camp Lubbock to provide security. Espy reassured his commander that all was well in hand. After the operation had ended at Boys Town around dawn, he'd explained to the men the reason for Duncan's departure. To a man, they'd demanded to drive down to the ranch to help, regardless of the consequences to Camp Lubbock.

Espy, emboldened by their unit's attitude, contacted their command at Fort Hood to advise them they had another mission, and they needed to pull some of the soldiers off the border fence detail to cover security at Camp Lubbock. Despite receiving pushback, Espy insisted they'd resign their posts if command didn't make it happen.

Duncan laughed as he told Espy he might be brought up on charges of desertion. Espy didn't care. His friendship with Duncan and the Armstrong family mattered most to him.

With his men's help, Duncan searched the entire ranch and surrounding areas, looking for stray commandos. After an hour, they were confident the ranch was safe, but Espy's men set up formidable perimeter security nonetheless.

After some much-needed rest, Major gathered his family in the living room of the ranch house. The furniture had been removed, and the blood had been scrubbed off the floors. A fire roared in the fireplace to allow some heat during the clear, crisp afternoon.

"Everyone, we need to bury our own today. This is a very difficult time for all of us, as well as those who fall within our care and live on the Armstrong Ranch. As you know, we have a family cemetery in the pecan grove down by the river near the windmill. In the history of our ranch, no one has been buried there unless they were an Armstrong. I propose to change that today."

Lucy, who was feeling much better after eight solid hours of sleep, was standing on her own with one arm in a sling and the other bandaged up to protect her burnt skin from exposure. She smiled and nodded at her husband to encourage him to continue.

"We lost seven ranch hands last night. Honest, hard-working men who came to Texas looking for a better life for their families. Some of them met their spouses here and raised their children as Americans right here on our soil. When the time came, they fought to protect this ranch, their families, and ours as well. They died heroes, in my opinion, and as such, they deserve to be buried on our ranch alongside our ancestors."

"I agree, Daddy," said Palmer. "I don't look at these families as employees. They're all my brothers and sisters. I've grown up with them and played together with many of them as a kid. Their sacrifice should be honored no differently than if they were one of us."

"Absolutely," added Riley. Cooper provided a thumbs-up, and Duncan simply nodded.

"It's settled, then," continued Major. "I know we're all exhausted regardless of the little bit of rest we managed this afternoon, but I think it would be appropriate for us to prepare their graves rather than calling on others. Do y'all agree?"

Everyone enthusiastically joined in the process. Palmer and Sook created wooden signs with the names of the dead written on them. Major and his sons dug the graves for the ranch hands, but they saved a special spot for Preacher nearest the windmill. After an hour, the graves were ready, and everyone on the ranch was invited to pay their final respects.

When the last shovel of dirt was reverently dropped on the last of the ranch hands, Major led everyone to Preacher's gravesite. Antonio had slipped away and hustled back to the ranch house alone. Inside the same old wagon he'd used to pull kids around the yard at Christmas, Preacher's body rested peacefully awaiting burial. The guys had retrieved one of his suits from his house as well as his well-worn Bible, which they tucked inside his jacket.

As everyone gathered around Preacher's grave, Antonio led Preacher's horse and the wagon along the driveway. The clippity-clop of the horse's hooves on the packed-gravel surface caught everyone's attention.

Major and his sons walked to the rear of the wagon and slid

Preacher's body onto a makeshift stretcher made of poles and canvas. The onlookers parted as the men carried his body to the grave and gently dropped him in. Once in place, Lucy, with the help of Palmer and Sook, approached the grave and knelt down. She gently placed Preacher's hat on his chest before she broke down in tears.

Lucy began to sob over the loss of a man who'd been the glue that had held the ranch together for years. She'd anticipated this moment all night, but now that it was upon her, the emotions overwhelmed her.

Major came to his wife's side and whispered in her ear, "He's with God now, my love. Let's take comfort in knowing he's watching over us and lending God a hand in making sure we stay strong."

Lucy looked into her husband's eyes and allowed a slight nod coupled with a smile. She raised her arm so Major could assist her to stand. She stayed by his side to give him strength to deliver the eulogy.

"Everyone, as a family, we have suffered terrible losses in the last day. Together, we're going through the process of saying goodbye to our loved ones, but it doesn't mean goodbye forever. We are simply saying that we'll miss them, and we will all be together again.

"Our life is different from others'. We are all Texans and cowboys. We're grateful for this earth, dependent upon it for survival, and thankful to God for providing us the opportunity to serve Him while here."

Major stopped as he became choked up. His eyes welled up in tears, and he quickly wiped them away with the thumb and forefinger of his right hand.

Lucy squeezed his arm and whispered to him, "It's okay, dear. Speak to us, and God, from the heart.

"I'm not too good at prayin', Lord, so you may not know me as well as Miss Lucy. I haven't been inside a church in a long time, but You have seen me through the eyes of my dearest friend, who I now lay to rest before You.

"Preacher was Your loyal, devoted follower, who was also my mentor in the Word. There was many a day when we would ride the ranch, discussing life and the Hereafter. Preacher taught me to turn my life over to You. To have comfort in the plans You had for me. To know that You'd always give me the strength to face any danger that faced my family.

"God, Preacher was right and truthful when he encouraged me with Your words. He was an unselfish man who always gave of himself. So much so, in fact, that one of the things he regretted most in life was also an act of kindness that saved the lives of a woman and her precious daughter. That experience, Lord, gave him the strength to minister to me, and to save the lives of everyone who stands around his body today."

Major stopped, look skyward, and took a deep breath before continuing. "Lord, Preacher has ridden his last dusty trail and run his last herd of cattle. He can no longer enjoy the smells of spring brought by Your bluebonnets, green grass, and fresh rain.

"With each hill and valley he's traveled, and all those miles of roamin' this ranch, Preacher has lived a life that brought our family joy. He's been our rock, steadfast in the Word and his trust in You. I can only pray that I might live my life to be half the man that our dear friend Preacher Caleb O'Malley has been."

Major began to sob once again as he fell to his knees at Preacher's grave. He began to slowly scoop up handfuls of dirt and allowed it to slip through his fingers onto Preacher's body. He sighed and found the emotional strength to finish.

"My friend, may your horse never stumble and your spurs never rust. I will miss you until we meet again. God bless."

Miss Lucy joined Major on the ground with Palmer's help. Soon, everyone was gathered around on their knees, sniffling and crying as they said their farewell to a man who'd brought them together and shared his heart with this extended family.

After his grave was filled and the goodbyes said, Major assisted Antonio in untying the reins of Preacher's horse from the back of the wagon. A saddle remained on the horse with Preacher's boots reversed in the stirrups. Duncan moved forward to rub the horse's ears and cheeks. As everyone gathered around, Duncan turned to speak.

"A riderless horse has long been a tribute to warriors and fallen soldiers in military parades. For centuries, placing a fallen comrade's boots in the stirrups of the riderless horse was done to honor those who've sacrificed their lives in battle.

"Preacher was a warrior worthy of this honor. He lived his life as a cowboy, and now he's buried like one. But he also stood strong against a powerful enemy when the odds were overwhelmingly against us. His quick thinking and unselfish bravery saved the lives of everyone standing here today.

"Preacher lived life the right way. He loved this land and the people who live on it. He stayed true to God and Texas. He was a man of his word and a warrior at heart. For these reasons, I salute him and honor his memory with his horse's final ride."

Duncan snuggled on Preacher's horse again and then took the reins. He began walking the riderless horse back toward the ranch house, with the group following close behind. As the sun began to set over West Texas, another day in the life of the Armstrong Family came to an end, culminating with their final farewell to an old friend.

PART TWO

CHAPTER 29

January 25
The Armstrong Ranch
Borden County, Texas

Major woke up first the next morning and made his way through the cold house to the kitchen. They didn't turn on the generators to create heat but opted instead to burrow under mounds of wool blankets accumulated over the years. The first order of business was to fire up the generator dedicated to the kitchen appliances so he could start a pot of coffee. Next up was a roaring fire to create some heat in the house.

With the fire beginning to grow in intensity and a hot mug of coffee in his hands, he stood at the glassless living room window and stared into the front yard at the remnants of the burned-out barn.

Where the heck do we start? Major thought to himself. It was easy to lose hope considering the circumstances and the resultant loss of life. From the moment he'd arrived to gunfire killing his state trooper escorts the evening before last until the burial of his best friend, it was hard to think about anything except the last *36 Hours*.

His priority was enduring the challenges presented by protecting his family and getting their home back. He was committed to one thing and one thing only—survival. Plans for the future, including the offer to become vice president of Texas, had not only been put on hold, but shut out of his mind completely. The last two days he'd focused on getting through from one hour to the next, as physical challenges on the field of battle gave way to emotional ones as the family dealt with death and loss.

Major took a deep breath, and his eyes adjusted to the rising sun. He tried to remind himself that all of the thoughts running through his mind were reasonable, practical, and totally understandable.

As he mindlessly stared, watching another day arrive, he heard sniffling behind him. Major turned and found Lucy bundled in her housecoat, standing at the foot of the stairs. She was crying.

Major rushed to her side. "Honey, what's wrong?"

"It's my job to make my husband coffee," she mumbled in between sniffles.

Right or wrong, sometimes reactions could be spontaneous. Major burst out laughing. It wasn't his intention to demean his adorable wife, but rather, in that moment, he thought she was cute as could be.

"Well, oh my gosh, Miss Lucy. For one day, I think we can cut you some slack on making coffee. For Pete's sake, you've made coffee for me every day for, I don't know, thirty thousand days or some such."

Lucy pouted and wiped her tears off on her robe. Major had purchased one of those plush, Nordic fleece robes that came with the Vermont Teddy Bear from PajamaGram one Christmas. He'd never forget the day he got the courage to *call the toll-free number on your television screen* after watching one of those sex kittens curled up in a pink onesie they called a *Hoodie Footie.* He was going to buy his wife one of those but opted instead for something she'd be more likely to wear. The Vermont Teddy Bear was a bonus, which had earned him more praise than the robe. Now, in her robe, crying and vulnerable, he'd never loved her more.

"I feel so worthless." Lucy continued to sniffle, but the teary eyes had begun to subside. "Major, there's so much to do, and I can't really help. Palmer and Sook have both warned me not to do too much."

Major kissed her on the cheek. "I really love you a lot today."

Lucy chuckled and managed a smile. "More than yesterday?"

"Yes, ma'am." Major, who was aware Lucy was having difficulty gripping things, wrapped his arm around her and helped her drink from his coffee mug. She took in the aroma before taking a sip.

The comfort, and *normalcy*, of a sip of morning brew seemed to wash away her melancholy mood. *Maybe that's the key*, Major thought to himself.

Lucy looked around the empty room where their furniture once stood. Even if they could remove the bloodstains from the chairs and couches, they didn't want the memories in their home. The guys had started a massive pile of furniture, bedding, and rugs away from the ranch house to be burned later in the day. Afterwards, Major would use the backhoe to dig a hole, bury all the debris from the barn and the house, and mound dirt over it as a grave reminder of what had happened.

They moved to the fireplace together, and Major helped her sit. He had decided to open up about his thoughts when she came downstairs.

"I've been thinking about all of this," he began as he waved around the room. "It seems so overwhelming, doesn't it?"

Lucy nodded and motioned toward the coffee.

Major helped her with another sip; then he continued. "We survived, and now it's time to rebuild. We have to believe that today is day one, where we establish some order out of the chaos, beauty out of the ugliness, and life where there has been death."

"Get back to normal," interjected Lucy.

"Yes, Miss Lucy. Exactly! We need to get some normality back into our lives. It's time to put the past behind us and look to the future."

Lucy frowned a little. "Dear, we can't hide from the realities we now face. I'm not talking about a lack of furniture. I'm referring to the fact that we've lost Preacher, who ran the ranch. We've lost many of our ranch hands, who helped him and acted as protection during these crazy times. Then there are the minor inconveniences like no windows and, yes, a lack of furniture."

"I don't disagree, and I'm not hiding from reality. All I'm saying is the universe has a way of creating beauty out of ashes. What we've just endured is a mere chapter in our book. It's by no means *the end*."

Lucy looked into Major's eyes and stretched her neck to get a kiss. "Okay, *mister profound author*, what's the next chapter look like?"

"Happily ever after," teased Major, which earned him a kick to the leg.

"Great," said Lucy with a laugh. "I could've written that. How do we get from tragedy to happy?"

Major had contemplated when he was going to tell his wife about President Burnett's offer. He was about to speak when the sounds of footsteps coming down the stairs interrupted him.

CHAPTER 30

January 25
The Armstrong Ranch
Borden County, Texas

"Good morning," announced Duncan as he arrived at the foot of the stairs. He was wearing jeans and a plaid flannel shirt, a look that was totally out of the ordinary for him. His uniform had been soaked with blood and was soaking in a wash bucket outside.

"Good morning, my son the rancher," quipped Lucy. "This is a different look for you."

"Yeah, I had to raid my brothers' closets looking for clothes. Coop's Wranglers fit me better, and Riley's flannel shirts gave me more room in the chest."

"When you think about it, Duncan, over the last five or six years, the ranch was more of a stopover for you than it was a home. Gradually, more and more of your clothing left when you did for another assignment."

Cooper and Riley emerged from the downstairs bedrooms. "Good morning, y'all!"

Everyone greeted them, and finally, the girls descended the stairs to join the morning gathering.

"Well, I reckon everyone should grab some coffee and a chair from wherever you can find one," said Major. He patted Lucy on the thigh and told her he'd be back with a refill. After some conversation in the kitchen regarding replacement windows, everyone joined the Armstrong matriarch of the family.

"Miss Lucy, I must change your bandages soon," said Sook, who sat on the hearth next to her patient. "Are you having pains?"

"No, no pains. Only frustrations."

Sook appeared puzzled but then smiled. "I understand. Palmer and I are here for you."

Dining chairs were slid into the room, and the Armstrong children formed a semicircle around the fire. Major was the last one to take his seat.

"I woke up this morning thinking about my day, as I always do. For the first time, I was at a loss. Usually, I can reel off five or six *must-dos* and another dozen *wanna-dos.* When the list of *must-dos* exceeds twenty, it's easy to lose count and priorities. Just before your momma joined me this morning, I had a revelation of sorts. I decided to bring back a sense of normalcy to the ranch."

Palmer jumped in. "A routine, right, Daddy?"

"Yes, honey, a routine. But it will be a new normal."

"That's confusing as heck, husband," said Lucy.

Major set his coffee to the side and wiped his face with both hands. He wasn't tired, as he'd rested well the night before. The magnitude of what he was about to say was beginning to overwhelm him.

"I have every confidence in this family's ability to pull itself out of this crisis and make a life for ourselves under the circumstances God has put before us. But I also believe that an opportunity has presented itself that can make our lives much easier, and safer."

His children looked to one another in surprise and confusion. Lucy never took her eyes off Major's. She knew him well and was beginning to realize that he'd withheld something from her.

He decided to just blurt it out. "While I was in Austin the day before yesterday, Marion asked me to accept the position as the vice president of Texas."

"Wow!" shouted an exuberant Riley, who immediately exchanged high-fives with Cooper. "Daddy's gonna be runnin' things!"

The boys' excitement died down when they realized that nobody else was dancing in the streets with them.

"Have you already accepted her offer?" asked a perturbed Lucy.

Major knew he was treading on thin ice by not telling her sooner, but he'd honestly put it out of his mind under the circumstances, and he hadn't wanted to overshadow yesterday's emotional burial ceremony. "No, honey. I haven't responded, although Marion is expecting an answer from me today."

"What's your answer gonna be?" Lucy asked. Major knew she was angry with him.

"That's up to all of us to decide. As a family." Major looked to Duncan, who was the most mature contribution to the conversation.

He picked up on his cue to help. "Dad, are you in a position to ask for conditions of employment? You know, perks beyond a paycheck?"

Major had given this a lot of consideration. "I think I am. I haven't raised any of these issues with Marion, and in light of what has happened here, I'm in a strong position to write my own meal ticket."

"Enhanced security?" asked Lucy, whose mind was starting to consider the possibilities.

"Exactly," added Duncan. "Think back to pre-EMP days and the security detail assigned to presidents and vice presidents. President Bush's ranch was protected like a military installation during and after his days in office. Why should Texas treat its leadership team any different?"

"Are you applying for the job, son?" asked Major.

"Well, um, not necessarily. But I sure would like to help set the security team up."

Major thought for a moment, and then Palmer asked, "Daddy, would you live here or in Austin?"

"Not sure," he replied. "It depends a lot on what she will have me doing."

"Maybe you can dictate that as well." Lucy was now fully engaged and appeared to be over her hurt feelings as the possibilities began to be bantered about.

"I've thought about that as well. My first inclination was to request an important role with the military. I hit it off with the generals at both the funeral and during one of my trips to the

Mansion. However, at the end of the day, I'd always defer to the generals' judgment, and I wouldn't have that much of an impact."

Duncan issued a reminder. "Dad, there's still General Lee and his commandos to deal with. If we could track him down, you know, cut off the head of the snake, the rest of the Lightning Death Squads would flounder, especially in Texas."

"Same question as before," started Major. "Are you applying for the job of hunting down General Lee?"

"I'd do it as a service to my country, without pay or accolades," said Duncan with a lowered voice. "Let me pick my team, which will include Sook, of course."

Palmer pounced on his last statement. "What? C'mon, Duncan. You can't take her away from us to fight these guys."

"Hold on. Hear me out. Yesterday, as Espy's men rounded up the bodies, they also gathered up all the radios. Further, under light interrogation—"

Duncan was interrupted by laughter. He'd never fully described his techniques in detail, but because he always got results, the family assumed his repertoire was extensive.

He continued as he held his hands up in surrender. "I swear. The guy Riley hog-tied told us everything he knew about Lee's next move. With Sook's interpretive abilities, we can track Lee down and end this."

"I, for one, don't want to look over our shoulders anymore," added Cooper.

Sook reached for Duncan's hand and held it tight. Apparently, he'd caught her off guard with the proposal, but her devotion to him was obvious. If he asked, she'd join him in battle again.

"So far, I'm losing two of my men and my new daughter to the government," said Lucy. Everyone grew tense and quiet, as they expected Lucy to use her all-powerful veto. She surprised them. "For years, we've stayed out of politics other than complain' about it when the news was on or sendin' the occasional check to a politician's coffers. That said, I believe that you two are best suited for the jobs you described."

"Thank you, honey. I just wanna add this. I plan on going to Austin to make a real difference in the Texas recovery effort. I trust Duncan to create the utmost security for our ranch, and I will insist that Marion give him everything he needs so we can all sleep at night. In exchange, he will offer his services to rid our new nation from these killers who've destroyed our power grid and put fear in every Texan."

"Daddy, what do you plan on doin' as vice president?" asked Cooper.

"I'm gonna spearhead the recovery effort. I will free up Marion to deal with Washington and the administrative roles that she understands. Let me use the organizational and preparedness skills we've used at the ranch and apply it on a larger scale to the nation."

Lucy struggled to stand, and Major helped her. Her approval was powerful.

"If I'm going to commit the lives of my husband and oldest son, together with his fiancée, to a cause, let that cause be Texas!"

CHAPTER 31

January 25
The Armstrong Ranch
Borden County, Texas

The ranch was bustling with activity as snow flurries filled the air. It had been a dry winter and not all that cold. Thus far, they'd avoided the nasty weather, which could descend into West Texas from the Rockies quickly. Duncan worked with Espy to get in contact with President Burnett's chief of staff. Major took over from there and explained what had happened. He also asked to be picked up as soon as possible because he had an answer for the president on her offer but needed to discuss it with her in person. He also insisted Duncan be allowed to make the trip with him.

While they waited for the helicopter to arrive, Duncan filled in Espy on his proposal to the president. Without giving him the information about his father becoming vice president, Duncan let Espy know there was an opportunity for him to head up the security detail at the ranch. He warned Espy it might be boring in many respects, especially in light of the action they'd seen with the TX-QRF around Lubbock.

Espy, however, didn't hesitate to jump at the offer. He and Duncan really meshed as a team, and Espy had grown fond of Palmer. He wasn't timid about broaching the subject with her oldest brother either. Short of asking Major for his daughter's hand in marriage, Espy knew gaining the permission of his commanding officer to court his sister was an important prerequisite to pursuing a relationship with Palmer.

Espy was thrilled following the conversation, in which Duncan gave the green light to the relationship. He did give Espy some friendly advice. His sister was a beautiful woman on the outside, but she was a wildcat underneath, just like her mother. If Espy crossed her, then he'd have momma bear to deal with and most likely Sook comin' at him from behind.

After seeing the look on the young man's face, Duncan didn't think it was necessary to throw in what the Armstrong menfolk might do. He patted his sergeant on the back and let him get back to work. He caught up with his dad and brothers, who'd gathered around some sawhorses and plywood sitting out in the front yard.

"What's goin' on, Dad?" he asked.

"Son, I think I'll let Coop explain."

Duncan and Riley reached into the horse-drawn wagon and removed a large sheet of plate glass. They grunted a little as they carefully set the heavy glass on top of the plywood table they'd created with the sawhorses. Then the guys donned a pair of safety goggles and stood opposite one another around the glass.

Cooper changed gloves from the leather ones he used around the ranch to a pair with a mesh back and rubber grips. As he did, he described their project. "This is the first of the fixed-glass windows we'll be removing from the Reinecke buildings. We lost a lot of windows, obviously, during the fight. With cold weather moving in, Riley and I decided it would make sense to get our shelter secured first, and then focus on the other things on our mental to-do list."

"You're gonna make your own windows?" asked Duncan, who was somewhat skeptical.

"Yeah, and without a glass cutter, too," replied Riley. "First, we cleaned out the windowsills and surrounds. After measuring, we took the wagon over to Reinecke and identified windows that could be removed as replacements for our broken ones."

"What's that for?" asked Major. He pointed to the ground at a sheet of plywood with a two-by-four surround nailed to its edges. The guys had a large piece of eight-millimeter plastic sheeting inside it, which created a makeshift bladder filled with water.

"That's the next step," replied Cooper. "Watch. First, we measure for our cuts and mark the line with a Sharpie. Then Riley will use this carbide-tipped saw blade as a scoring tool. Once he's dug in enough to get us a good cut, I'll tie this kite string around the glass to match up with our initial cut."

"Are you gonna snap it like a chalk line?" asked Major. "I don't think that'll do it, boys."

Cooper laughed and shook his head. "No, Daddy. Watch. Ready, Riley?"

"Let's do it."

Cooper and Riley wrapped the string around the glass so that it matched up with the scored indentation. Cooper reached into his pocket and retrieved a lighter. He set fire to the string and it began to burn across the top of the glass. As soon as the string was entirely ablaze, Cooper shouted, "Now!"

The guys quickly lifted the glass and set it into the water trough. They placed a cut two by four just below the cut line and simultaneously thumped it with the back of their fist. The glass broke along the score and snapped cleanly.

"Wow! Would ya look at that?" exclaimed Major.

"So what did the water do, exactly?" asked Duncan, who was impressed and now curious about the process they followed.

Cooper responded, "Setting it in the water does two things. For one, the blow was softer and more evenly distributed to avoid shattering. The water also lessened the vibrations through the glass so that we end up with two clean pieces."

He and Riley pulled the smaller of the two pieces out of the water and set it back on the table. They slid it to the edge so the cut side could be polished with a whetstone, which was kept around the barns to sharpen knives.

"We'll cut some strips off these two by fours to frame the window and hold the glass in place. We have several rolls of weather stripping lying around from past projects and a tube of clear window sealant, which was used to replace broken windows in the storage buildings."

"Okay, boys, I've gotta ask," started Major. "I know you didn't jump on the internet and watch a YouTube video to figure this out."

"You're right, Daddy," said Cooper. "We learned it from Preacher one afternoon. He got tired of running clear to Midland to buy replacement glass every time a pane got busted out of the buildings. He started to keep smaller pieces around to make repairs, and he taught us how."

Duncan walked over and gave each of the guys a fist bump. "Y'all, I'm impressed. I'll be glad to dump all of those wool blankets off my bed tonight."

The distinctive thumping of a helicopter in the distance grabbed everyone's attention. Even Lucy heard it, causing her to come out onto the front porch. A doctor was coming to check on her and Antonio as part of Major's agreement for them to fly to Austin. He'd stay at the ranch during the day while the guys were in Austin. Major looked at the arrangement as a way to ensure they would send them both back via chopper.

Everyone said their goodbyes, and Lucy led the medical team inside. In addition to Antonio, she'd arranged for everyone on the ranch to get a quick checkup. She planned on getting her money's worth out of the doctor and his nurse.

On the trip to the capital, Duncan spoke with Major about how impressed he was with Cooper and Riley's project. "They've learned a lot around the ranch, haven't they?"

"I'll be honest, son. I had no idea they'd been paying such close attention to our operations. I thought they spent their days dreamin' of rodeos and buckle bunnies. They've really picked up a lot, it seems."

"Dad, have you talked with them about their new roles once you take the V-P job?"

"No, but I want to make sure you approve. Cooper is best suited to run the ranch."

"I agree, and I'm not cut out for it. He's a great choice."

"Good. I didn't want you to feel slighted. You are the oldest."

Duncan laughed. "I've seen a lot now by the ripe old age of thirty. Unfortunately, running a ranch isn't on my résumé anywhere."

"Riley will be okay with it as well," said Major. "I'm gonna put him in charge of the livestock. He loves that aspect of ranching. I just wish he'd spent more time with Preacher on the financial side. I'll teach him what I know."

"What about Palmer and Sook?" asked Duncan.

As they approached the Mansion, Major pointed out the large military presence around the city. Armored personnel carriers were visible on most of the primary roads and highways. There was no evidence of unrest in Austin.

"I'm turning them over to Miss Lucy. They are three peas in a pod and will work well together."

The helicopter landed, and as the men waited for their doors to be opened, Major asked Duncan what he wanted to do.

"I don't know yet, Dad. I'll take care of Lee, and then I have some personal unfinished business to attend to. Then we'll see."

"Yeah," started Major, frowning as he immediately understood Duncan's meaning. "About that. We really—" Before he could finish his statement, the door opened, and they were warmly greeted by two uniformed officers.

"Welcome back to Austin, gentlemen."

CHAPTER 32

January 25
The Mansion
Austin, Texas

The reception Major received from the moment he touched down at the helipad until he reached President Burnett's office was markedly different from any of his previous visits, including the one of just a couple of days ago. The rumor mill apparently had kicked into high gear, as his name must've been leaked as one of the front-runners for the vice president slot. Without admitting it to Duncan, he was flattered by the outward show of respect from military personnel and political staffers alike.

"Come on in here, Major!" exclaimed the president when she caught a glimpse of him milling about outside her office.

Major reluctantly touched his son on the shoulder, and the two entered the president's office without an escort. "Madam President, thank you for seeing us on short notice."

"Hello, Duncan," greeted the president. "Would you mind closing the door behind you? I don't know where my secretary has disappeared to. But we're all capable of fending for ourselves, aren't we?"

Major scowled, wondering if the president had a hidden meaning behind her statement.

She continued and clarified what she said somewhat. "Major, I am truly sorry for what happened to you and your family since you were here on Monday. Did you lose anyone?"

"We did, Madam, um, Marion. My longtime friend and the head

of my ranch, Preacher Caleb O'Malley, died, as well as a number of ranch hands."

"The men who attacked you, were they part of the North Koreans who took down our grid?"

Duncan gave her a quick summary of the events in Lubbock followed by the attack on the ranch. After he was finished, President Burnett sat in her chair in stunned silence.

"Please, my goodness, gentlemen," she began to stammer. "Where are my manners? Would you like some coffee, a soda, or maybe a glass of water?"

"No, Marion, we're fine," replied Major.

"Also, please express my condolences to the families of those who lost someone."

The awkward beginning to the meeting was throwing him off balance. He'd imagined the conversation going a certain way, and he wanted to control the flow of the negotiation. Finding the president frazzled like this was out of character and, in turn, forced them off the topic at hand.

"How are things going for you? Has something changed since we last met?" Major began to wonder if she'd changed her mind about her offer.

She exhaled and sat forward in her chair. "I'll be up front with you, Major. Every day, I feel like I'm losing my grip on Texas. With much of the country without power, I now have a good understanding of what President Harman is going through in Washington. The difference between our situations is the border security. Americans are still lined up around our country, attempting to access what they think we have."

She hesitated for a moment, so Duncan added his appraisal of the situation. "The refugees continue to be emboldened by successful intrusions across the border. The attack on the Hobbs gate in West Texas led the refugees to believe they could do it elsewhere. My men at the TX-QRF quelled an uprising of armed refugees at Boys Town Monday evening, which lasted into Tuesday morning. The hostage-takers said word was being spread all up and down the border that our loss of power was rumor and part of a disinformation campaign to discourage them from entering Texas."

"How the heck am I supposed to prove to them that we're in a pickle just like they are?"

Duncan looked her in the eye. "You can't change your policy on the border. Many of these people have traveled for hundreds of miles to enter Texas. If you opened the borders, they'd all pour in because they have no place else to go."

"Washington needs to get their act together," mumbled the president. "But then, so do we. Major, I hope you have an answer for me. I can't do this alone, and Texas needs someone with a level head that can be trusted."

"Marion, I'm prepared to accept and give our country everything I've got, but the events of the last forty-eight hours have changed things quite a bit."

"How so?" she asked.

"My goals for Armstrong Ranch are the same you'd have for the Four Sixes, or Texas, for that matter," he replied. "I want to keep those within my charge safe and healthy."

"That goes without saying," said the president. "What do you have in mind?"

Major went on to express his concerns about security and his ideas for a secret service type of detail to reside permanently on the ranch. He insisted on commuting to Austin, but the president said his presence would be required all over the country. A dedicated helicopter and security detail associated with his travel was agreed upon. Major was also granted food, supplies, and medical necessities as part of his compensation package.

"When can you start?" she asked. Then she had another thought. "Well, let me add there are certain formalities to be followed, but the rolling-up-the-sleeves part can begin when you're ready."

"How about right this second?" said Major with a laugh.

President Burnett smiled, and a wave of relief seemed to come over her body. She was showing signs of the Marion he'd known on the campaign trail—confident and in charge.

She stood and shook hands with Major. "Thank you, Mr. Vice President–designate Armstrong. Where would you like to start?"

"Based upon our prior conversations and my understanding of the role Monty Gregg played in your administration, let me tell you how I can help the most. Clearly, I have no experience dealing with Washington. They'd eat me alive. Perhaps you can handle them?"

"With pleasure," said the president with a chuckle. "Monty was my military liaison, primarily because he promoted all those generals to their present positions at one time or another. You seemed to hit it off with them in your recent interactions."

"I will continue to do so. But I have a proposal."

"Go ahead," said the president, who gestured for Major to continue.

"This is where Duncan comes in. Marion, the North Koreans aren't done with us yet. I'll allow Duncan to explain." He nodded toward his son, and Duncan explained.

"Ma'am, we've captured some of their commandos and seized their communications gear. We've continuously monitored their transmissions to determine—"

The president interrupted him before he could continue. "They're North Korean, right? How can you understand them?"

Duncan squirmed in his chair and then responded, "My fiancée is North Korean. She has been listening in to their conversations, and we think they're going to strike oil refinery targets along the Gulf Coast."

President Burnett slumped in her chair and studied her guests. "Let's get to their targets in a moment. Please satisfy my curiosity. How did you meet this girl?"

Duncan looked uneasy, so Major placed his hand on his shoulder. "Full disclosure, son. If Marion has a problem with our family's background, best she hears it all from us now."

"You guys are worrying me," said the president, who suddenly appeared to be guarded.

Duncan looked at his dad and nodded. Then he turned his attention to the president. He explained everything to her except the part about Gregg's and Yancey's involvement. He'd never received the orders directly from them, so he wasn't prepared to disclose their role in the plot to assassinate Kim Jong-un.

"Marion, that's all of it," added Major. "We're not ashamed of Duncan for following the orders of his government. It shows his loyalty, and I hope it reassures you that he'd be similarly loyal to Texas as well."

"Even more so, Madam President. I was born here, and Texas blood runs through my veins. Now, I'm offering my services to you, as a fellow Texan, to rid our country of the Lightning Death Squads and this General Lee who commands them."

The president seemed to have accepted Duncan's explanation, and now she was intrigued. "What are you asking for?"

"Madam President, let me assemble a team to hunt down General Lee. Once he's been eliminated, I believe his operations in Texas will fall into disarray. Outside our borders, in the U.S., there may be a different command and control structure. As for Texas, he's the head of the snake."

"Okay, Duncan. You're in. I'll arrange for the adjutant general to join us to work out the details before you go back to the ranch. Major, that lands you in the most important position of all at this point—rebuilding Texas. I hope you're up for the task."

"I'm ready, Madam President."

CHAPTER 33

January 26
ExxonMobil Baytown Refinery
Baytown, Texas

Darkness had settled in as General Lee gathered his top lieutenants in a nondescript one-story brick home in Ginger Creek Estates, a neighborhood located in Baytown, Texas. Baytown was a bedroom community located just to the east of Houston on Trinity Bay. The small city of seventy-two thousand was culturally diverse and had a fairly large Asian population prior to the collapse. Its economy revolved around the petroleum industry.

The ExxonMobil Baytown Refinery was the second largest oil refinery in North America behind the Port Arthur, Texas, facility owned by Aramco, a Saudi Arabian Oil Company. Following the nuclear attack that had grazed Galveston to the south, this refinery remained the only facility that was fully operational other than Port Arthur, which had reduced its production due to security concerns.

As a result, Baytown Refinery had become the most important resource to Texas as the new nation coped with the collapse of the power grid. It was going to take lots of fuel to operate generators, transportation, and equipment as the Austin government tried to rebuild.

The field commanders of the Lightning Death Squads had performed admirably and were now en route to their next assignments. General Lee had split his commandos into two groups. An advance group was sent to Beaumont and Port Arthur to plan their attack upon the Aramco facility.

In addition, and just as important, they were requested to map out their escape from Texas and back into the United States. General Lee had abandoned his dream of overtaking the nuclear enrichment facility at the West Texas border with New Mexico. It was now apparent that his homeland had been destroyed by nuclear retaliatory attacks by the United States, and Dear Leader would no longer have a use for the nuclear material.

Instead, General Lee focused his efforts on their original task, which was to disrupt and destroy as much of the North American critical infrastructure as he could. He still held out hope that a North Korean invasion force would be forthcoming and that he'd be rewarded for his successes.

General Lee had created a crude map out of a bedsheet and a permanent marker. He spread it out on top of a large dining table. He had marked certain identifiable landmarks within the twenty-four-hundred-acre refinery complex, including security stations, vehicle checkpoints, and administrative offices.

Over the next several days, his men would sneak into the complex under cover of darkness and fill in more points of interest on the map. They needed to confirm the administrative offices in order to destroy their computer systems and manual operational overrides. There were also key components of the refinery process that needed to be rendered permanently inoperative.

Oil refineries like Baytown were large sprawling industrial complexes with extensive piping running throughout the facility, carrying streams of crude oil and refined gasoline products from one massive storage container to another. Baytown was capable of refining six hundred thousand barrels of oil into gasoline daily.

Taking away this resource would cripple Texas. The secondary attack on Port Arthur would put the nail in the coffin.

General Lee knew very little about the inner workings of an oil refinery, but common sense told him that the crude oil entered one side of the plant and exited the other in the form of gasoline. Tonight, he and his commandos would infiltrate Baytown Refinery and begin to generate a flow diagram of its operations.

After his teams were in position, and following some well-deserved rest, they'd be ready to strike efficiently and then race to their next target at Port Arthur, barely sixty miles away.

CHAPTER 34

January 27
The White House
Washington, DC

"The way I see it, the first phase is complete," began Chief of Staff Charles Acton as he commiserated with Billy Yancey about the recent events in Texas. "Their grid is down, and mighty Marion Burnett has been knocked off her steed."

The two men who had previously met on park benches in the dead of winter were now more comfortable meeting within the cozy confines of the White House as they continued their destructive plans for the Burnett administration and Texas.

"I have to caution you, however," began Yancey, "these Texans are a resilient bunch. I'm getting feedback from my moles within the Austin government that Marion plans on bringing in an outsider to replace Monty Gregg."

"Who?" asked Acton.

"I've met him. A rancher named Armstrong. He's an old friend of Marion's and a highly respected former lawman. He headed Company C of the Texas Rangers."

"What's his political experience?"

"None, but that's not what he's on board for," replied Yancey. "She's looking for someone who she can trust implicitly while taking the burden off her shoulders to an extent. I'm hearing that Armstrong will focus his efforts on relations with the military and their own rebuilding effort."

Acton continued his questioning. "Does he know what he's doing?"

"Jury's still out on that," replied Yancey. "He's achieved his most important role thus far. He's provided Marion a trusted ally, which gives her strength. Inner confidence is her most admirable trait. Without it, as we saw following Monty's death, Texas flails about without a leader."

Acton lifted himself out of his chair and walked around his office. He took a quick glance toward the South Lawn of the White House as yet another snowfall blanketed the grounds. He gathered his thoughts and shared them with Yancey.

"Has he been officially sworn in?"

Yancey shrugged. "Not yet. I don't know if a date's been set, but it'll likely be within a week or so."

"Hmm. That means there's still time to throw a wrench in the works."

Yancey turned in his chair to address Acton. "Yes. What do you have in mind?"

Acton continued to stare out across the South Lawn. "It sounds like this Armstrong guy has no experience in government and has been brought on board simply to bolster Marion's confidence. She trusts him. How can we change her opinion?"

Acton turned to Yancey, who immediately came up with an idea. "Armstrong's son. We undermine his credibility by exposing his son's involvement in the North Korean matter."

"How do we get the information to her?" Acton asked.

"Let me give it some thought, but my initial thought i the indirect approach using the Texas adjutant general as an unwilling pawn. I'll brief our operative Pauline Hart and have her leak the information to her brother-in-law."

Acton interrupted with a suggestion. "Or I could take the more direct approach. I could use it as a tool to get into her good graces. We'll expose the Armstrongs as part of our plan to woo Texas back into the union. It's a little riskier that way, but it gets my foot in the door so I can mess with Marion's head a little."

Yancey stood to leave. "Before we do anything, let me run the scenarios through my mind a couple of times. We'll only get one shot at this without raising Marion's antennae. She's not stupid, but the timing is right because she's overwhelmed."

"Two days, Billy. We need to move on this quickly."

CHAPTER 35

January 27
1st Cavalry Division
Fort Hood, Texas

After meeting with the leadership command of the TX-QRF headquartered at Fort Hood, Duncan joined Colonel Sanderson, the officer who originally met with Duncan at the ranch when he was recruited. Sanderson had continued to follow Duncan's activities at Camp Lubbock and was impressed. When he received word from Austin that Duncan was given the opportunity to handpick his team to hunt down General Lee, Sanderson voiced his approval.

"Commander, 1st Cavalry has a storied history," Sanderson began as he led Duncan to a personnel building where a conference room containing a stack of files awaited. Sanderson had had his subordinates choose from hundreds of candidates to join Duncan's newly formed unit. He was given the parameters by Duncan in advance—Delta Force training, combat experience, and, lastly, the ability to operate in stressful situations.

Sanderson continued. "They've fought in World War II, the Korean War and Vietnam. Recently, it was 1st Cavalry that controlled Bagram Airfield and supported our forces during Operation Freedom Sentinel, which dealt heavy losses to the Taliban. These guys know how to fight."

"That's what I need, Colonel," said Duncan as they reached the personnel building. "Let me tell you more of what I've learned once we're in the conference room. Then I'll start picking out my team."

They entered the personnel center, and Duncan was introduced to several officers in the 1st Cavalry who were familiar with the soldiers who fit the specifications requirements. They were made available to Duncan if he had any questions or if he wanted to interview the candidates in person.

The colonel closed the door behind them, and then he opened the conversation. "How reliable is your intel, Commander? I've heard about your interrogation of the two men captured at Camp Lubbock. I have to say there are some who, under other circumstances, might disagree with your tactics."

Duncan chuckled. "Maybe so. Usually those who criticize interrogation techniques are not the ones responsible for keeping their friends and neighbors safe from the enemy. I get results, Colonel, and I'll follow the same methods if the situation arises."

The colonel leaned back and held up his hands. "No argument from me. Are you sure of the reliability of the intel?"

"I have a second way to confirm General Lee's plans. We've been monitoring his satellite two-way communications."

"What about the language barrier?" asked the colonel.

"I have an expert North Korean interpreter. Our intel shows Lee plans on attacking a target near Baytown and also in the Beaumont-Port Arthur area."

"Refineries," muttered Colonel Sanderson.

"Yes, sir. If what we're gathering is correct, refineries in these two towns will be hit within the next several days. While I'd love to lead a team of Apache choppers and armored vehicles in there, we'd only force them into hiding so they can regroup around another target."

"What do you propose?"

"I want to embed my team within the security and operations personnel of each facility. We'll equip them with advanced comms, night vision, and tactical weaponry."

"You want to allow the attack to commence?" asked the colonel.

"Yes, sir," replied Duncan with confidence. "I want to give them a false sense of security. Suck them in and catch them off guard. While our unit is eliminating the commandos who enter the facility, I'll locate General Lee and personally bring his operation to a halt in Texas."

The colonel leaned back in his chair and folded his arms. "What's your anticipated rate of success?"

"One hundred percent, sir."

"Spoken like a true operator." Colonel Sanderson laughed. "You guys are supremely self-confident most of the time, often to the point of arrogance."

"It's a survival mechanism, sir. As I play out an operation in my mind, every shot finds its mark and every member of the unit goes home to their family. There simply is no other way."

Sanderson added his thoughts. "Operators hate to lose. I've seen it. Losing is not an option. At anything. In any circumstance. Ever. A jog with a buddy ends up in a sprint to the finish for you guys."

"Yes, sir. We only know one speed, and that's full throttle. There's no such thing as a friendly game of anything. Likewise, on the battlefield, there are no rules that allow for a friendly firefight. Losing means death. Winning means we come home to our families."

"Commander Armstrong, with confidence comes courage. Courage is the first trait of a warrior. I have no doubt you'll succeed, and I'll give you whatever it takes to help."

Duncan smiled and reached for the file folders. "Let me find some fellow warriors."

CHAPTER 36

January 28
The Armstrong Ranch
Borden County, Texas

Duncan and his father took a casual ride around the ranch early that morning to observe the security measures established by Espy and the rest of Duncan's former unit from Camp Lubbock. They watched in amazement as soldiers from the 36th Engineer Group from Fort Bliss erected housing units for the security detachment assigned to Armstrong Ranch. Their expert teams of engineers and construction personnel were able to begin building two twelve-hundred-square-foot buildings in the first day of their deployment to the ranch.

"Pretty dang impressive," said Major as he pulled his horse to a stop to admire the roofers nailing on the dimensional shingles.

Duncan nodded and relaxed in his saddle. "They'll be dried-in by the end of the day, and tomorrow another group will arrive to wire and plumb the buildings. On day three, interior finishes will be installed, and on day four, a furniture truck will arrive to supply beds, tables, sofas, etcetera."

"Maybe I can have them throw an extra set on the truck for Miss Lucy?"

Duncan laughed. "One step ahead of you, Dad. I've already made the request."

"Thank you, son. Your mom's putting her best face on each day, but deep down, she's struggling with what happened in our home. The fresh paint, cleaned floors, and the window installation by your brothers helped a lot. New furniture should do the trick."

"And the passage of time," interjected Duncan.

"That too."

They continued their ride back toward the ranch house, where the two helicopters came into view. Major pointed toward them. "A strange sight, don't you think?"

"True, but a welcome one also. Your chopper is made for speed and comfort. Mine is made for speed and killing. They're both versions of the Sikorsky SH-60, but vastly different in their purpose."

Major was introspective during their ride. He finally spoke about what was on his mind. "Son, we're doing the right thing by getting involved. The timing is horrible considering what our family has been through. Yet God put these challenges before us to nudge us in the direction that may have been our calling."

"Hey, you don't have to convince me. I think we are absolutely doing the right thing. I can't think of anything more important right now than driving this enemy out of Texas. And I can't think of a better man for the job of reuniting Texans behind a common goal than you. Dad, you're not a politician. You're one of us. One of them. People will listen to you, and from what I've heard at Fort Hood, your help has arrived just in time."

Major had a puzzled look on his face. "What have you heard, and why haven't you mentioned anything to me before now?"

"Dad, I've been waiting to be alone with you. Listen, parts of Texas are in real trouble. Other than the occasional skirmish with refugees on the eastern border, the Panhandle and North Texas are fairly under control. The story is much different in other parts of the country."

Major pulled his horse to a stop once again as they got closer to the house. Several military personnel were taking orders from Espy. "For example?"

"El Paso is a war zone. There is no other way to describe it. Border breaches are commonplace. Many times, the breakdowns are assisted by gang members who've been residing in El Paso for years."

"I've heard. It's the first priority for me. What else?"

"Sunnyside, located south of Houston off Texas 288, has become a war zone. Violence has spilled over into Southeast Houston toward

Houston-Hobby airport. Colonel Sanderson tells me his troops won't go into the area south of the Interstate 610 loop without heavy artillery."

"Just the one area?"

"No. The other hotspot is Houston's Third Ward. It's an historic area near downtown where both the University of Houston and Texas Southern is located. The problem is that heavily armed gangs have spread throughout the neighborhoods, killing at will and establishing territories as they loot homes and businesses. Like Sunnyside, the Texas Guard refuses to enter the Third Ward because they're not prepared to engage in guerilla warfare with the locals."

Major shook his head and sighed. "This is totally opposite of what we saw in Austin. It seemed calmer after the grid collapsed than before."

"Dad, the commanders, in somewhat muted terms, blamed the president for that. She placed a significant emphasis on DFW and Austin for crowd control. El Paso was already a lost cause in her mind. Houston's northern suburbs, like The Woodlands, got protection. The rest of the city had to rely upon local law enforcement, who quickly threw their hands up in frustration."

"Okay, thanks for the heads-up," Major said as he urged his horse forward toward the house. "Before we meet with Espy, let me ask you about something."

"Sure."

"Are you totally confident in his ability to protect our family? You and I are going to be away a lot in the coming days and weeks. We're putting a lot of stock in this young man."

Duncan's response was quick and unequivocal. "Dad, I trust him with all of our lives. He's practically family in my mind, and his loyalty will always be to our best interests."

"Okay, that's all I need to hear. I will absolutely trust your judgment. Now, next question. Is he sweet on my daughter?"

Duncan gulped and thought about his answer. "Dad, I'm not gonna lie. He's already talked to me about dating Palmer, or courting, or whatever that looks like in times like these. I've given him my approval with the caveat that (a) he'll have his hands full with her, and (b) one misstep and there'll be a line full of Armstrongs to deal with."

"I couldn't have said it better myself."

CHAPTER 37

February 1
The Mansion
Austin, Texas

After an hour-long meeting with key members of her cabinet, President Burnett asked Adjutant General Deur to join her in her office. Deur indicated he had some important information to relay to her from the deputy director of clandestine services, Pauline Hart. After she made a quick phone call, the two settled in by the fire to discuss what Deur had learned.

"Madam President, you asked me to be involved in the vetting process of your vice president candidates and, with the minimal resources I have available, provide you the best possible background report on each of them."

"Yes, Kregg. The information was more than sufficient, and as I announced yesterday, a decision has been made."

Deur cleared his throat and continued. "Yes, ma'am. Something has come to my attention overnight from my sister-in-law, Pauline. She contacted me in an unofficial capacity, so it didn't raise the eyebrows of anyone else within my department."

"Sounds ominous, Kregg. What is this about?"

"She came to me unofficially because the information was obtained through clandestine channels she's maintained in Washington. Revealing her sources to me, or to you, Madam President, would not only expose her source, but it would quite possibly ruin any hope of gaining intelligence in the future."

"Fine, Kregg. What has she found out?"

Deur fidgeted nervously in his seat. "It's about the vice president–

designate's son, Duncan Armstrong. Apparently, um, he was a CIA operative in southeast Asia. He went rogue while he was there. His handlers lost track of his whereabouts, and he cut off all contact with his family during the time frame in question."

President Burnett intently listened to her adjutant general's explanation of what Duncan was being accused of. The story he told matched what the young man had explained to her just the day before. Finding it odd that the information was coming through a leak out of Washington, she didn't let on that she knew about the details. Then Deur added one additional detail that caught her off guard.

"Madam President, Pauline's source also indicated that it was Duncan Armstrong who used his sniper abilities to kill Vice President Gregg."

"Why would he do that?" asked the president.

"Apparently it had to do with some vendetta he had against Gregg, which arose during the time he was the Secretary of Defense. Pauline didn't provide any additional details."

As President Burnett contemplated this last wrinkle, her secretary lightly knocked on the door and stuck her head into the office. "Madam President, I am so sorry for the intrusion. There's a phone call for you from President Harman's chief of staff—Mr. Acton. He says its important."

The president rose and made her way behind her desk. She decided to dismiss Deur for the time being until she took this call and then contemplated the information he'd given her. After Deur left, she began speaking with Acton.

The two covered several mundane subjects regarding the United Nations relief supplies and proposed agreements regarding trade over the coming months. President Burnett was uneasy about the conversation. Acton was not his usual smug, condescending self. He was professional and at times complimentary. The turnaround was too abrupt.

Then something else dawned on her. The topics of conversation were not necessarily urgent, as he'd led her secretary to believe. It was as if he was softening her up for a request or accommodation. With her defenses fully engaged, she waited to see what Acton was up to.

"Madam President," said Acton, a term he'd rarely used in their prior conversations unless he wanted something, "President Harman and I agree that it is not up to us to meddle in the affairs of any other nation, especially yours, under these unusual circumstances. That said, I would be remiss if I didn't pass along some information to you."

Here we go.

"What is it?" asked President Burnett.

"We've heard through international media reports that you've chosen a replacement for Vice President Gregg. There is something you may not have considered regarding your choice."

"Is there something about Major Armstrong that you need to tell me?" she asked.

"No. Rather, it's about his son. We have an extensive file on him at the Pentagon that I'd like to share with you. I can send it down by courier, if you'd like."

Careful, Marion. Do not trust these people.

"Well, I didn't ask his son to be my veep."

"That's true, but under the circumstances, I think you should look at the dossier created by our intelligence community."

"Charles, I'd like to see the file, but could you please bottom-line this for me?"

"I will, Madam President. Our analysts verily believe that Duncan Armstrong, who recently went rogue on a mission, had a vendetta against Monty Gregg and may have possibly pulled the trigger that killed him."

President Burnett fell back in her chair and became silent.

After half a minute, Acton began speaking again. "Madam President, are you still there?"

"Yes, Charles. I am. I don't know what to say, but would you please deliver the dossier to me as soon as possible?"

"I will, Madam President. I am sorry to be the bearer of bad news."

No, you're not.

"Thank you, Charles. I'll look into this further," she said as she disconnected the call.

The president walked over to her beverage cart and found a Dr. Pepper. As she popped the top, she decided against a glass and took a big gulp of the Texas staple. After allowing herself a slight burp, she stared out at the cityscape of Austin.

"How many foxes do I have in my henhouse anyway?"

PART THREE

CHAPTER 38

January 30
The Mansion
Austin, Texas

Major was summoned by President Burnett to Austin, ostensibly to go over his thoughts about the recovery effort. He braved the icy wind, which had accompanied a cold front's arrival the night before. Over the past few centuries, the art of weather predicting changed from the spiritual to the mathematical to the current-day scientific methods.

Commensurate with the collapse of the power grid, life in North America was thrown back to the nineteenth century in many respects. Gone were the days of triple-Doppler radar graphics, twenty-four-seven weather channels, and predictors of hurricane activity that were remarkably accurate months in advance.

On the farms and ranches of Texas, those schooled in the ancient art of weather prognostication practiced during the 1800s studied things like the color of the sky. Greenish hues of the sky near the horizon was a predictor of wet weather. Whereas, in the fall, a purple haze at sunset was often a sign of continued fine weather.

At night, when the moon took on a fiery red color, like copper, then wind could be expected, while a pale moon with ragged edges was a predictor of rain.

As Major made his way to the front entrance of the Mansion, escorted by his security detail, he took a quick glance at the sky. The clouds had formed into an anvil-like shape, and said anvil was pointing directly at Austin.

One of the security guards opened the door for him, and he was making his way inside when the sound of another helicopter landing grabbed his attention. He couldn't identify it from a distance, but it appeared to belong to the military. Major shrugged and continued to the president's office.

He milled about, making small talk with President Burnett's secretary and a few other staffers who stopped by to wish him congratulations. Major accepted a black cup of coffee and began to sip it when he was suddenly joined by Duncan.

"Hey, son. What are you doing here?"

Duncan leaned forward and whispered to his dad, "I was told the president wanted to speak with me directly about the, quote, *North Korean problem*." Duncan used the index and middle fingers of both hands to create air quotes.

Major whispered back, "This is no coincidence. Let me do the talking, okay?"

"Please do."

The secretary interrupted them. "Gentlemen, the president will see you now." She stood and opened the door for Major and Duncan.

Before either of them could greet President Burnett, she spoke in an unusually loud, gruff voice. "Gentlemen, I'm gonna get straight to the point. Please sit. And shut that door! I don't want to be disturbed!"

Duncan shot his dad a glance, and Major lowered his brows to indicate his concern. There was something wrong.

As soon as the door was shut, the president stood and put her right index finger to her lips to indicate the guys should be quiet. She nodded her head and pointed toward the couches. Now Major was really confused. *What's with all the cloak and dagger?*

As they found a spot on the sofa, the president reached out and touched them both on their hands. "Sorry, boys. That was all for show. We've got a real problem."

"What is it?" asked Major.

"Yesterday, I was approached by my adjutant general to inform me of supposedly *credible information* as it relates to Duncan.

Information that was damaging enough to derail your consideration as my vice president."

"Like what?" asked a perturbed Duncan.

"Hear me out, Duncan," said the president reassuringly. "Kregg claimed to have received information from his deputy director of clandestine affairs, Pauline Hart, who also happened to work for the CIA. Let me add one more thing about this attractive young woman. She's Kregg's sister-in-law."

"What did she do with the CIA?" asked Duncan.

"I don't know. All I remember from the introductions was that she was qualified for the position in my government based upon her past duties in Washington."

"Let's get her checked out," insisted Duncan. "I've still got some friends who owe me a favor. I just need to see if they're still around."

Major patted Duncan on the leg and spoke up. "Son, let's see what this is about before we go digging around the CIA, shall we?"

The president continued. "Basically, Kregg relayed to me everything that you guys have told me already about Duncan's mission in North Korea except he characterized it as a *rogue operation,* unauthorized by Washington."

"How would he know? Based upon this Hart woman's allegations?"

"Hold on, son," Major tried to encourage Duncan to tone down his rhetoric. "Turn your boil down to a simmer. Let Marion finish."

The president gave an appreciative smile to her future vice president. "Duncan, trust me. I ain't buyin' any of this BS. Let me finish; then we'll discuss what to do about it."

Duncan took a deep breath and nodded. He remained quiet as the president laid out the sequence of events from yesterday.

"Kregg relayed what Hart said, which not only included the phrase *rogue operation*, but also implied you pulled the trigger that killed Monty based upon some *vendetta*."

The president sensed that Duncan was about to react, but she held her hands up to calm him down. "This is where it gets *curiouser and curiouser*, as Alice in Wonderland said. A few hours later, I get an extremely *cordial* phone call from Charles Acton, President Harman's chief of staff. Now, keep in mind, this man hates me. Yesterday, however, he was sooo peaches and cream it made me wanna puke. Seriously. After we discussed a few mundane matters about intergovernmental cooperation, blah-blah-blah, he hits me with this friendly advice. Using the same lingo that Hart, via Kregg, used, he called you a rogue operator and also accused you of killing Monty for a vendetta."

"Same words. Unbelievable," said Major. "Marion, I know my son, and I can assure you he told the entire truth the other day. Someone in Washington is trying to torpedo my nomination to be your VP."

"Yes, they are," said the president. "They are very threatened by you and especially the two of us as a team. I'm starting to see a pattern emerging. It's one that points to a logical conclusion—they want us to fail."

"They want us back," interjected Major.

"Bingo. Well, it ain't gonna happen."

Duncan leaned forward and interrupted. "Madam President, I wasn't one hundred percent truthful with you. I was angry with Secretary Gregg. I believe he was one of two people who gave the order to cancel the extraction of me and my partner from North Korea. They left us there to die, and Park did. I guarantee you, Gregg and Billy Yancey, who planned the operation, either gave the order or knew of it."

Major added, "That's consistent with Monty's final words to his wife before he died. He said *tell Armstrong it was Yancey.*"

"Do you believe he was referring to Duncan's situation, or the hiring of the sniper to kill him?" asked the president.

"I believe he was referring to Duncan and here's why. In that dying moment, he'd have no idea that I'd be assigned by you to investigate his shooting. It is likely he was feeling remorseful over leaving my son stranded in North Korea. I watched his body language the day the four of us met here, in your office. He was extremely nervous. I believe he knew exactly who Duncan was, and after meeting him in person, he felt guilty for leaving a man behind on the battlefield."

President Burnett turned to Duncan. "Do you agree with your dad's assessment?"

"Yes, ma'am. I do. Yancey's job at the CIA is regime change, and it's possible Pauline Hart works for him in some capacity. They've screwed up by sticking to the script too closely. How often do you hear the words *rogue operator* and *vendetta* used? They were used at the same time and originated from a single voice, in my opinion."

"Billy Yancey," the president surmised.

"Yes, ma'am," said Duncan.

President Burnett leaned back on the settee and crossed her legs. She tapped her knees with her fingers as she digested the conversation.

"Okay," she began. "I suspected something was wrong about the conversations from yesterday, which is why I wanted to put on a façade as you entered my office. I don't know who to trust outside this room. I wanna believe that Kregg is a loyal soldier, but he did express some reservations early on when the concept of secession was discussed. He's also been hesitant at times to use force to protect our borders. That said, he has never given me reason to doubt his loyalty until his sister-in-law entered the picture."

"Ma'am, if she works for Billy Yancey, she's a master of manipulation. Your adjutant general is likely blinded by the family relationship too."

"I hope you're right, young man. Either way, I have to be careful what Kregg's made privy to in the short term. Let me ask you something. Do you want revenge on Billy Yancey for what he did to you and your partner?"

"Now more than ever," replied Duncan.

She turned her attention to Major. "Nothing leaves this room. Ever. You gotta swear to me, Major."

"Marion, I swear my loyalty, so help me God."

The president of Texas looked at Duncan. "You take care of this North Korean problem for me, and I will give your father every resource at my disposal for you to settle your score with Yancey. Frankly, I don't know which is a bigger threat to our nation—the devil we know or the devil we don't."

Duncan looked his president in the eyes, and then he whispered to her, "The devil works best in the dark. Unfortunately for him, so do I."

CHAPTER 39

January 30
The Armstrong Ranch
Borden County, Texas

Cooper was not unlike any new manager inserted into a business operation. He had to demonstrate to his team that he was capable of leading them in a manner they respected. He couldn't come in heavy-handed, as that might alienate them. He couldn't pretend to still be one of them, as they might not afford his decision making the requisite deference. Cooper's job was further complicated by the fact that half of his team were family, one was the fiancée of his older brother, and the fourth had worked under his predecessor for many years.

He decided to follow his daddy's sage advice. *Don't ask them to do anything that you're not willing to do yourself.* And with that principle guiding his daily interaction with everyone, Cooper set about filling the mighty big shoes of Preacher.

The challenges began on day one as they made the decision to consolidate the herd back at the ranch. With Espy's men on constant patrol, they no longer had to worry about marauders trying to steal their cattle. The day before, he'd informed Antonio and Riley that first thing this morning, he wanted to drive the steers from the eastern part of the ranch back up to their grazing fields nearest the barn.

This morning, however, Riley elected to sleep in. This resulted in an argument as Cooper tried to roust his brother out of bed. Although he was successful in herding his brother out the front door, Riley repaid his brother with a fussy demeanor the entire day. After two days in charge, Cooper had managed to turn his director of livestock management into a *dude with a 'tude.*

The next order of business was to clean out the Slaughters' house over at the Reinecke operation. Cooper called upon Palmer and Sook for assistance. Sook was more than willing, but Palmer thought the brutal cold weather moving in meant the clean-out job could wait for another few days.

Cooper got half of the dynamic duo to help. Palmer stubbornly remained in the house while Sook joined Cooper and a couple of the ranch hands' wives in the cleanup process. Cooper wanted to prepare the home for guests or newly hired ranch hands to move into, as the homes on the ranch were occupied by existing families and soldiers.

Except for Preacher's home. Lucy and Major insisted they'd package up his things and make the home available to Espy, who'd asked to live at the ranch full-time. While his men would rotate between their homes, Camp Lubbock, and the temporary quarters at the ranch, Espy preferred to be there all day, every day.

The Armstrong family was better prepared than most because they'd made the effort to study preparedness websites and sacrificed expenditures on other, frivolous items in favor of the necessities of shelter, water, food, and security. As a result, once they'd survived the attack upon their ranch by the commandos, returning to a normal life was easier.

Granted, the presence of the security team gave them the peace of mind to go about their daily activities without fear of getting injured or killed. But the building blocks Lucy and Major had laid certainly expedited their return to normalcy.

By the end of his fourth day running the ranch, Cooper, utilizing the organizational skills learned from his mother, had returned the operations of the ranch back to a normal routine. Now his biggest challenge was finding warm bodies to work the ranch in order to get it ready for spring.

Fields needed to be tilled. Fences were in a state of disrepair following the attack. He and Lucy had discussed tripling the size of their gardens in order to feed the soldiers who were stationed there.

Despite the president's promises of additional food supplies, Major warned that the Texas food supply was greatly diminished, and they'd have to continue to grow their own.

Cooper considered his options in adding to the ranch's workforce. He could travel to nearby cattle ranchers and ask if they had anyone they could spare. He considered riding into Lubbock with Espy one day to look for potential workers. He was concerned that the people he would bring on board were unknowns. He had no ability to check their backgrounds, so he decided against it.

After he finished locking up the Reinecke property, he walked through the milking machines, which had been reinstalled from the Slaughters' ranch. He either needed to move this entire dairy operation to the protected confines of the Armstrong Ranch, or he'd need to widen Espy's secured perimeter to include the oil fields and the Reinecke buildings. That wasn't a long-term solution because he assumed, at some point, the company that owned the property would return.

To return to the ranch, he decided to retrace the route he and Riley had taken the night they had fought the commandos at the south gate guard tower. Everything that had happened was fresh in his mind, including how different the firefight was from what he'd seen in movies. He recalled how loud the shooting was. His ears were still ringing for days afterwards.

Also, the stop-and-go aspect of the shooting seemed odd to him. When the commandos had shot at him, it sounded like a bunch of angry bees whizzing by his head. Then the shooting would stop, and the world became deathly silent. In those few seconds between volleys, the ranch looked different to Cooper. He saw the sky differently. He could hear the winds blow through the tall grasses. His senses had kicked into overdrive.

Then the oncoming vehicles amped his adrenaline into overdrive as threats closed on him from two directions. The concept of dying became very real for Cooper at that point. That was when he fell in love with his rifle. Duncan always referred to it as a tool, but Cooper began to see it as his lifeline. Without it, he was going to die. He even recalled saying a prayer thanking God for his rifle, and then he chuckled to himself when he wondered if God was pro-Second Amendment.

As the battle had raged on, Cooper learned several things about himself. He discovered he was capable of killing. When his bullets tore into the commandos, he didn't see them as human beings but rather as machines hell-bent on his destruction. A coldness had washed over him as he transitioned from mid-twenties rodeo star to soldier.

His acceptance of killing had culminated with his asking Riley why he didn't just shoot the last commando they'd chased through the field. Riley's response was meant to be humorous when he replied that he missed steer wrestling. What struck Cooper the most was that in the moment when the two brothers risked death, they remained calm and capable of carrying on a somewhat casual conversation in the face of mortal danger.

They'd both evolved from rodeo kids raised on a ranch to hardened soldiers taught on the battlefield. Now they'd have to find a way to turn back into ranchers.

CHAPTER 40

January 30
The Armstrong Ranch
Borden County, Texas

Palmer told her mother she was going to ride over to the Slaughter property to check on Sook and Cooper when she happened upon Espy meeting with two of his men. She remained a respectful distance away to allow him to complete his instructions; then she moseyed closer to his Humvee. Palmer blushed as a huge genuine smile came over Espy's face when she caught his eye. The butterflies in her stomach told her the feeling was mutual.

"How're ya holdin' up?" Espy asked as he helped Palmer dismount from her horse.

"Good, actually," she replied.

He took the reins and tied them to a black handle on the hood of the truck. The hood of a Humvee opened with the hinges positioned near the front grille, requiring the handles to pull the heavy piece of steel forward. "I was fixin' to ride over to Reinecke's to check on Coop and Sook when I saw you. I just thought I'd stop by and say hi."

"I'm glad you did. Um, I've been meaning to talk with you alone, but sometimes that's hard to do with so many people around, you know?"

"Yeah." Palmer felt a little nervous. The more she was around Espy, the more she could tell she had feelings for him. The question she kept asking herself was what to do about it. The whole situation was awkward. Espy technically worked for her brother, but he was also the head of the detail assigned to protect her father, the vice president. A relationship would be complicated.

"It's gettin' cold. You wanna sit inside?"

"Sure," Palmer replied as she walked around to the passenger's side. Espy hustled around her and opened the door to help her in. He gently pushed the door closed so it didn't slam. Palmer tried to recall if any other guy she was sweet on ever opened the truck door for her. Usually their lack of manners resembled something along the lines of *git in the truck*.

Palmer got settled in and surveyed the spartan interior. The military Humvees were short on luxury and geared toward simplicity. Even the seats were somewhat uncomfortable. She imagined what a date would look like in a military vehicle like this one. She glanced up at the turret, which led to the fifty-caliber machine gun. Then she laughed a little. They'd have no problem getting a parking space near the front door.

After Espy settled in, they made small talk about the weather and laughed about Riley's grumpy attitude, which had quickly spread around the ranch. It was a reminder to Palmer of how close-knit the entire group had become in a short period of time.

Finally, she could tell Espy was easing into the point of his wanting to speak with her alone. He was nervous, and she was enjoying watching him squirm.

"Palmer, I really like you. You know what I mean? It's just kinda weird with how we met and, you know, all of this."

Palmer tucked a leg under her and turned to face Espy. She reached forward and fiddled with a handheld radio that had been left on the truck's armrest. Apprehensive, she began to rotate it in a circle. With each successive effort, the radio spun a little more on its axis.

"I really like you, too. This whole world is convoluted. How do you act normal when any minute we could be getting shot at?"

Espy chuckled. "What is normal anymore? I tried to be normal once. It was the worst three minutes of my life!"

His joke took the edge off, and Palmer responded with a hearty laugh. She playfully swatted at his shoulder, and he pretended to defend himself. In reality, Palmer knew that Espy wanted her to touch him, even if it was a playful brush across his uniform.

"I grew up living in the moment," she began. "Normal was waking up, spending time with my brothers, and thinking about rodeos. If anything, the EMP and then the attack the other day has forced me to grow up. Espy, I've killed people, and I didn't bat an eye. Oddly, I have zero remorse for taking another human being's life because they were trying to kill all of us. It's not something I dwell on. Every day since, I've gotten out of bed, helped Momma around the house, and thought about what our future looks like."

"I believe your future is brighter today than it was a week ago," said Espy. "Your dad is going to be the new vice president. Duncan, who I love like a brother, will be a national hero after he drives the North Koreans out of here. Can you see that?"

"Yes, but honestly, that's their lives. I think about my future too. Truthfully, I never have before in a serious way. It's always been about the next rodeo or state fair. Not about the important things in life."

"Like relationships?" Espy went for it.

Palmer stopped twirling the radio. With her head still tilted downward, she looked up at Espy with her blue eyes. Then she smiled. "Yeah, like relationships," she replied with a soft voice. She hesitated and gave him a smile as she asked, "So, you wanna play spin the radio?"

Espy beamed. "You betcha. As I see it, I can't lose."

Without spinning, Palmer set aside the radio and leaned forward to kiss him. She closed her eyes, and a feeling came over her that she'd never forget. In that moment, she fell in love for the first time.

CHAPTER 41

January 30
The Armstrong Ranch
Borden County, Texas

It took a few days for Major and Lucy to have the time, and the courage, to enter Preacher's home and pack up his things. Neither had visited him there in some time, and they were astonished at how simply he lived. There were very few photos, mementos, or collectibles in sight. His space was filled mostly with books.

Major had learned over the years that Preacher was a reader who admitted to enjoying disaster thrillers and post-apocalyptic fiction. During their rides around the ranch, Preacher would often cite something he'd read in fictional accounts of end-of-the-world scenarios. He'd once posited that one way to learn what to expect during the apocalypse was through well-written prepper fiction. Apparently, he'd taken it to heart.

"I guess he liked this guy the most, since he's filled up three bookshelves," Major said as he directed Lucy's attention to the built-in containing books, a few photos, and a television.

Lucy laughed as she picked up a book and showed it to her husband. "He didn't think too much of the guys in this stack on the floor. Look, he even wrote *CRAP* in big letters across the front covers."

Major chuckled and shook his head as he ran his fingers across the three dozen titles on the shelf. "Look here, Miss Lucy. This set is about Texas. Maybe we should read it to see how it turns out?"

"Forget it, *Mr. Vice President–designate*, or whatever your official title is. You best be studyin' up on your grandparentin' skills."

"What? Do you know something I don't know?"

"No, Sook's not pregnant. She's savin' herself for her wedding night. But we don't have any birth control around here 'cause, frankly, I didn't think we'd need it anytime soon. Big mistake on my part for overlooking such a simple thing."

"Well, you didn't know Duncan would be bringing his future wife back to the ranch. Do you think they'll have kids right away?"

"Maybe. She's excited about the prospect of having babies with Duncan, but she hasn't discussed it with him. Sook's very levelheaded, and after the last several days, she understands the impracticality of bringing a child into this world."

Major set the boxes on the kitchen table and began to remove Preacher's clothes from the closet, leaving the hangers behind. With each piece of clothing, he paused as he tried to remember when his old friend wore the item last.

He snapped back into the present and continued. "We didn't think it was practical to have a baby right away either. Do you remember?"

"Yes, of course, but this is a lot different," Lucy replied. "Although, our security situation is entirely better now. Perhaps a wedding will bring joy to the ranch, and then a baby on the way will make us all realize what life is truly all about."

"We'll let them work it out, and I'll be there to advise them both if requested. You and I have done a great job in not meddling in the kids' decision making in the past. I believe they've grown up into well-rounded, mature adults as a result."

Lucy continued to use her right hand to load the *crap books* into boxes. She planned on offering them to the soldiers to pass the time, but out of reverence to Preacher, Lucy wanted to leave his favorites on the shelf.

She looked over to Major and asked, "Have you mentioned to Espy that we're going to suggest he live here?"

"Not yet. I need to have a talk with him about something else."

"Related to security?" Lucy asked.

"No, not exactly. A personal matter."

Lucy stopped again and approached Major. "Don't you scare that young man away from our daughter."

"How did you know that was what I was referring to?"

Lucy quickly replied, "Your tone of voice changed from husband to father."

"No tone," he protested.

"Yes, dear. You had a tone. Palmer is a grown woman, and she can take care of herself. Don't meddle, remember?"

Major shook his head and stopped for a moment. He reached to hug his wife, and she stepped backwards to avoid his clutches. "Miss Lucy, I'm gonna be polite. I want to honor him with this home, but I wanna make it abundantly clear that the words *Love Shack* aren't written across the front door. He needs to respect my daughter while he's here."

"Major, you listen to me. I don't even know if those two have told each other how they feel yet. I may be missing the signals, but Espy may not be interested."

"Oh yes, he is interested. He's already asked Duncan for permission to court Palmer."

"See, he's a gentleman. Have any of her other boyfriends come along to ask for permission to take our daughter on a date?"

Major crossed his arms. "She's never had any boyfriends. In fact, I asked the boys if—"

"Yeah, I heard about that conversation. You're lucky I didn't give you a whoopin' for that. Major, they'll be fine. I'll have a talk with Palmer when the time's right."

"How will you know?" asked Major.

"Mothers just know."

CHAPTER 42

January 31
The Armstrong Ranch
Borden County, Texas

Duncan didn't have to stress the importance of monitoring General Lee's communications to Sook. She understood and was so committed to her duties that it was disrupting her ability to sleep. Finally, just before dawn, there had been a breakthrough.

During the past couple of days, she and Duncan had talked about the attack on the ranch and their battle to take it back. Sook had confirmed to Duncan what he'd already suspected—Holloway's men were a far cry from the commandos under General Lee's command.

Sook explained that many of the soldiers in the Korean People's Army were simply peasants with a uniform on. They were used to bolster numbers in the eyes of the world. In reality, they were more likely to carry a hoe in the fields than a rifle on the shoulder.

However, those trained for military service, especially the commandos, were rabid fighters who'd die for Dear Leader or simply to honor their family. Holloway's men were criminals, not the type of soldiers trained for combat like Lee's men.

Duncan was beginning to understand the plan designed by Dear Leader many years ago. He just wasn't sure how Holloway and his men fit into the overall scheme, not that it mattered at this point. He was focused on finding Lee and driving him out of Texas or, better yet, killing him.

When Sook had gently tapped on his door this morning, he was already lying awake thinking about his day. He was tired of waiting for Lee to make a move, and he considered pressing the fight.

Duncan wrestled with his options and in the end convinced himself moving on Lee prematurely might force him to go into hiding. Then the frightened general would be a far more challenging adversary.

Duncan opened the door and allowed Sook into his room. She was carrying one of the MSAT G2 push-to-talk satellite radios utilized by the commandos. The devices were ideal for instant communications, but also had email capability, the ability to transfer files, and could download weather reports in areas where cellular service was unavailable.

"Good morning," Duncan whispered so he didn't wake up his parents. He and Sook exchanged a kiss. He turned on the kerosene lamp next to his bed and pushed the door to where it was barely ajar. At night, they didn't run the generators to cut down on noise and save on fuel. "Come, sit down."

"Duncan, I heard General Lee. I am sure of it. They didn't use his name. They called him *jeongbogja*, which means conqueror. It is a term of great honor in North Korean history."

Duncan repeated her pronunciation of the word. "Tsun-book-sah."

"Yes, *jeongbogja*. He is in Baytown. Do you know this place?"

Suddenly excited, Duncan leaned over and gave Sook another kiss. "Did he say anything else?"

"Yes, he talked of another place. Arthurport? I am not certain."

"Port Arthur. Very good. What did he say about Port Arthur?"

Sook referred to her notes. "He notified second unit to be ready at Arthurport, um, Port Arthur. First unit is located at Baytown."

"Thank you. Thank you." He kissed her a third time.

Sook giggled. "You are welcome, Duncan. I think you just like kissing me."

After another kiss, he added, "I sure do. I have to call Fort Hood."

Duncan grabbed his satellite phone and contacted the captain of his unit at Fort Hood. He put the team on full alert to move out to the two predetermined rally points outside the visible perimeter of the refineries. He instructed their liaison to contact the management teams of the Baytown and Aramco facilities and have them route all incoming employees through the rally points.

Once there, his men would replace the employees in their vehicles and make the drive into work as always. He believed Lee was very observant and would see through any change in routine. If Lee had the facility under surveillance, he was most likely tracking incoming and outgoing traffic. If his men followed the employees' typical routine, then a petroleum engineer would be replaced by a highly trained ex-Delta Force operative.

After disconnecting the call, he asked Sook, "Are you sure you want to come with me? You can monitor the radio from here."

"I made a promise to help you and my new country. I want to come with you."

"Okay then, soldier. Get your gear ready. We pull out in fifteen minutes. I love you."

"I love you, too," Sook said as she quickly exited his room.

Duncan watched Sook as she made her way through the darkened hallway. He was amazed at her dedication and unselfishness. He moved to the closet and retrieved his clothing. Anticipating an evening assault on the facility, he wore dark clothing and prepared his favorite tools of battle—two knives, a full-size sidearm, a concealed weapon strapped to his ankle, and his battle rifle.

As he walked out of the room, he caught a glimpse of himself in the mirror. He mumbled to himself, "You're not indestructible, you know."

Duncan chuckled as he walked into the hallway.

I am today.

*****

The entire Armstrong family got up to see Duncan and Sook off. The powerful helicopter threw dust and debris around the front yard of the ranch house as it lifted off to make the long flight to the rally point in Baytown.

His captain had chosen the Houston Raceway on the east side of the peninsula that jutted into Trinity Bay. The refinery was located on the water, and the bridge from South Houston to the facility could be easily monitored by Lee's men.

Duncan's unit traveled through Houston on Interstate 10. If Lee had scouts watching for troop movements, it would appear to the casual observer that a convoy was headed to their east. Once the convoy was past Baytown, part of the unit split off and backtracked to the racetrack while the rest made their way to Port Arthur, sixty miles to the east at the Louisiana border.

As he rode in the helicopter, he studied a map of the region. First, he tried to get in Lee's head as to the goal following the attacks on the refineries. The I-10 bridge into Louisiana was heavily guarded, and Lee most likely knew that. There was a two-lane causeway that crossed Sabine Lake into Louisiana only a few miles from the Aramco refinery.

If he was the general, he'd attack Aramco second, creating a diversion. Hopefully, any security detail blocking the Sabine Lake Causeway would be drawn toward the activity to lend assistance. Even if they didn't leave their post, Lee and his men could easily overpower the nominally guarded border crossing and make their escape into Louisiana.

This line of thought was bolstered by Lee's reference to his Port Arthur team as *second unit*. The first target was Baytown. That was where Duncan would join the fight. Throughout the afternoon, he and his men would make their way into the facility and take up defensive positions around pipelines, critical operations systems, and in hidden positions to cut off Lee's escape.

Duncan wanted to personally lop off the head of the snake and feed its carcass to the gators.

After he arrived at the racetrack, the captain assembled the men in the covered grandstand to avoid the slight drizzle, which preceded the cold air approaching the region. He studied the men he'd handpicked out of hundreds of personnel at Fort Hood. These guys were the best of the best and proud to be a part of the effort.

For the military personnel across Texas, fighting their former countrymen from the U.S. was difficult. They were used to deployments where the enemy, although difficult to define at times, spoke a language foreign to them and lived a lifestyle different from what they knew back home.

Guarding the borders against Americans entering proved emotionally difficult for them. But with the downing of the Texas power grid, subduing their fellow Texans from rioting and looting was worse. It was a welcome change of pace for these highly trained soldiers to battle an enemy who was easily identifiable by appearance and language.

"Gentlemen, a little over two weeks ago, North Koreans attacked Texas. They ambushed our border patrols, leaving their families without a parent. They set about to murder innocent civilians who were simply doing their jobs of keeping the lights on for our fellow Texans. Then, in an act of terrorism in furtherance of their undeclared war against us, they destroyed the lifeblood of any nation—the power supply.

"We have credible information that attacks on the two largest oil refineries in Texas are imminent. I believe the first attack by General Lee, the leader of the DPRK Lightning Death Squads, will be initiated six miles down the road from here at the Baytown Refinery.

"This unit is here to end this war. The hopes of Texas rest on our shoulders as we do what it takes to protect our nation's most valuable fuel resource. And we are the ones who will avenge the deaths of our brothers and the innocents who've lost their lives at the hands of Lee's commandos."

Duncan paused as the voices hollered, "Hooah!"

"Alright, gentlemen. We start this operation in two hours. Police your gear and get your heads right. Dismissed."

CHAPTER 43

January 31
Baytown Refinery
Baytown, Texas

General Kyoung-Joo Lee, formerly a commander in North Korea's Lightning Death Squads and now in charge of the entirety of the invasion forces within the continental United States and Texas, had spent the better part of a decade studying the habits and idiosyncrasies of Americans. His overall opinion was that Americans tended to overreact to a perceived crisis, and then as interest waned, so did their ability to respond.

An isolated occurrence of a politician's use of words resulted in tens of thousands of opponents taking to the street in protest. They created chants, slogans, and signs, all of which vowed to throw the bum out at the next election. Within a few days, a new media-driven crisis was created and theirs was quickly forgotten.

Lee, who was a student of history, continued his fascination with America once he began sneaking his operatives across the country's northern border. The America of today was nowhere near the America of World War II. The young adults of that time period were known as the Greatest Generation. Born in the twenties, they had endured the deprivation of the Great Depression and then patriotically volunteered to fight in World War II or make sacrifices at home to help the war effort.

Once the war was over, the men who survived the battles returned to create the most dynamic industrial economic base in the world. Over the decades, however, that changed. America became soft and distracted.

Matters of importance gave way to matters of emotion. The conversations in Washington turned from national security and economic prosperity to culture wars.

Lee's study of the American psyche served him well as he carried forward the mission of Dear Leader over the years. Today, even without Pyongyang's guidance, the leader of the Lightning Death Squads remained focused on the task at hand.

Lee also studied Sun Tzu, who posited in *The Art of War, know thy self, know thy enemy—a thousand battles, a thousand victories.*

Lee had spent hours studying the activities of the security personnel and the employees of the Baytown Refinery. They were going through the motions. To be sure, at the beginning of their assignment to this facility, they had probably practiced a heightened state of awareness. But over time, no threat materialized, and their routine became mundane.

He pulled his jacket closer around his chest to ward off the cold wind, which swept down the deserted street. A wintry mix of rain and sleet had reached as far south as the Houston area throughout the day. While many Texans who lived in the area lamented the nasty weather, Lee cheered it. The security personnel at the refinery would be distracted and more interested in staying warm than fighting a battle. His men, on the other hand, fought for a cause. They were trained to fight with passion and grit. Tonight, he would succeed and bring glory to Dear Leader.

Before he sent his men into the cold drizzle, he gave them one final warning.

"Our enemy does not have the courage and conviction that you hold in your heart. But do not underestimate your foe. In Texas, the enemy may dress like a deer, but they will kill like a lion. My honorable warriors, every battle is won before it is fought through preparation. Move swiftly, yet quietly. Position yourself as we've discussed. When the time comes, we will attack, remembering our Dear Leader expects victory!"

CHAPTER 44

January 31
Baytown Refinery
Baytown, Texas

"Alpha One, Foxtrot Two. Over." The radio contact from the perimeter patrols designated Foxtrot startled Duncan. He'd expected Lee to make his move on the refinery in the early morning hours. Then he considered the big picture. Lee expected to quickly launch the attack, destroy the refinery operations and join his second unit at Port Arthur. Duncan was immediately glad he'd placed his men in position during the four o'clock afternoon shift change.

"Go ahead, Foxtrot Two."

"We have movement along the western security line at Ashby Street. Four hostiles on foot."

"Roger that, Foxtrot Two. Stand by."

Duncan turned to the team of engineers who were prepared to assist Duncan in identifying possible targets. They studied a wall-size map, which provided a flowchart of the refinery's operations.

"What's the most likely target on the west side of the complex?" Duncan asked.

"Our operation flows from west to east. Raw crude comes into the area your man referenced at Ashby Street. It is then submitted to atmospheric distillation at these large fractioning towers located here and here." The engineer used a pointer to direct Duncan's attention.

"Have you shut down the system in these fractioning towers?"

"Yes, per your instructions. None of the facility is operating at the moment, as we instituted Category 3 Hurricane protocols after your captain phoned us. When major hurricanes are forecast for the

Galveston Bay area, we empty all pipelines between the towers, the hydrotreaters, and the final processors, which make the conversion to gasoline, diesel, and other petroleum byproducts."

Duncan rubbed his temples. It would take some heavy-duty explosives to take down the fractioning towers. Reports indicated that Lee had used RPGs at the nuclear power plant, but he had utilized construction-grade TNT to take down the large transmission towers as well.

His captain interrupted his thoughts. "Sir, Foxtrot Two is still waiting for his orders."

"Yeah, I know. I don't know what General Lee's understanding of refineries is. Do they even have oil refineries in North Korea?"

Another engineer stepped forward. He was of Asian descent but spoke English without an accent. "Sir, if I may. The largest oil refinery in North Korea, located in Sinuiju at the Chinese border, may be known to the general of whom you speak."

"Sinuiju?" asked Duncan.

"Yes."

Duncan shot a sly grin at Sook, who smiled back as she continued monitoring the radio with an earpiece. "I know it well."

Duncan took to the radio. "Foxtrot Two, Alpha One. Over."

"Go ahead, Alpha One."

"Targets are likely the three large towers on your western perimeter. Possible use of explosives. Eliminate targets immediately."

The action was starting to pick up, and the other Foxtrot patrols were advising Duncan of the commandos' entrance into secured areas of the Baytown Refinery. The entire complex covered over twenty-four hundred acres, and its perimeter was secured by an eight-foot-tall chain-link fence topped with barbed wire. However, the dual-entry gates to parking areas could easily be breached, giving quick access to the complex. After that, the commandos had a more difficult task in their quest to destroy the facility.

A refinery consists of three basic operations to convert crude oil to refined petroleum products like asphalt, coke, liquid petroleum gas, and of course, transportation fuels for jets, trucks, and automobiles. The first phase, which starts with the fractioning towers, is part of the separation process. The finishing process is an interim step primarily required for the creation of gasoline. Finally, the conversion phase produces the final product.

Duncan had discussed these processes with the engineers as soon as they had assembled in the main operations building earlier that afternoon. He'd also warned them that building would be a likely target of Lee and his men. They were willing to take the risk in order to help.

"Alpha One, Foxtrot One. Over."

"Go ahead, Foxtrot One."

"A dozen bogeys are running northbound along San Jacinto Avenue toward the center of the refinery complex."

"Roger that, Foxtrot One. Stand by."

Duncan studied the map again. One of the engineers assisted him in identifying San Jacinto Avenue.

"Commander, several of our gasoline hydrotreaters are located along this road. It's possible they're going to—"

The crackle of the radio interrupted his sentence. "Alpha One, Foxtrot One. They are peeling off in teams of two at each cross intersection. Confirmed. Six teams of two. Over."

Duncan turned and asked, "How would you disable these hydrotreaters? What are they?"

"Their goal would not be the catalyst systems themselves but rather the mechanical rooms associated with each of the catalysts. First, they'd have to identify them. They're all bolt-locked and require a torch or small explosive to remove the doors. Then the computer and manual operations could be vandalized in any number of ways."

"What do the buildings look like?"

"They're all the same except their identifying numbers are different. In this part of the flow, they are simply S-J one through six. The S-J represents San Jacinto."

Duncan returned to the radio and immediately provided the Foxtrot One team the information. His men had the benefit of night vision as well as the ability to quickly find their way to the potential target sought by Lee's men. Foxtrot One would be able to lie in wait as the commandos entered their trap.

Duncan nervously paced the operations center of the refinery. He touched base with his team at Port Arthur, who were in position to fire upon the commandos the moment they entered the perimeter fencing. Unlike Baytown, where Duncan was attempting to capture the North Korean commander, Port Arthur was strictly a search and destroy mission against the commandos. Duncan wasn't interested in prisoners. He wanted a high body count to bring this to an end.

After a few more excruciating minutes, he reached out to his security detail, which surrounded the Eco Services Operations Center where he was located. He switched the communications channel to the one dedicated to Bravo team.

"Bravo One, Alpha One. Over."

After there was no response, Duncan tried again. "Repeat. Bravo One, Alpha One. Over."

There was still no answer. He turned to his captain, who also had a concerned look on his face. Duncan tried to hail any of the three units assigned to Bravo team.

"Bravo team, Alpha One. Over."

Duncan took a deep breath and exhaled. "Sook, have you heard any radio chatter at all?"

She shook her head and frowned.

Duncan turned to his officer. "Captain, you coordinate the Foxtrot teams. I'll remain on Bravo's channel as its team leader. Lock and barricade the door after I leave." He shot a reassuring smile in Sook's direction, grabbed his rifle, and exited into the dimly lit hallway.

The two soldiers guarding the operations center entryway were given instructions to monitor Bravo's dedicated channel and to remain at their post no matter what they might hear. Their job was to protect the occupants of that room.

"I'll handle the rest," growled Duncan as he left through the side emergency exit of the building.

CHAPTER 45

January 31
Baytown Refinery
Baytown, Texas

Duncan stopped and pressed his back against the brick wall, allowing his body to transition from the warm confines of the operations building to the cold, damp evening air. Lee had chosen the perfect night to undertake his assault upon the refinery. The weather was unusual for Houston, and most of the security staff would've spent their time inside guard shacks and enclosed buildings. Lee probably expected little resistance as his men snuck about the operations of the refinery in search of targets to disable or destroy.

At this point, however, Lee had most certainly been alerted to the enhanced security measures put into place by Duncan. If Bravo team had been compromised, Lee and his commandos would realize they were not up against run-of-the-mill security personnel.

Duncan learned something as well. Lee's men had eliminated the six fine-tuned killing machines assigned to Bravo team. If that was the case, Duncan would have to be on his game to defend Sook and the men inside the building.

The staccato sound of gunfire could be heard from the south end of the complex, where Foxtrot was protecting the hydrotreaters. Duncan didn't need to understand what all of the facets of the refining process were. He just knew that losing the ability to produce fuel would throw Texas into a tailspin from which recovery would be long and ugly.

He adjusted his night-vision goggles, readied his rifle, and went hunting. The operations center was open on the front to a parking lot, which contained half a dozen cars. The side emergency exit he used emptied into a labyrinth of pipes and metal structures that were connected by more pipes branching off in three directions. Every square foot of this high-dollar, bayfront real estate was utilized. There was no room for picnic tables or walking trails. The refinery was a jungle of asphalt, concrete, and steel.

Each side of the operations building had a door, but only the front entrance could be accessed from the outside. The three emergency exits had no exterior door handles. This helped Duncan in his positioning, as he knew Lee had to approach the facility with a full-frontal attack.

With the elimination of Bravo team, and the extended firefight heard from the rear of the building, Duncan knew Lee would be making his move soon. Even if his commandos were unsuccessful in damaging the rest of the facility, destruction of the operations center would bring the Baytown Refinery to a screeching halt.

He edged his way to the front of the building and searched for any form of movement through his night-vision goggles. He decided to move within the adjacent pipelines using the twelve-inch wide pipes as cover. With his head rotating on a one-hundred-eighty-degree swivel, Duncan moved toward the parking area and the block wall that separated the courtyard-style entrance from the asphalt parking lot.

Suddenly, a figure appeared over the wall and made a throwing motion. He heard the distinctive sound of a grenade clanking against the concrete entryway and bouncing against the plate glass.

The resulting blast from the grenade's impact with the glass was deafening. The entire front entrance was obliterated as glass flew in all directions. Duncan moved into position and dropped to the ground. Lee's men wouldn't wait long to move in. Duncan had to be patient. All of his targets needed to reveal themselves before he opened fire.

"Come on out, boys," Duncan mumbled to himself as he focused his aim on the sidewalk closest to the block wall.

There you are, he thought to himself as two groups of men raced along the sidewalk toward the front door. They opened fire on the entry on the chance that someone was waiting on the other side of the cloud of dust and debris. They never thought to look for trouble on their left flank.

Duncan had silenced his rifle, and the spitting sound couldn't be heard over the combination of the commandos' gunfire and the burning front entrance. The commandos, however, felt the bullets tearing through their bodies. He sprayed them with four quick bursts, immediately killing them or knocking them to the sidewalk. If their bodies made the slightest movement, Duncan filled them with a couple more *insurance* rounds.

Even though the tracer rounds had not yet appeared, meaning he had several rounds of ammunition left, Duncan switched to a full magazine. This battle still had one primary target to locate—General Lee, their *conqueror.*

Duncan slipped back into the protection of the pipeline maze and worked his way toward the parking lot. He took a moment to raise his captain on the radio.

"Alpha One, Bravo team leader. Over."

"Go, Bravo team leader."

"Four kills at front door. Sitrep."

"Lost one. All others secure. Foxtrot team's mopping up hostiles."

"Roger that. Still on watch for the conqueror and more hostiles."

"Repeat, Bravo team leader."

"Never mind. Bravo team leader out."

Duncan looked in all directions. *Am I wrong? Would Lee sit this one out in favor of making a quick escape to Port Arthur?*

Still puzzled, he worked his way through the pipes and then emerged in the parking lot. As he cleared the last bit of cover, he instinctively lowered his profile into a crouch. The move saved his life.

Automatic gunfire released a barrage of bullets over his head, striking the now empty pipes, but the deafening sound caused his ears to ring. Duncan, still recovering somewhat from the concussive blast in his Humvee a week ago, crawled forward and then ran at a low crouch toward an old Chevy Suburban in the parking lot. A trail of bullets tore up the turf behind him as he went.

He caught his breath and remained in a crouch as he pressed his body against the SUV's front fender. He listened for his adversary. The attacker knew where he was, but Duncan couldn't risk breaking cover to stick his head up for a better look. He decided to lure him out with psychological warfare.

"*Jeongbogja! Jeongbogja!* Isn't that what they call you, General Lee?"

There was no answer, and he was starting to think that Lee had escaped after firing upon Duncan. He decided to try again.

"How about it, conqueror?" Duncan asked sarcastically. "Why don't you and I have a chat? I'm sure you speak English."

Duncan listened and drew his knife out of his pocket. He gently set his rifle against the tire and then used the knife to jimmy the side mirror off the door.

Duncan pulled his sidearm and inched his way to the back of the Suburban. Using the mirror, he positioned himself so he could see the open parking lot. There was a single vehicle, a smallish four-door sedan, parked nearest the street. At least seven cars were parked along the block half-wall separating the courtyard from the parking lot.

After holstering his pistol, he pulled the partially emptied magazine from his pouch and prepared to throw it like a boomerang toward the parked sedan. He decided to taunt Lee one more time before making a second attempt to draw him out.

"Hello, *Jeongbogja! Jeongbogja!*"

With his left hand, Duncan slung the magazine, which sailed across the parking. It skipped once before bouncing up and hitting the front bumper. Duncan kept the mirror in place, and when Lee immediately opened fire, the muzzle flash gave away his position.

Without hesitating, Duncan spun around and raced toward the front of the Suburban, picking up his rifle as he went. As he ran toward the sixth parked car nearest the sidewalk entrance, he trained his rifle on the target. He used his speed and the element of surprise to catch Lee off guard.

When Lee didn't show himself, Duncan dropped to one knee and sent bullets skipping under the vehicle until they struck flesh. Lee groaned and fired wildly over Duncan's head. Duncan retreated one vehicle and circled it toward the rear, anticipating that Lee would focus his attention toward the operations center where Duncan's gunfire had come from.

As he approached from the rear, Duncan could hear Lee's heavy breathing and moans of pain. The animal was wounded, and it was time to put him out of his misery.

Duncan crouched down and saw Lee's left arm stretched out to support his body. Duncan immediately fired, the powerful AR-10 rounds splintering the man's forearm and then embedding themselves in his left hip.

Lee rolled across the pavement, writhing in pain. Duncan was around the rear of the vehicle before Lee could raise his other arm and beg for mercy. Duncan didn't want to give the man the satisfaction of the final word. He shot him twice in the forehead. It was over.

"Alpha One, Bravo team leader. Front secured. Conqueror KIA. Over."

"Roger, Bravo team leader. All hostiles KIA by Foxtrot. Over."

"Alpha One. Advise Port Arthur. They are a green light, go. Over and out."

As a precaution, Duncan worked his way past all the parked cars and then to the other side of the operations center building. There, he found the six dead members of Bravo team. Each of their throats had been slit, as the commandos had managed to catch them by surprise. He shook his head in disbelief as he considered the loss of their lives. He'd never know how they were compromised to allow Lee's men close enough to kill them in that manner.

After saying a brief prayer for them, he made his way to the front entrance, where the surviving soldier from the hallway detail led Sook through the destroyed front entry. She was bleeding from her forehead.

He shouldered his rifle and pulled out his shemagh to apply pressure to the wound. "Hey, what happened? Let me look at that." Duncan wiped away the blood and kissed her on the cheek.

Sook smiled. "I'm okay. The explosion knocked a large metal box off a shelf, and it hit me on the head."

She hugged him and held tight for nearly a minute. The feeling that they were finally safe to pursue their lives together hit them both at the same time. Relief and joy came over the couple, causing them to shed a few tears as they stood alone in the misty rain.

PART FOUR

CHAPTER 46

February 1
The Armstrong Ranch
Borden County, Texas

By noon, the entire Armstrong family had gathered around the dining table to enjoy a large dinner prepared by Lucy and Palmer. Duncan and Sook, who'd arrived home just before dawn, had slept for seven hours before stirring awake from the smell of barbecue pork, ranch-style beans, and mashed potatoes. Lucy also opened up two boxes of Krusteaz Blueberry Muffins to be prepared as dessert.

This was a big day for the family in many respects. Most importantly, at one o'clock, voting would begin pursuant to the Texas Constitution in both chambers of the legislature to confirm Major as the second vice president of Texas. Like the U.S. Constitution, whenever there was a vacancy in the office of the vice president, the president nominates a successor, who shall officially be confirmed by a simple majority vote in both Houses of Congress.

Major had learned that opposition to his nomination was minimal, other than the direct pressure put upon the president by Washington and its subordinates. Even Patrick Linkletter, the former mayor of Austin and new Senate Minority Leader of Texas, used toned-down rhetoric in voicing his opposition. His preferred candidate would be anybody from across the proverbial aisle to show Texans their government was unified. Naturally, President Burnett rejected that notion. In her years as a politician, calls for reaching across the aisle always came from one side—theirs. Linkletter's party had never compromised when they were in power. As far as the president was concerned, neither should she.

The conversation at dinner centered around Duncan and Sook's success at Baytown. The Port Arthur operation had been much sloppier, but Duncan had expected that. Once Duncan had caught General Lee hiding in the parking lot, he was unable to radio his second unit at Port Arthur without giving away his position. With Lee's death, the second unit of commandos waited for their instructions, not knowing that Duncan's team, with the support of the Beaumont TX-QRF, were closing in.

A fierce gun battle erupted around the perimeter of the Aramco facility, but its security fences were never breached. A few of the North Koreans attempted to fight their way through the checkpoint on the Sabine Lake causeway but quickly found themselves boxed in. Most were killed, but a couple jumped into the icy cold waters below. Using their infrared night scopes, Duncan's men killed them as they floated away.

While there was no way of knowing whether additional commandos were at work within Texas, Duncan's efforts gave Texans the unsung hero they so desperately needed. During their meal, he recalled his thoughts when his team had first arrived in Lamesa a couple of weeks ago.

"I was really pissed off that the local county judge paraded us through town like we were their saviors," he continued to relay his thoughts to his family. "Regrettably, I was kinda rude to him."

"He could've given you a heads-up, son," interjected Major.

"That's true, Dad. But I would've told him to forget it. He knew the needs of his citizens better than I did. They were on the brink of despair anyway, and adding to their troubles, friends and families were being held hostage at a place designed to be safe for those in need. They needed a hero, and he was looking to me to provide them a ray of hope. In the end, did it really matter if the local dignitaries took credit as long as the public was inspired to survive another day?"

Major started laughing, which puzzled everyone at the dinner table.

"What's so funny, dear?"

Major pulled a small spiral notebook and a pen out of his shirt pocket. He opened up the front cover to display the contents for everyone to see.

"Well, the good Lord willin', I'll be confirmed as the new vice president in a couple of hours. Early in the morning, I'll return to Austin to be sworn in. Afterwards, Marion and I will address the nation."

"Your first speech, ever," quipped Palmer. "No pressure, Daddy."

"Yeah, no kiddin'. After listening to what Duncan said, I'm beginning to think the wrong Armstrong will be takin' the microphone tomorrow. So, son, care to write down what you just said?" He playfully pushed the notepad and pencil in Duncan's direction, who immediately recoiled as if a rattlesnake was bearing its venomous fangs.

"No way! Get that thing away from me!"

The Armstrongs broke out in laughter as Duncan pretended to be afraid of a notepad. Lucy reached across her husband and pulled the notepad back in front of her husband.

"Dear, you don't need this. What you need to do is speak from the heart like Duncan just did. You're not a speechmaker, but that's not what Texas needs right now. Texans need to listen to someone with heart and soul. Someone who understands what they're going through. In a way, it's like Duncan said. They're gonna be looking for a hero to give them hope."

The table grew silent, and Major stared at the notepad for a moment. Then he grinned and slyly attempted to slide it in front of his wife.

"Can you write that down for me?"

Boom, the laughter erupted again.

CHAPTER 47

February 2
Joint Session of the Texas Congress
The Capitol Building
Austin, Texas

Throughout history, politicians have risen to the occasion to provide the citizens of their country uplifting words of wisdom and encouragement in times of struggle. Major believed the best way to judge a politician was by the speeches they gave during the worst of times. Speeches given during a crisis revealed more about someone than any campaign stump speech.

As he flew into Austin that morning, he reflected on the magnitude of the day. He'd easily won confirmation as the next vice president, and the swearing-in ceremony, with its pomp and circumstance, was more than a formality. It was a symbol of a democratic nation's ability to maintain stability in government following the death of a high-ranking official.

Major was an unknown in the Texas political world. He was well known in the law enforcement circles and was highly respected. Fellow ranchers around the country knew of his family and their accomplishments at the Armstrong Ranch. But they knew nothing of Major's view on politics, especially in light of the challenges the new nation faced.

He'd never given a speech of this magnitude. He'd addressed conventions of law enforcement personnel in the past. When he'd led Company C of the Texas Rangers, Major was known to gather his top personnel frequently to address concerns and dole out accolades.

Major didn't know it, but he had the innate ability to truly touch people. He didn't connect with his fellow law enforcement officers because his words were particularly heartwarming or emotive. His words came from his soul in a way that only someone who means it could say.

As his helicopter approached Austin, Major thought of a speech that had touched him. In January 1986, Major was a teenager at the time and fascinated with space. He remembered sitting around the television with Pops as the Space Shuttle *Challenger* exploded less than two minutes after takeoff.

He was devastated as he thought of the lost lives of the men and women he revered. That evening, President Ronald Reagan was slated to make his State of the Union Address to the Joint Session of Congress. He cancelled it and, instead, spoke from the Oval Office to a nation in mourning.

Major remembered the speech given by President Reagan. They were exactly the right words delivered in exactly the right way. President Reagan had the unenviable job of explaining to the country what had happened and how America, as a nation, could move on from the tragedy.

Today, Major had to speak to eight-year-old children as well as eighty-year-old elderly listeners. Every Texan was represented by the administration he'd just joined and the Texas Constitution he'd sworn to uphold. It was going to be a call to action that encouraged every Texan to reach out to their neighbors to assist. It was also going to be a warning to those who sought to take advantage of their fellow Texans in a brief moment of weakness—be prepared to face the consequences of your actions.

Major's day continued, and he found himself growing more comfortable with being thrust into the limelight. He'd always been an unassuming man, dedicated to God, family, and his job. He didn't seek the microphone when a significant criminal investigation crossed his desk. Nor did he expect pats on the back when a particular year's herd yielded excellent prices at auction. That wasn't who he was.

Eventually, after the hands were shook and the last glass of sweet tea was toasted, he and President Burnett entered a sound studio created at the Mansion by the Recording Conservatory of Austin. Without the ability to broadcast via television, AM radio was the only available means to reach Texans across the country. The engineers from the sound studio also established a simulcast of this speech over the emergency broadcast network and multiple ham radio frequencies. If a Texan had access to power- or battery-operated radios, they'd be able to listen to Major's words.

After they were settled in, precisely at three o'clock that afternoon, President Burnett made some introductory remarks and introduced Major to the people of Texas. Major was nervous at first, and then he recalled Lucy's words at dinner the day before.

Texans need to listen to someone with heart and soul.

He looked into the microphone as if he were staring into the eyes of every Texan. After some introductory remarks, he spoke from the heart.

"Following a disaster of any kind, its normal for people to feel stunned, disoriented, or unable to comprehend the magnitude of what has happened to them. None of these feelings make you a weak person. They simply mean that you're human.

"Be aware of your common, unpredictable feelings, such as anxiety, nervousness, and irritability. Once you recognize these new feelings, make sure you don't act irrationally by projecting them onto others. Other folks have stresses too, and under these difficult circumstances, conflicts can arise. This is a time to come together, not fight one another.

"President John F. Kennedy once said in his inaugural speech, *ask not what your country can do for you, ask what you can do for your country.* What you can do for Texas is help your neighbor. Help them hold on to hope. Help them avoid dying. Help them while we work diligently to help you.

"Here's what your country can do for you. Texas, like no other nation, prepared in advance for this type of attack. The ERCOT power grid did suffer significant damage, but unknown to our attackers, Texas leaders had the forethought to plan many years ago.

Throughout Texas, redundancies have been built in to replace damaged transformers. Backup computer systems and manually operated devices needed to manage our electricity substations have been safely stored for just this type of situation.

"Engineers, ERCOT workers, and civilian volunteers have worked tirelessly over the past ten days to restore power to the country. In order to help the greatest number of people at once, substation damage in the major metropolitan areas will be assisted first. This also serves to open up our food distribution warehouses once again. Trucks are being requisitioned from businesses around Texas to join in this effort.

"With electricity being gradually restored, it's time to look toward a new normal in Texas. One of the first steps is to reestablish our monetary system. Toward that end, we are expanding on President Burnett's initial steps in this regard by creating a system of banks throughout Texas, where you can exchange your precious metals for the gold-backed monetary instruments created by the Texas Treasury. You'll need this new form of money to shop in the local marketplaces that will be established in mid-size and larger communities around the country. The barter markets may continue. However, it is my goal to provide a more traditional method of shopping. And you will have the benefit of security as you shop via local law enforcement and our military.

"Now, let me discuss your security. After we were attacked two weeks ago, our nation rallied to find the perpetrators. As an old lawman, I know the dedication and commitment of those officers I worked with when they looked for those responsible for committing a crime. In terms of the people responsible for attacking the ERCOT power grid, I can say from firsthand experience that the men and women of our military sacrificed their own blood to hunt down those responsible for this unprovoked attack.

"I am pleased to report to you that two days ago, an assault upon our two largest oil refineries in Texas was thwarted, and the leader of the men responsible for these heinous attacks met the ultimate form of justice—death. While this immediate threat is behind us, it is still in all of our best interests to be vigilant. Remain aware of your surroundings. If something seems out of sorts, contact your nearest law enforcement office or member of the Texas Guard.

"We still have work to do, and one of my pledges is to work with the president to communicate with you via broadcasts of this type more often. Let me add in closing.

"I am making this commitment to you as I join President Burnett in bringing Texas back to glory. Know this. Texas is not just a place on a map. It's in our blood, our hearts, and in our soul. Texas is free, and so are you. Texas is strong, and so are you, my fellow Texans.

"God bless you and God bless Texas."

CHAPTER 48

February 3
The Armstrong Ranch
Borden County, Texas

"Hey, son, I've got something you might be interested in," started Major as he joined Duncan, who was drinking coffee on the front porch of the ranch house. Duncan was mindlessly staring across the snow-covered ground in the direction of the cattle, which had been moved closer to the barn for feeding. He'd just finished a conversation with Cooper about their hay supply. They needed to make one final run to the Slaughters' old place for the remaining stored hay. Duncan had insisted they take at least one of the Humvees with the fifty-caliber machine gun mounted on top.

As a defensive precaution, anytime someone left the perimeter fence line of the ranch, a military escort had to accompany them. When the guys had brought the cattle from the abandoned property east of their ranch, two of Espy's men had escorted them up the trail with their automatic weapons at the ready.

Duncan turned and greeted his father. "Good mornin'. Great speech, Dad. I hope folks paid attention."

"It'll take time, son. Not everybody heard it, and those who did may not necessarily be on board. We're gonna go through a period where people are desperate. If we can show them ways to make do, hopefully we can set the country on the right path before it falls apart at the seams."

Major reached into his coat pocket and gave Duncan an envelope. He opened it. Enclosed was a legal-size document stapled together in a blue manuscript cover. Duncan ran his fingers across the large gold seal embossed with the seal of the nation of Texas.

"Proclamation?" Duncan said inquisitively.

"Yes. It's pretty self-explanatory. Go ahead and read it."

"Lots of *whereases* and *therefores* in this thing?"

Major chuckled. "Lawyers get paid by the word. Even the ones who work for the government."

Duncan smiled and read portions aloud. "Whereas, Duncan Armstrong Jr. and Rhee Sook-hae are desirous of entering into the bonds of holy matrimony. Whereas, Borden County is without an official marriage officiant at this time. Now, therefore, by the power vested in me as President of Texas, I declare this document to act as an official marriage license and further declare Vice President Duncan Armstrong as being authorized to perform a valid marriage ceremony under the laws of Texas."

His hands began to shake from nervous excitement. "You got this for us?"

"I did," replied Major. "It was one big old lovefest yesterday, so I asked Marion if she could help us out. I am sure there were other ways to solve the problem, but I'd be honored if you'd let me marry the two of you."

Duncan, who ordinarily remained stoic regardless of the circumstances, rushed to hug his dad. It was an emotional moment for the two men as they both teared up.

"Gee, I really don't know what to say, Dad. I was standing out here this morning, staring out across the ranch, wondering what happens next. I've never been settled before, you know? I mean, the ranch is my home, but I always knew I'd be sent off to some part of the world on a moment's notice."

"I get it, son. All of our lives have changed dramatically, needless to say. With this proclamation from the president, you and Sook can now make plans for a wedding and your future. You know, when the time's right. No pressure. Okay?"

Duncan folded the proclamation and shoved it into his pocket. "Are you kiddin' me? Let's call the family together and do this right now. I wanna be married to Sook right this minute."

Duncan started toward the house, and Major grabbed his arm. "Now, son, hold on a minute. Let me give you some sage advice. In your pocket is the legal authority to get married, and Sook has accepted your proposal. But a wedding is the most important day in a woman's life except for when their kids are born. You need to give Sook time to think about the ceremony, reception, etcetera."

"Yeah, Dad. You're right. I don't want to rush it. This needs to be a special day for Sook. I think I'll go tell her now, if that's okay. There's no way I can sit on this!"

"I get it. Go. Give her the good news, and you might as well gather up your momma and Palmer. Those three will jump into the planning headfirst. Enjoy the moment, son."

Duncan shook hands with his father and gave him another hug. Then he ran into the house, shouting for Sook. She replied from the kitchen, and Duncan ran to embrace her. After twirling her around a couple of times, Lucy made him stop before he crashed her into the table.

"What's going on?" asked Palmer.

All three of them waited as Duncan struggled to find the words. He finally exhaled and pulled the proclamation out of his pocket and handed it to his mother.

"Oh my," she said as she covered her mouth, and tears began to stream down her cheeks. She shook the proclamation in the air. "This is why I love your father. With everything going on, he remembered this."

Palmer was losing patience. "What, Momma? Are you gonna tell us?"

Lucy regained her composure. "Your daddy has been authorized to marry Duncan and Sook. We can plan the wedding!"

Sook and Palmer squealed in delight. They grabbed each other's hands and began jumping up and down in the kitchen. With each jump, the loose boards bounced the wooden kitchen chairs in the air, but Lucy didn't complain. She moved to hug her son, and the group shared a tender moment.

"There's so much to do!" shouted Palmer.

"What will I wear?" asked Sook.

"We need to decide where the ceremony will be. And what about a reception?" Lucy fired off her questions.

The three women looked at each other's frenzied faces. Lucy and Palmer said in unison, "We've gotta get started!"

Within seconds, the women had raced out of the kitchen and chased each other up the stairs. Duncan, the groom-to-be, stood alone, mouth open, wondering what the heck just happened.

CHAPTER 49

February 4
The Armstrong Ranch
Borden County, Texas

Palmer was in her element, utterly surprising her mother. Lucy would never admit that she'd always looked upon her beautiful daughter as one of the boys. After giving birth to four sons, when this cherub of a baby was born with sparkly blue eyes, she was secretly thrilled that she wouldn't be alone in a world full of cowboys. Major was stricken with the thunderbolt as well. He was proud of his sons, but Palmer would always be his baby girl.

Growing up, Palmer couldn't help but be a tomboy. The family's life revolved around the ranch and rodeo. When Duncan and Dallas went off to war, Cooper, Riley, and Palmer became inseparable. She looked up to her older brothers and was honored when they included her in their ranch activities.

Soon, Palmer became a skilled rider. She won her first event at the Greeley Stampede in Colorado, and after that, Lucy's rodeo kids spent their days planning their next rodeo.

So Lucy was shocked when at three in the morning in May of 2018, Palmer gently shook her awake to watch the royal wedding between Prince Harry and the American actress Meghan Markle.

Lucy, in her half-sleepy state, recalled asking Palmer, "Who are you?"

Palmer had assured her the daughter she loved wasn't possessed and truly wanted to enjoy the pomp and circumstance of the royal nuptials.

When the guys stirred awake, some playful ribbing occurred,

followed by moans and groans when they realized they had to fend for themselves to make breakfast. Lucy and Palmer were glued to the television, occasionally envisioning what Palmer's wedding would be like.

For nearly five hours, the Armstrong women flipped through the channels, alternating between the UK version of the ceremony on BBC America and various American networks, who spent more time talking about the bride's ethnicity than they described the pageantry surrounding the event at Windsor Castle. Regardless of the future Duchess of Suffolk's background, Palmer said at the time, she appeared to be welcomed into the royal family with open arms.

Palmer and Lucy were determined to give Sook that same feeling of warmth and love for her upcoming nuptials. After the excitement died down and the initial frantic planning sessions passed, Palmer sat down with Sook to talk about what she wanted for her wedding day. Palmer remembered the visuals from the royal wedding as she relayed her recollection to Sook over breakfast that morning.

"Sook, it was all about the bride. Once everyone was seated in St. George's Chapel, they became quiet and turned their attention to her as she came into the church. All cameras focused on her beautiful wedding gown as she walked down the aisle. She was the center of attention, as all brides should be. Tomorrow, we want the wedding ceremony to be all about you."

Sook smiled shyly and then made an admission. "I have never been to a wedding. Most ceremonies are for the elite in Pyongyang. I have seen pictures."

Palmer reached out and touched her hand. "That's not a problem. Tell me about what you know of North Korean weddings. Is there something you can recall that you might like for tomorrow?"

"Okay. Miss Lucy has shown me her wedding gown. Thank you for allowing me to wear it before you do."

"You're welcome. You are the same size as Momma when she married my daddy. It is an almost perfect fit."

"In North Korea, the bride wears a *hanbok*. Some are white with colorful embroidered flowers while others are a combination of bright pinks, reds, and yellows. The elites were entitled to have fantastic weddings in hotels and gardens. For the average couple, the wedding is usually in the bride's home."

"What about flowers?" asked Palmer.

"Yes, a simple bouquet. In Pyongyang, the bride and groom visit the statue of the Great Leader to bestow their flowers."

Palmer smiled. "Okay. In Texas, the bride will throw the flowers to the single women attending the wedding. The tradition says that the woman who catches the bouquet will be the next to get married."

Sook shrugged at this concept, so Palmer continued.

"Is there anything about the North Korean wedding ceremony that you want for yours?"

"We did not have Christian weddings, as they were forbidden. One of the traditions is to wrap a live hen and a rooster in blue and red cloths to be set on the ceremonial table. During the wedding, guests place flowers and dates into the hen's beak. The rooster's beak gets stuffed with red chilis."

Palmer stifled a laugh. She didn't want to be disrespectful, but the tradition seemed odd to her. "Sook, would you like to do that as well? I mean, um, we certainly have the chickens and roosters. I don't know about—"

Sook interrupted Palmer and shook her head. "No, thank you. I want a Texas wedding. I want to be a Texan."

Palmer finally was able to emit a hearty a laugh. "Excellent. Then we shall throw you the finest Texas wedding that's ever been!"

"Yes, Palmer. A Texas wedding, please."

Lucy came downstairs and joined the wedding planners. "How's it goin'?"

"Momma, Sook wants a bona fide Texas wedding."

Lucy sat next to Sook at the table and grasped her hand. "That's a great idea. We are very casual in Texas. Anything goes. Our guys wear cowboy boots instead of dress shoes. We have country-western music and line dancin'. The food is spicy, and the desserts are sweet. I think I even have a case of the official drink of Texas in the smokehouse—Dr. Pepper."

"Whoa, you are goin' all out, Momma!" exclaimed Palmer.

Palmer and her mother exchanged high fives.

"Yes, we are," continued Lucy. "With the weather warming, I think an afternoon wedding in the barn would be nice. We can include the ranch families as well as some of the off-duty soldiers if you want."

"I could see if any of them can play the guitar," interjected Palmer.

"Good idea," said Lucy. "I'm thinkin' the guys should wear black jeans and pressed white shirts."

"Black hats and boots too," added Palmer. "I'll make sure they polish them."

"Boots for me, too?" asked Sook.

Palmer chuckled and looked at her mother. "Why not, right, Momma? We also need a garter for Duncan to remove."

"I've got something that will work," replied Lucy as she stifled a laugh. "You'll see."

"What is a garter?" asked Sook.

Palmer allowed her mother to take that question.

"In the olden days, women wore socks or hose that came above their knees. To keep their stockings from rolling down, an elastic strap was used to hold the stockings to a woman's legs." Lucy hesitated and then shrugged before continuing. "After the wedding ceremony, the husband and wife were expected to consummate their marriage."

"Consummate?" asked Sook, who appeared unsure of the meaning.

"I'll explain later, dear," replied Lucy with a smile.

"In the medieval days, the guests went into the bedroom to watch, didn't they, Momma?"

"Yeah, and thank goodness they don't do that anymore," said an embarrassed Lucy. "Instead, the new husband will remove the garter belt from his new bride's thigh."

Sook blushed. "Does everyone watch this?"

"Um, yes. It's a tradition. Then he flicks it at the eligible bachelors to wish good luck to whomever catches it."

Sook shook her head. "I thought stuffed hens and roosters was odd."

CHAPTER 50

February 5
The Armstrong Ranch
Borden County, Texas

There was no reason to rush Duncan and Sook to the altar other than they loved each other dearly, and in an uncertain world, there was no time like the present. Besides, everyone pitched in to help as excitement about the ceremony lifted spirits around the ranch. The barn was cleaned out, and tables were set up similar to their Christmas gathering. The opening located at the southern end of the barn was decorated and would serve as the spot for the actual ceremony. This allowed the sun to shine upon the bride and groom as they said their vows.

Duncan and Sook wanted to speak to one another from the heart and without formalities. Major reminded them he had to follow certain minimum requirements to make their bond in matrimony legal, but otherwise, this was their special day.

The guests consisted of the ranch families and their children. Antonio was instrumental in making the barn a beautiful setting while the women helped Lucy prepare the wedding reception food and desserts. The Armstrongs' extended family was anxious to put the horror of that night behind them, finish mourning the loss of their loved ones, and look to a better future. The wedding of the Armstrongs' oldest son to a young woman who had escaped a brutal regime was a fairy-tale start to a new life for all of them.

Espy was also in attendance. That morning, he got together with Palmer and Cooper to discuss music. It had been a while, but Espy said he was capable of playing several songs, including the guitar version of "There is Love," first performed in the late sixties by Peter, Paul, and Mary.

Cooper offered to play a few songs on his harmonica. They found a couple that Espy could perform on his guitar, so with Palmer handling the vocals, the trio practiced them together.

Everyone was settled in their seats. Duncan joined Major, as did Cooper and Riley, who acted as his groomsmen. Lucy and Palmer were Sook's bridesmaids. It was a beautiful scene as Espy began to strum his guitar. All heads turned to the back of the barn.

When Sook rounded the corner, a hush fell over the attendees, who stood in unison to take in the bride's beauty. Lucy's dress was perfect for Sook. It was a white V-neck with a ruffled tiered skirt. Its dainty design wasn't overwhelmed with an excess of lace and organza. The cap sleeves revealed Sook's buff arms, and the slightly shorter length revealed a pair of white cowboy boots Lucy had stored at the top of her closet for decades.

As Espy strummed "There is Love" on the guitar, Sook walked slowly toward the Armstrong family, who took in her beauty. Duncan, Major, and Cooper had huge smiles across their faces. Lucy, Palmer, and Riley made a feeble attempt to fight back tears of joy. This was indeed Sook's day, and she strode toward her groom with confidence and flair.

Once Sook arrived in front of Major, he gave her a smile and nodded to everyone, encouraging them to take a seat. He then directed his attention to the bride and groom.

"Today, it is with great joy that we come together to celebrate the marriage of my son, Duncan, to this beautiful, young woman, Sook. Please join me in prayer.

"Dear Father, we humbly invite Your presence and Your blessings to be upon Sook and Duncan as they enter into the ceremony that will unite them in the bonds of holy matrimony. Impress upon them the solemnness and the impact of their actions today that will set the course for their lives into eternity. Amen."

Major looked up for a moment and then wiped a tear from his eye. "It is with a somewhat heavy heart that I stand before you instead of our dearly departed friend Preacher. He would've been proud to join you two in marriage. I'm sure he would've known all the right words to say and when. I know what's required by Texas law, but you two know what's in your heart."

"You're doin' great, Dad," whispered Duncan.

"Thank you, son. Why don't you tell Sook how you feel?"

Duncan and Sook faced one another and held hands. Their smiles were so big that one wondered if their faces might break.

"Sook, you saved my life. I have never told you this before, but I was awake at times while you were nursing me back to health. At first, I thought you were an angel of mercy. It didn't take long for me to realize that you were much more. You became my best friend and partner as we fought to survive. When you were in danger, I fought to protect you. When I went into battle, you stood shoulder to shoulder by my side.

"Our burdens, our joy, and our lives became one. As your husband, I promise to continue protecting you during times of sorrow and struggle. When times are good, I promise to laugh with you and enjoy every moment of our time together. You will always have my respect, my trust, and my love. This I promise with all my heart. I love you."

Duncan squeezed both of her hands and turned to his father.

"Duncan, do you take Sook to be your lawfully wedded wife, forsaking all others, in good times and bad, for so long as you both shall live?"

"I do."

Major smiled and turned to Sook. "Is there anything you'd like to say to Duncan?"

Sook shyly looked down, and then her eyes met Duncan's. "Yes, please. Duncan, because of you, I laugh. I smile. I dare to dream of my future. I am thankful to God that I am able to spend the rest of my life as your wife, and a member of this wonderful family."

Sook paused to make eye contact with all of the Armstrongs before continuing. "I promise to nurture you and be there when you need me. I will love and cherish you with my heart and soul. My devotion to you comes from my heart and the prayers that have been answered by God. I make these commitments in love and strengthened by faith. I will love you forever."

They stared lovingly at each other for a moment, and then Major asked, "Sook, do you take Duncan to be your lawfully wedded husband, forsaking all others, in good times and bad, for so long as you both shall live?"

"I do, y'all!" exclaimed Sook to the delight of everyone. Overwhelmed with emotion, Duncan swept Sook off her feet, and the two kissed.

"Hey, I think I'm supposed to give you permission to do that, or something," said Major with a chuckle. As they continued their embrace, Major stood to the side to address the attendees. "I now declare these two lovebirds to be husband and wife. They're already kissing, so let me just present to you Mr. and Mrs. Duncan Armstrong Junior!"

The barn erupted in applause and even a few whistles of congratulations. Duncan and Sook broke their embrace in order to receive congratulations from the entire Armstrong family. They spent the next fifteen minutes greeting everyone and talking about their future together.

While Duncan and Sook accepted the well wishes, Palmer and Lucy recruited the guys to help bring out the food. They'd spent the morning fixing a Tex-Mex menu of taquitos, enchiladas, burritos, and a variety of desserts. There was plenty of food for everyone and some leftovers for the members of the military who continued to stand guard during the festivities.

After eating, the party really swung into high gear as Espy, Cooper, and Palmer made their debut as a country trio. They only had a set of three songs, but they played them all twice. Their biggest hit was their rendition of John Denver's "Take Me Home, Country Roads." Every time they sang the lyrics, those who sang along substituted *West Texas* in place of *West Virginia.*

The whirlwind of events exhausted everyone. As the afternoon came to a close and the sun dropped on the western horizon, the final two wedding traditions took place.

At first, Sook hesitated to relinquish her bouquet of bluebonnets. Although it was early February, bluebonnets had begun blooming in parts of the Big Bend area of West Texas. Espy had arranged for a supply convoy headed to Camp Lubbock from Fort Bliss to pick the flowers. One of the camp's soldiers had made the special delivery in time for Duncan's wedding.

Sook gave them a final look and prepared to fulfill the wedding tradition. The bouquet toss should have been anticlimactic, as Palmer was the only single woman in attendance. With a knowing glance from Palmer to Espy, Sook turned her back to Palmer and heaved the bouquet over her head.

She overpowered the throw, and the flowers flew through the air, beyond the outstretched hands of Palmer, and hit Riley squarely in the chest.

Boy, it was awwwn then.

The laughter and teasing was relentless as Riley turned fifty shades of beet red. He didn't know what to do. At first it appeared he was gonna throw the bouquet of bluebonnets back at Sook to give her a second try. Thinking better of it, he sheepishly walked over to Palmer and presented them to her. She immediately danced in circles as if she'd just won both showcases on *The Price is Right.*

Next up was the ceremonial removal of the garter. Sook had been warned in advance of the two options available to her new husband. Duncan could respectfully remove the garter before flicking it toward the eligible bachelors. Or he could take the cruder approach and pull it off her thigh with his teeth. After hearing both choices, Sook was calm when she issued her instructions to Palmer.

She'd said, "Tell your brother if he takes off this garter thing with his teeth, I will unleash all the fury of my taekwondo training upon him, which might prevent us from having children someday."

With that settled and Duncan forewarned, he carefully removed the garter in front of their guests, making certain he respected Sook's modesty and kept his teeth to himself.

After she gave him a gentle kiss as her way of saying thanks, he turned to the eligible, unmarried guys—Cooper, Riley, and Espy—lined up next to each other. They eagerly awaited Duncan's stretching of the elastic garment to let it fly.

Duncan wrapped one end around his left thumb and pulled the other side back with his right hand. He set his aim for the eagerly awaiting bachelors.

The resulting toss was less of a flick and more of a rocket projectile. *Operators, go full throttle.* It came at the guys so quickly that none of them were able to react before the garter smacked Riley in the chin.

"Ouch!" Riley shouted as he snatched the garter out of the air before it hit the ground.

"Way to go, bro!" shouted Cooper. "This is the first time in history the garter and the bouquet were snagged by the same person!"

"Yeah, no fair!" shouted Espy.

As everyone laughed, Duncan piled on. "Would the Riley wedding party please step forward? Riley, party of one!"

Riley playfully charged his brother before their dad intervened.

"Son, this will be difficult to explain to the president, but I'd be glad to get you a marriage proclamation the next time I'm in Austin."

Riley had had enough. "Come on, y'all. I'm not the marrying kind anyway."

It was Lucy's turn. "Really? Neither one of you? Surely there's a groom or bride in there somewhere."

And the laughter reached a crescendo.

CHAPTER 51

February 7
The Reinecke Caretaker's Home
The Armstrong Ranch
Borden County, Texas

As a wedding gift to Duncan and Sook, everyone had worked together to create a bungalow getaway of sorts at the former caretaker's home located on the Reinecke property adjacent to the ranch. Formerly occupied by the Slaughters prior to Holloway's attack of two weeks prior, the home was cleaned, decorated, and stocked with food to allow a brief honeymoon for the newlyweds. The plan was to get away from it all for three nights before returning to the ranch to start their new life together. Somehow, the lone rider on horseback approaching from the ranch that morning was an indicator the honeymoon might be over.

Duncan quickly dressed and greeted Cooper as he arrived at the backyard. He had a serious look on his face and was carrying one of the satellite phones that connected the ranch to Major at all times.

Duncan shielded his eyes for a moment so they could adjust to the rising sun. "Hey, Coop. Is everything alright?"

Cooper didn't bother to dismount and rode up alongside of Duncan. He tipped his hat and caught his breath. "Mornin', Duncan. Dad said it wasn't an emergency, but he does need you to call him right away. He sent me over to bring you this."

He leaned over the side of his horse and handed the satellite phone to his brother.

Duncan took it and looked up. "Did he say what it's about?"

"Nah, just that you need to call," replied Cooper, who changed the subject as a disheveled Sook emerged on the back stoop. "Hey, Sook! Y'all need anything?"

Sook shook her head and retreated to the house. Duncan thanked Cooper again and returned inside to call his dad. He stopped for a moment. He shouted to Cooper, who'd already turned his horse around and was about to ride off.

"Hey, Coop! Tell Momma we'll be home for dinner, okay?"

"Uh, sure. Are ya gonna cut your time away short?"

"I don't want to, but I've gotta hunch. We can always come back. I kinda like it over here. It's quiet, ya know?"

"Are the cows botherin' y'all?" asked Cooper.

"Nope. They're all pretty happy. We only hear them lowing occasionally. I'd better make this call." Duncan held the satellite phone up and then waved goodbye. He'd dialed his dad, and the two were talking before he was back inside the house.

"Son, we have addressed this subject lately, but I wanted to make you aware of something."

"What is it, Dad?"

"I was in a meeting today with the adjutant general and his sister-in-law, the spy. I'm still leery of her."

"Yeah, me too," said Duncan. "Did something come up?"

Major hesitated for a moment and then continued. "Sorry about that. Someone walked by, and I didn't want to be overheard. Listen. I'm told by Pauline Hart that Billy Yancey arrived in Texas last night."

"How did he get here? Can he just fly in and out of Texas as he pleases?"

"He has a ranch on the west end of Greenbelt Lake outside Clarendon," replied Major. "You know where that is, right? It's about an hour southeast of Amarillo."

"Yeah, I vaguely remember. Dad, when you think about it, we're not exactly patrolling our airspace, are we? What would stop someone from flying in and out with nobody noticing?"

"You're right." Major seemed to be in a hurry. "Son, I'm not going to tell you what to do at this point. I don't know if the information is reliable or not. Yancey's place is on the reservoir at the end of a road called Reservoir Way. Whatever you decide, be careful and know that I love you, son."

"I love you too, Dad."

Duncan disconnected the call and tossed the phone on the sofa. Sook was in the galley-style kitchen, making them some coffee. Although she only heard Duncan's side of the conversation, she could tell it affected him emotionally.

"Is your father okay?"

Duncan didn't answer right away as he paced the floor. The home was small, so he was able to cover the distance from the front door to the back door in five paces.

"Duncan?"

He forcibly shook his head to shake the hundreds of thoughts that were racing around inside. The first thing he needed to decide was whether he should confide in Sook about Yancey's presence in Texas. She knew about the anger Duncan held against the CIA man who had left him and Park behind. She also was aware Duncan had placed Yancey on the short list of people that her husband wanted dead.

"I'm sorry, Sook." He joined her in the kitchen and wrapped his arms around her. He gently kissed her on the neck before he reached for the mug of coffee she'd just poured for him. Duncan took a deep breath and then pointed toward the couch. "Let's sit down for a moment."

"Okay."

He drank some of his coffee, hoping the caffeine would help give him clarity. Sook was an excellent listener and had proved to be a reliable sounding board in the past. Duncan sighed and then laid it out for her.

"You know how I feel about this man with the CIA, Billy Yancey."

"Yes. You want him dead."

Duncan tilted his head back and forth and smiled. "You don't mince words, do you?"

"Mince words?" she asked with a puzzled look on her face. "Is that the same as not beating around the bush? Palmer taught me that."

"This is why I love you. Yes, it's the same."

"Okay. Is he in Texas now?"

Duncan nodded. "Dad was given information that Yancey arrived in Texas last night. If it's true, he may still be at his home north of here."

"Are you going to kill him?" she asked, once again not mincing words.

Duncan shrugged. "Sook, things have changed for me now. I'm a different person. I am still a soldier, but I'm not a killer."

"My husband, you will always be a killer, and you should not stop being one because we are married. We need both Duncans—husband and killer."

"Okay, I can do that. But what I'm considering is different from fighting an enemy. I *am* getting even. I *am* killing for revenge, which is something I have never done." Duncan emphasized the word *am* with each sentence.

"Is it still important to get revenge against Yancey?"

Duncan flopped against the back of the couch. "I honestly don't know."

Sook turned toward her husband and massaged his shoulders. "There is only one way. You must look this man in the eyes. Then you will know."

CHAPTER 52

February 8
Greenbelt Lake
Near Clarendon, Texas

After Duncan got Sook settled in from their shortened honeymoon, he summoned Espy to help him make his travel arrangements. Espy only asked his commander once about the nature of the trip. Duncan curtly, but politely, told his newly promoted lieutenant that this was one operation he wanted no part of. Content with Duncan's explanation, Espy arranged for a civilian vehicle to be ready for his commander at the Amarillo International Airport. The arrival of Duncan's helicopter there wouldn't raise any eyebrows.

It was likely going to take most of that Wednesday afternoon to locate the ranch and then identify the subject. Duncan had only a vague recollection of what Billy Yancey looked like, which he coupled with the description his father had given him previously.

Duncan packed light for the trip. He didn't bring his sniper rifle, the weapon of choice when assassinating one of his targets. With his deadly accuracy, he could achieve his goal and have a one-mile head start on any pursuers.

This time, Duncan needed to get up close and personal with Yancey. He agreed with Sook's advice. Not because he needed to determine Yancey's level of guilt in giving the order leading to Park's death and almost the loss of his own life. His suspicions coupled with Gregg's dying words gave him an answer on that count.

Duncan was now wrestling with a far greater issue. Was he still a cold-blooded killer?

As he traveled alone from Amarillo to Clarendon along Highway

287, he alternated between being angry with Yancey for the betrayal and visions of life at the ranch with Sook. Each time he tried to weigh the pros and cons, his mind went off on a tangent.

As he thought of his new wife, he envisioned summer in West Texas. Signs of life were everywhere as the ranch began to look like the days before the attack on North America. He could visualize himself walking along the river with Sook, a tiny baby bump barely visible under a flowery summer dress.

Duncan turned off a deserted county road and headed due north toward the reservoir. His recollection of Greenbelt Lake was that every side of the reservoir except the west end was surrounded by lakefront homes and a marina. If Yancey had a place tucked away, it was most likely at the end of Greenbelt Way where the Salt Fork Red River opened up into the lake.

As the paved surface changed to packed gravel, Duncan could tell from the transition that he was getting close. The rougher terrain was symbolic of his state of mind as his mind switched back to that cold, dark morning on the mountain of Sinmi-do.

He remembered Park getting injured and how he'd hoisted his friend and partner onto his back to flee the pursuing North Korean soldiers. As the road narrowed and a gated driveway came into view, Duncan subconsciously flinched as his body recalled the bullets riddling Park's back, knocking them both to the ground, where Duncan slid over the edge of a cliff to the icy waters of the river below. Park had unknowingly saved Duncan's life that day, and as a result, Duncan felt he should honor Park with revenge against the man who caused his death.

As the anger returned, the visions of a pregnant Sook were quickly replaced with thoughts of his powerful hands wrapped around Yancey's throat.

Duncan briefly closed his eyes as he pulled the vehicle into a thicket of brush and trees. He heard his voice in his head, hissing at Yancey, *This is for Park.*

Duncan took a deep breath before gathering his things. A man of Yancey's training wasn't likely to leave his driveway unprotected or at least unmonitored. Duncan would have to hike through the woods along the ridgeline overlooking the driveway, which ran parallel to the small river.

He had some comfort in knowing that Yancey's position with the CIA didn't warrant his own security detail. Yancey's background and history within the intelligence community had most likely prompted him to install security measures, which would remain in place in a grid-down scenario.

As Duncan ascended the ridge and began his slow jog toward the end of the gravel driveway, he considered the outcome. *Do I really care if Yancey detected my approach? Let him fire on me. It'll make my decision easier.*

He slowed his jog to a fast walk after thirty minutes. The CIA must pay this guy well, Duncan thought to himself as he considered how far he'd traveled from where his car was parked. The deserted area suited him, however. It provided him several points of view to study his prey and little chance of detection once the deed was done.

After another fifteen minutes of hiking through the woods, Duncan spied a clearing up ahead. The land was fenced and cross-fenced, but there was no indication of any livestock in the fields.

He pulled out his binoculars to take a closer look at the buildings within the compound. A single-story ranch-style residence was located in the center. A barn was well to the rear of the home, and a four-car garage was set off to the side. Two of the garage doors were open. One contained a pickup truck, and the other bay was empty. A second pickup was parked in the driveway near the garage.

Suddenly, Duncan heard the faint rumble of some type of machine coming from the far side of the compound. He stood and inched closer, finding a fallen tree to use as cover. He searched through his binoculars, trying to catch a glimpse of what was making the noise, which was growing louder.

"There!" he muttered to himself as he caught a glimpse of a camouflaged four-wheeler appearing out of the woods near the river. Then a second one emerged from the same trail.

Duncan followed their path as the two riders came into view and sped onto the circular driveway. The lead driver stopped his ATV, stood on the sides of the all-terrain vehicle, and raised his arms over his head.

"I am still the best!" the voice proclaimed as the second rider waved his arm at the self-proclaimed champion.

Duncan focused on the men's faces. The rider who stood victorious was a younger man in his mid-twenties. The second rider was much older, Duncan surmised, from the graying hair and the pudgy middle-age belly that protruded under his sweatshirt.

"You're right, son!" he shouted back. "Do it again tomorrow?"

"For sure!"

Duncan shifted his binoculars to the front porch as a woman appeared. "Hey, guys, chili is ready when you are!"

She appeared to be in her mid-twenties—perhaps a sister or wife to the younger man. Duncan realized he knew nothing about his mark. He didn't know if Yancey was married or not. *Are these his kids? Are there more inside*? So many unanswered questions, which was dangerous for someone in his line of work.

Duncan put away the binoculars and crouched below a nearby tree. It was beginning to get dark, and as the light faded, Duncan waited. Darkness was the assassin's ally.

CHAPTER 53

February 8
Greenbelt Lake
Near Clarendon, Texas

After it was dark, Duncan moved closer to the ranch house. Lights were turned on throughout the home as Duncan made several trips around the perimeter of the compound. He was comfortable with his determination that there were only the three occupants he'd identified earlier. Further, based upon the interaction between the younger man and woman, he determined that they were romantically connected.

After the three shared a meal in a breakfast nook, which was located at the side of the kitchen, they made their way into an open family room, where they sat around a fire and played a board game, which appeared to be Yahtzee.

Duncan checked his watch. It was approaching nine when the group began to turn in for the night. The younger couple went to a bedroom located at the far-right side of the house nearest the river. The older man moved into what appeared to be the master bedroom. Yancey's house, Yancey's master bedroom.

Yancey shuffled about his bedroom, and Duncan used the opportunity of the distraction to move closer to the house. He reached the side of the home adjacent to the kitchen. There was only a single rear exit, and that was located nearest the bedroom occupied by the couple. If he was going to take Yancey out, he'd have to do it through the front door.

He inched toward the front porch, and as he reached the front corner, an exterior floodlight turned on. Duncan froze and looked straight up. It was a motion-sensor light immediately over his head.

I'm a lousy burglar, he thought to himself as he quickly retreated to the cover of the pickup truck parked near the garage. He forced himself to breathe slowly, as the clear night produced cool temperatures, which caused condensation as he breathed.

The front door slowly opened, and Yancey walked out onto the porch. He was carrying a shotgun. First, he walked along the porch in the direction of Duncan's position. Then he descended the steps and began walking into the front yard toward the four-wheelers.

Duncan's heart raced as he removed his sidearm and reached in his pocket for the silencer. He glanced through the pickup's cab to watch Yancey's movements as he spun the silencer into place.

Yancey stopped, and then the corner floodlight turned off. He stood there in the darkness, and Duncan considered moving on him.

"Hey, Dad! Is everything okay?" The man's voice came from the front door. *Yancey's son.*

Yancey didn't respond at first, and then he began walking backwards towards the house. His movement caught the attention of the motion sensor, causing the floodlight to illuminate once again. Startled, he immediately swung around and pointed the shotgun toward the garage and the open space between them.

"Who's out there?" he shouted.

Duncan detected that Yancey was frightened and even paranoid. This would make Duncan's job more difficult.

"Dad, it's probably nothing. You set off the motion sensor light when you came back toward the house. Why don't you come in out of the cold?"

Yancey took another look around, and then his body relaxed. He cradled the shotgun under his armpit and walked back toward the house. "You know what, son? I think I'll hang out here and have a cigar. Would you grab me a glass of brandy to keep my bones warm?"

"Of course, but you can smoke inside, you know. Since Mom passed away, we've kinda relaxed the rules around here." *Widower. Father. Scumbag.*

Yancey laughed. "Well, I'm sure she's still watching us. I'd better stay out here just to be safe."

Duncan relaxed and looked at the stars, which filled the sky. It was a beautiful night, and he was watching a father and son discuss their deceased loved one while they enjoyed a tender moment together. Now the man whom Duncan came here to kill was settling in on the front porch of his family's home with a cigar and a brandy.

He considered his options. If he attempted to charge Yancey, the motion-sensor light would turn on immediately, and even an untrained homeowner could manage to point the shotgun at Duncan and pepper him with buckshot.

Duncan dropped to a crouch and approached the truck's tailgate. He calculated the distance and angle to the target. He could pull off the shot. At the worst, the bullets would imbed in the decking, startling Yancey while Armstrong charged forward. The best case, besides a kill shot, would be a hit to the torso, again enabling Duncan to rush his target.

But neither of these options provided Duncan the closure he needed. He closed his eyes, took a deep breath, and stood up where he could be seen. Duncan walked several steps toward Yancey, who was calmly smoking his cigar, when the floodlight caught his motion and lit up the front yard.

To Duncan's surprise, Yancey didn't react. He calmly took another sip of brandy and a long drag on his cigar. As he exhaled, three rings of smoke floated into the air until a slight breeze carried them away.

"You're trespassing, Armstrong," said Yancey calmly.

Duncan stopped, and his eyes darted back and forth, looking for an ambush. *Have I unknowingly walked into a trap? Did Yancey cunningly lead me out into the open? But how did he know?*

"Hands away from the gun," Duncan snarled. "Keep them both where I can see them."

"Fine," said Yancey, who continued to avoid eye contact with Duncan. He took another puff of his cigar. "You're a long way from home, Armstrong. Shouldn't you be watching over your father, the new vice president?"

"He's in good hands," said Duncan, who was uneasy playing Yancey's game. The man was a snake and couldn't be trusted. He wanted to change the dynamic. He continued to approach Yancey, with his gun trained on the man's chest. "Get up. Let's take a walk."

"Nah. No, thanks. I'm comfortable right here. If you're gonna kill me, let it be on my doorstep. I'm not gonna let you drag me out in the woods like some animal."

Duncan got frustrated. "I'm not playin' games with you, Yancey. Let's go."

"Listen up, Armstrong. I'm not surprised that you're here. I personally leaked my plan to come home so that it would reach your father's ear. I know what Monty said to his wife as he died. It was a matter of time before you and I had this conversation."

"Let's talk, then," growled Duncan. He continued to be keenly aware of his surroundings. He listened for broken twigs or noise from the forest. His eyes constantly looked for movement inside the house, where Yancey's son could be preparing to take a shot at him.

"This won't take long," continued Yancey. "When I'm done, either you'll kill me, or you won't. As you're about to learn, it's just the business we're in. All I ask is that you keep my son and his wife out of this. This is between you and me."

"I'm not a murderer," Duncan shot back.

"I know that. I used to be you, Armstrong. I was the guy that got the cryptic messages and the sealed dossiers from couriers in the middle of the night. I was the one who slipped out of my wife's bed to an awaiting jet, whose crew told me where we were going *after* we landed."

"Let's get straight to the point, then," started Duncan. "Why'd you leave us behind?"

Yancey finished his brandy and set the glass to the side. Duncan continued to watch his hands carefully. The shotgun was in plain view, but a pocket-sized handgun could be retrieved easily.

Yancey responded to his question after inhaling his cigar. The cigar was also a potential distraction, but Duncan remained focused.

"Monty and I made a business decision, just like the one you're about to make. We couldn't get a team in there without being discovered. Even if you'd been successful, the mission would've been blown by the discovery of our extraction team. The magnitude of the international outrage over the incident would have destroyed America's credibility and severely damaged our relationship with our allies."

Duncan was incredulous. "Come on. You knew the extraction plan before you sent us in. Why didn't you give us a plan B?"

"You sell yourself short, Armstrong. You and Park were our best operatives. If anyone could find their way out of North Korea, it was you two. Frankly, after you killed the wrong guy, it was a wonder the two of you made it out of Kusong alive."

"Yeah, about that. What happened? Did you set us up for failure?"

Yancey chuckled and took another puff. *Just two old friends having a chat on a crisp evening in the Panhandle of Texas.* Duncan didn't like the nature of the drawn-out conversation. He was exposed, and that might prove to be a fatal mistake.

"No, we were double-crossed by Kim's sister. I don't know when she had the change of heart, but at some point, she alerted her brother of the planned assassination. I was frankly amazed that he didn't use it to his advantage from a geopolitical standpoint. The EMP, in my opinion, was a brilliant strategic move on his part."

Duncan had heard enough. Monty and Yancey had planned to extract them and then changed their minds. There was never intended to be a plan B other than he and Park using their own experience to find a way out of the country. He was starting to feel the pressure of time.

"There was no *business reason*, as you call it, for leaving us to die. If we were captured, the DPRK would've tortured us until one of us broke. You knew—"

"Plausible deniability, Armstrong. Two rogue agents with a grudge against Kim and his regime. We would've documented your file and manipulated the media before your parents were notified of their loss. Make no mistake. The CIA is always one step ahead of everyone else."

"They would have publicly executed us for the world to see!"

"Maybe, but if they did, we would have reacted with force."

"And start a hot war?"

"You bet, Armstrong. Don't be naïve. People like me within our government wanted a war with North Korea, just on our terms, not theirs. It turned out this way because Kim got the jump on us. The only reason we held back all these years is because we thought he was just crazy enough to push that button."

"Heckuva way to conduct international diplomacy," Duncan scoffed.

"Come on, Armstrong. Think about it. Reagan always pushed the concept of peace through strength. Yet the media accused him of being a madman in charge of the nuclear football. They said the same thing about Trump. You can throw Putin and Khrushchev into the group, along with Kim. The world's nuclear powers have held back for decades because of peace through strength, plus the fear a madman may lose it and push the button."

"So you wanted a nuclear war?" asked Duncan.

"No, but we should've used the power of our Pacific Fleet to stop Kim's nuclear program in its tracks. Kim's assassination, if successful, would've brought peace to the Korean Peninsula. Frankly, your capture and the aftermath would've given us the excuse to attack militarily."

Duncan had had enough conversation, so he stepped forward. The fact that he was being used as a political pawn didn't bode well for Yancey's chances of survival.

"Why shouldn't I just kill you and walk into the woods?"

"You probably should," replied Yancey dryly. He took another puff on the cigar, which was approaching the end of its useful life. In the moment, Duncan wondered what Yancey would do when his cigar was spent—get up and go to bed, leaving him on the front porch alone?

Yancey sensed Duncan was conflicted. He saw an opening and he went for it. "Armstrong, you're starting a new life now. I suspect your career as an operator is over since you've chosen Texas over the United States. I doubt Texas will need a man of your talents in the near future. You and your family have full-time military protection, so the days of battling bad guys is done."

"Maybe, maybe not," Duncan interrupted, but Yancey continued.

"Do you realize, for the rest of your life, there are two kills you'll replay over and over again in your head? Your first and your last. Your first kill will be a burden upon your soul because it opened the door for the darkness to enter you. After the first, it always gets easier.

"Your last kill will be the one that makes you the proudest. Not just because it was the last time you took another human being's life. But because it will be replayed over and over again in your mind to the point that you have to justify the kill.

"So ask yourself. Right here. Right now. Who was your last kill? And then look me in the eyes and ask if you'll be prouder to put a bullet between them. But, Armstrong, make a decision, because I'm tired and I'm going to bed."

Duncan had experienced visions as he'd neared death in the freezing waters of Sinmi-do before he was rescued by Sook and her father. Near-death experiences had a way of accelerating moments in your life in a fast-forward manner.

As he stared down Yancey, he was experiencing similar visions of Sook, his family, and life at the ranch. Then his last kill surfaced. The one that he could arguably tell his grandchildren about someday. The kill that ended the North Koreans' assault on their new nation. The death of a great warrior who'd challenged him and Texas during the early days of the collapse.

And then he focused on the CIA man who had nonchalantly orchestrated regime change in foreign lands like most people would decide which shirt to wear with their jeans. In the end, Duncan knew Yancey was right. It was business. Both he and Park had known it when they signed on for every operation. There was always the threat they'd be left behind, on their own, and with the potential to disappear without a trace.

That night, if he and Park had only walked a little slower, or faster, to avoid detection by those soldiers. If he'd only darted to the left or the right as he'd descended that creek bed, Park wouldn't have been shot. So many variables played a part on that fateful evening. It was easy for Duncan to assign blame and seek revenge. But would it really make him feel better at this point?

Yancey cautiously rose to a point where he stood over Duncan. "I think we're done here, right, Armstrong?"

Duncan continued to point the gun at Yancey's head. His finger slowly slid toward the trigger. For the first time, he felt his hand quiver ever so slightly. Then he exhaled.

"We're done."

Yancey made no effort to pick up the shotgun or his glass. He dropped his cigar onto the porch and stamped it out with his foot. He turned his back to Duncan and walked into the house, where he gently pushed the door closed, barely making an audible click.

Duncan continued to stand in the front yard of Yancey's house, staring as the final lights turned out in the CIA man's bedroom. He casually unscrewed the silencer and returned it to his pocket before he holstered his weapon.

For Duncan, a new life was awaiting him. Park's death and the circumstances surrounding it, while a tragedy, could no longer be a burden upon him. Duncan would've never known true happiness until he let it go and moved on. Adding Yancey's blood to his already stained hands wouldn't bring Park back. It would only add to the burdens Duncan carried.

In that moment, Duncan learned that to heal a wound, you have to stop touching it. He slowly turned around and began the long road home, at peace with himself.

CHAPTER 54

February 9
The Armstrong Ranch
Borden County, Texas

Lucy finally sat down at the dinner table to her husband's right and reached for his hand. "Honey, would you mind saying the blessing?"

Major squeezed her hand and smiled. He immediately bowed his head, and everyone at the table joined him. For the first time in many days, all of the Armstrongs, including the newest addition to the family, Sook, was present. Even Espy was invited, and he had proudly taken a seat between Lucy and Palmer.

"Heavenly Father, thank You for the nourishment You have provided us on this afternoon. Thank You for keeping us safe during these trying times and for meeting our physical needs of health, hunger, and thirst.

"Forgive us for taking this simple meal for granted when there are those who live in starvation and sickness. We ask that You bless and relieve the starvation of those who hunger, and inspire our hearts to seek out ways that we can help from our abundance.

"Especially, on this day, Father, thank You for bringing us together as a family, free from the worldly burdens that can stain our souls from time to time.

"We thank You for all of the gifts and talents You have provided us around this table. Help each member of our family use these gifts to Your glory. Guide our mealtime conversations and our family time together in order to steer our hearts for Your purpose. In Jesus' name, amen."

"Thank you, Daddy," said Palmer, who looked at Espy and

smiled. The two of them continued to hold hands longer than others at the table, an act that didn't go unnoticed by anyone except Riley, who was the first to reach for the bowl of mashed potatoes.

"Yes, thank you, dear," said Lucy as she leaned over to kiss Major. She turned her attention to Espy. "Espy, I'm glad that you joined us. There's always a seat at our dinner table for you."

Espy, who was always in uniform, smiled and replied, "Thank you, Miss Lucy. I've come to know all of you and consider you my friends. It's an honor to be with you."

"Did y'all know Espy was promoted to lieutenant the other day?" asked Palmer as she passed the green beans toward Sook, who sat to her right.

"That's right," interjected Duncan. "He's on the fast track to general. Heck, just a little while ago when we met, he was a corporal. At this rate, he'll be runnin' Fort Hood by Christmas."

Everyone laughed, and Major shook his head as he wiped his mouth. "Trust me, Espy, you don't want that job. That command has its hands full."

"It can't be worse than the stresses Fort Bliss is under in El Paso, can it?" asked Duncan.

"Not quite as bad, but at least the soldiers trying to defend El Paso can sleep in their own quarters at night," replied Major.

"Defend? That's an interesting use of words, Daddy," said Cooper.

Major took another bite of beef barbecue and responded, "That's what it has come down to, Coop. The border between Mexico and New Mexico is nonexistent. The Fort Bliss command has to fight two fronts—Mexican drug cartels to the south and New Mexico refugees on the west. Coupled with the unrest in the city itself, it truly is a war zone there."

"Dad, where are the Fort Hood units deployed?" asked Duncan.

"Well, San Antonio has been contained. That's the good news. Houston, on the other hand, is burning out of control in certain parts of the city. The unrest is spreading to suburbs where folks used to live a safe, comfortable lifestyle. Now they're being attacked by large mobs of desperate people led by inner-city gangs."

"Does Austin have a plan to get Houston under control?" asked Espy.

"Yes, but it's come down to the use of force. Urban warfare has taken over, and a lot of innocent civilians are getting caught in the crossfire. It's gonna take a tremendous surge of military personnel to clean out the trash and restore peace in the city."

Everyone sat silently for a moment as they ate their dinner. Living in a remote area of West Texas, the challenges facing big cities during the apocalypse were unknown to them.

Duncan had seen firsthand what kind of chaos could be achieved by organized opportunists hell-bent on destruction or looting. "Dad, if you look at the city of Houston as a whole, it's easy to get overwhelmed by the geographic size and the two million population."

"You're right, son. The problem is the lack of geographic boundaries. There's no logical way to approach the problem. We can't box them in or even force them into a corner geographically. We don't have enough troops to encircle them and drive them to the middle of an area. Remember, we've still got a few of the personnel assigned to defend our borders."

"Has that settled down?" asked Lucy.

"Somewhat," replied Major. "Through attrition, refugees have sadly died waiting to get into Texas. Others have given up and gone home. Washington has finally taken the steps to provide relief supplies in areas nearby as well as promises of transportation, using Texas school buses, to take folks back to where they came from."

"Is that working?" asked Palmer.

"Not as well as we hoped, honey. It's a terrible humanitarian problem, but things are turning around in that regard. The UN is now airlifting supplies into the United States and dropping them at remote airfields. Hopefully, the refugees attempting to enter Texas will move to the new refugee centers being established by FEMA in the States."

Dinner was almost over, and the subject turned to the power grid. Cooper raised the issue first. "How's ERCOT coming along?"

"Now that the threat has been eliminated, thanks to Duncan," Major began to reply, nodding to Duncan, who sat at the other end of the table, "ERCOT workers have felt comfortable to systematically repair the substations. What I'm most proud of is the response of our fellow Texans."

"In what way?" asked Cooper.

"Son, the response to my address the other day has been nothing short of remarkable. Folks began to seek out work sites and were standing in line to do anything they could. They cleared debris. Near Waco, they toted heavy transmission lines by hand. There was supposedly a line of a hundred people threading the lines down the side of a hill so it could be hoisted up to a tower."

"That's great, dear," added Lucy. "It sounds like your speech had a real impact."

"I think so. I met with church leaders from around the country yesterday. They've offered up their sanctuaries as temporary medical facilities to replace those that have been looted or damaged in their communities. High school administrators came up with the idea of using their football stadiums for the new marketplaces I've suggested. Texans have begun to adopt that sense of pride and community we've been known for. It's gonna make a real difference."

Lucy leaned over and kissed Major. "You've provided Texas the spark necessary to move forward."

"Thank you, dear." Major stood and reached for her empty plate. "The thought of rebuilding Texas was beyond my comprehension until I realized that we can only do it one brick at a time."

"Well said, Dad," said Duncan, who also stood to gather plates.

"Hey, y'all, it's really a beautiful afternoon outside," started Lucy. "Whadya think about a ride around the ranch together? I feel like we should go pay our respects at the cemetery and then remind ourselves of what we've fought so hard for. Who's in?"

The vote of approval was unanimous.

CHAPTER 55

February 9
The Armstrong Ranch
Borden County, Texas

While Major and Duncan joined Lucy in the kitchen to clean the dishes, the rest of the group made their way to the barn to ready the horses. It was an unseasonably warm afternoon in which the temperatures had risen into the low sixties. Espy radioed his men and advised them that the group would be riding the perimeter of the ranch on horseback. He told his men to be aware of the family riding through their security areas. He also ordered mobile patrols to exit the ranch at both the north and south gates to look for any approaching vehicles. The Armstrong family had earned its place in Texas on a par with the founders of any new nation. Espy took his job of protecting each of them very seriously. The fact that he'd fallen in love with their youngest member was just added incentive for him to do his job well.

While they waited for the last three riders, Cooper and Riley discussed ranch operations. Any sibling rivalry they might have had in the past was left behind with Preacher's death. They had both been thrust into roles of great responsibility at the ranch. Riley was not in the least resentful of Cooper's rise to the head of ranch operations. He was quite content taking care of the cattle and the other livestock located at the barnyard.

Likewise, Palmer and Sook immediately took to their new roles assisting Lucy with the all-important task of organizing their food and medical supplies. While Lucy was proud of her husband's initial accomplishments as vice president on a national level, it would still be some time before all of North America was on solid footing. She planned on continuing their self-reliant lifestyle that didn't count on additional provisions from Austin.

She also planned on marshalling their assets with an eye toward long-term sustainability. The spring would look a lot different around Armstrong Ranch with a new emphasis on expanding their gardening operations.

Lucy used to say that the ability to grow your own food was like growing your own money. In a post-apocalyptic world, the ability to plant and harvest crops simply allowed you to live longer. The concept of gardening took on a whole new meaning when your life depended on it.

Major, Lucy, and Duncan joined the group, and they mounted their horses for a leisurely ride around the ranch. Their first stop was the cemetery.

Everyone dismounted and found a spot to tie off their horses. They paid their respects to the hands who had given their lives in the defense of Armstrong Ranch. Major and Lucy pledged to take care of their families for so long as they wanted to remain on the ranch.

They made their way to the grave of Pops, who had been laid to rest years ago next to Major's mother under an oak tree.

Major spoke from the heart. "Pops, we all miss you. I don't think you have any idea the mark you made on this family. I swell up with pride when I hear the kids, your grandchildren, make reference to the things you taught them. I'm amazed at how much Miss Lucy learned from you, which encouraged her to get prepared for these frightening times.

"You were a success in so many ways. You raised your family well. You taught us to laugh and love. You had the respect of your fellow ranchers. Pops, you always looked for the best in others and gave the best you had to offer. There is no doubt in my mind that you left this world in a better place than how you entered it. God bless you."

Major bowed his head and said a prayer in silence. His sniffling caused Lucy to join him and rub his shoulders.

She whispered into his ear, "Dear, know this. You are your

father's son. You should be proud."

Major nodded and gathered himself before standing. As they walked toward Dallas's grave, Duncan joined him and patted him on the shoulder.

"Mom, Dad, may I speak about Dallas?"

"Of course, son," replied Lucy. She gave him a smile of encouragement and wiped the tears from her eyes.

Duncan led the group to the grave and dropped down to one knee. "Dallas, you were a true hero and a patriot. You made the ultimate sacrifice in defense of your country, and I want you to know we will forever remember what you've done for us.

"I'll never forget the phone conversation we had when I was deployed in one part of Afghanistan while you were in another. Your words were simple. *Duncan, what the heck are we doin' here?* And I replied, *Dang good question.*"

The group chuckled a little at Duncan's recollection of the conversation.

"Dallas, you and I both had a desire to fight for our country. When the national anthem was sung at a football game, we joined in loud and proud despite the fact we couldn't sing a lick. I remember walking around the ranch with you as teenagers, talking about what was happening in Iraq and Afghanistan.

"Do you remember how many movies we'd watch together, like *Red Dawn*? We'd shout at the TV *don't do this* or *go that way!* Remember? It was in our blood from somewhere, and going into the service was our calling.

"Dallas, I've carried a lot of guilt for not discouraging you from enlisting. I knew what war was really like. It wasn't anything like the movies you and I watched."

Duncan began to get emotional as he teared up. Cooper joined his side and offered him encouragement, so Duncan continued.

"When I heard that you'd died, something changed inside me. Suddenly, every time I was deployed, every hostile was the one that caused your death. I lost part of myself as I tried to ease my own guilt for not stopping you.

"I carried that guilt until recently when Cooper forgave me. He proved to me that families can set aside differences through love. I've applied that same *let it go and move on* principle in the last few days, and I'm a better man for it.

"You're a true hero, Dallas. You will always be in our prayers and missed."

At this point, Sook and Palmer were crying. Riley was sniffling in the background as he pulled his hat down over his eyes. The Armstrong family had seen loss. Some was from natural causes, others from the throes of war both abroad and at home. But they were alive and together because of the heroics of a man who had his own cross to bear.

The group moved along to the final stop. Major dropped to both knees at Preacher's grave. "Old friend, I don't know what else to say that hasn't been said already. Your presence is still everywhere around this ranch and in my soul. When I'm in Austin, dealing with the president or cabinet members or military leaders, your words echo in my ears more than anyone realizes.

"We've had so many conversations over the years. Our talks ranged from pigs to politics and what does the end of the world as we know it look like. We experienced it all, old friend. It is because of your bravery and sacrifice that our family is still alive. No amount of words or deeds could ever express my eternal gratitude for that.

"Just know this. I will continue to love and protect them as you did. I will never take for granted what you did for us, and I promise that I will make every effort to fill your shoes. God bless, my friend."

"Very nice, Daddy," said Palmer as she moved to help him stand. The trip had been very emotional for Major, and he found himself a little weak as a result.

"Come on, y'all," said Riley cheerfully. "Let's ride and let the horses do the heavy liftin' for a little while."

Major kissed the top of Palmer's head and thanked her for helping him to his feet. He smiled in Riley's direction. "I agree, son."

The guys helped Lucy and the girls onto their horses, and then the entourage rode along the river and past the windmill and the busy beavers, who were getting ready for the spring floods. Major quipped that the beavers didn't need The Weather Channel or a calendar app to know when it was time to shore up the dam.

The sun was beginning to drop on the horizon, and the sky slowly turned from blue to a combination of purple and orange. The clouds began to throw interesting shadows, which even produced a pink tint at times.

As they reached the top of a rise at the westernmost end of the ranch, Major brought his horse to a stop.

Lucy was the first to comment on the sky. "This is amazing, isn't it? If you look back toward the ranch house, the sun is reflecting across the fields, turning them almost pink. Over toward the Rockies, it's bright orange."

After they admired the sunset for a moment, Palmer asked, "Daddy, what happens next? I mean, I don't want to get too comfortable, but it seems like now that we're all together, life might get back to normal."

Major adjusted his seat in the saddle, removed his hat, and ran his hands through his thinning hair. His silhouette was darkened against the backdrop of the setting sun. "I have to say I feel more at peace today than at any time since this whole thing started last year. It's time to live our lives based upon this new normal. We'll focus on the ranch and do our part to help Texas."

"I agree, Dad," said Duncan. "Texas will be challenged as a nation, and it's possible that our family will be as well. We've managed to persevere through times of trouble, and I believe we've gathered strength from the distress we've endured."

Major nodded. "Son, when bad things happen in life, we have a few choices. We can let them define us and change who we are. We can let them destroy us. Or as I believe has happened in the last few months to this family, it can make us all stronger."

"Texas Strong," added Lucy proudly.

"That's right, Miss Lucy."

Everyone joined in and yelled, "Texas Strong!"

THANK YOU FOR READING *SUICIDE SIX*!

If you enjoyed it, I'd be grateful if you'd take a moment to write a short review (just a few words are needed) and post it on Amazon. Amazon uses complicated algorithms to determine what books are recommended to readers. Sales are, of course, a factor, but so are the quantities of reviews my books get. By taking a few seconds to leave a review, you help me out and also help new readers learn about my work.

And before you go …

SIGN UP for Bobby Akart's mailing list to receive special offers, bonus content, and you'll be the first to receive news about my upcoming new series, as well as more information about the Lone Star series, the Pandemic series, the Blackout series, the Boston Brahmin series and the Prepping for Tomorrow series—all of which includes over twenty Amazon #1 Bestsellers in forty-plus fiction and non-fiction genres. Visit Bobby Akart's website for informative blog entries on preparedness, his novels, and his latest new project.

www.BobbyAkart.com

If you enjoyed the EMP aspect of The Lone Star Series, I invite you to try The Blackout Series which portrays a grid down scenario as a result of a massive solar flare.

www.ingramcontent.com/pod-product-compliance
Lightning Source LLC
Chambersburg PA
CBHW020933310726
48980CB00007B/757/J

* 9 7 8 0 6 9 2 1 3 4 9 9 3 *